SATYANWESHI

IN EXILE

ADVAITA BHUSHAN

Made with ♥ on the Notion Press Platform
www.notionpress.com

Contents

Note: This story has been written based on true events

Acknowledgements

This book is dedicated to my father, an Indian army officer, **MR. Puldas Venkateshwar,** and to the generations of my family who have dedicated their lives to serving our nation. Coming from a lineage of freedom fighters, our family has always prioritized the welfare of the people and the fight for freedom. My grandfather and father both served in the defence of our nation, and their values have shaped me for who I am today. My father always taught me, "Family first," but he also emphasized that the nation must come before everything else, even family. It is a lesson I carry with me every day: that true responsibility lies in serving a great cause. I would like to share an incident that still holds tears in my eyes, One night, I was feeling unwell with a fever, and my dad repeatedly offered to take me to the hospital. I reassured him that I was fine, insisting it was just a fever and nothing serious. Despite my refusal, he told me to wake him up if I started feeling worse during the night. He said, "I might be in a deep sleep, but don't hesitate—just kick me in the face to wake me up if you need to. We'll rush to the hospital right away." His words made me think of Sandeep Reddy Vanga's writing: "My father is the best father in the world." At that moment, I felt an overwhelming sense of gratitude for having such a caring and selfless father. My father turned me from a boy to a man. Dad, you are always my idol and inspiration, and I am forever grateful to you.

At the same time, while my father served the nation, it was my mother who kept our family strong and grounded. Her unwavering support and care are what held us together through the years. I owe my parents everything—the privileges, the ethics, and the values they instilled in me. I hope and believe someday I can live up to all the love and care that you have consciously showered on me I wish to prove worthy of all they've given me and to make them proud.

I would also like to express my heartfelt thanks to my love, you have been a constant source of support. You made countless sacrifices to give me the time and space I needed to focus on my work, even when it meant putting your needs aside. I'm sorry I couldn't give you all the time that you deserved, but I want you to know, that your support and understanding mean the world to me. Our love, built on respect and mutual freedom, will remain timeless, even after I am no longer here.

A special acknowledgment goes to Khaja, my brother from another mother. I've never met anyone like him—his selflessness and willingness to help others, often putting their needs above his own, are truly remarkable. He has always stood by me like a shadow, a shadow that never vanishes even in the deepest dark with no source of light around. You have always been by my time of need, and I am forever grateful for his friendship and unwavering loyalty.

I would also like to extend my deepest gratitude to Srilekhya Grandhi, the editor of this book. Srilekhya's insights, dedication, and attention to detail were invaluable in shaping the structure and flow of this work. Her contributions have elevated this book to its fullest potential.

Lastly, I want to acknowledge and thank the women who have come into my life and played a significant role in my personal growth. Their influence has been a key source of the positive changes I've seen in myself, and I respect and honor each one of them for helping me become a better person.

Thank you all for being a part of this journey.

Prologue

Fear of the Unknown

There's a certain kind of fear which has no face of its own. It lurks in the shadows, hides in the silence, and creeps into your mind when you're alone in the dark. It's the fear of what you can't see, what you can't explain. "The fear of the unknown." To the farthest that I can remember, I was once clenched by the same kind of fear

Just like any other, I had my own irrational phobias.

As a child, I was terrified of the dark. I'd convince myself that there was something lurking just beyond the edges of the shadows in my room, waiting for me to fall asleep so it could strike on me. As I grew older, the fear didn't fade away, it just took on new forms. Spirits, Unclear shadows, strange noises during the night, the feeling of being watched. Even when there was nothing around, my mind created monsters to fill the silence.

But there is a thing about fear, it feeds on what we don't understand. The less you know, the more your mind fills in the blanks, with the worst possible scenarios. That is why people are afraid of the dark, scared of the unknown. It is not the darkness alone that terrifies them, it is the idea of what could be hiding within it.

I used to be constantly scared of the shadows, of what might be lurking just out of sight. I used to believe that a few scratches of fear would never leave me. But then things changed due to that one incident. Something that made me question everything, I thought I knew about fear. And an incident proved to me that fear isn't real, it's a trick played by the mind, an illusion that is born from what we don't understand.

And that incident took life in a place called ABK township.

The day I stepped into ABK township Fear hugged/ welcomed me again.

I remember the first time I visited Khaja there. It was a humid evening, the kind where the air felt heavy and the sky looms with the promise of rain. The apartment complex stands tall against the darkening sky, a quiet, looming structure at the edge of the city. From the outside, it looked like any other high-rise—impersonal, sterile, a place where people come and go without knowing each other's names. Yet, something about it felt wrong, even before I crossed its threshold.

The moment I walked in, I felt it—an unwinding chill circulated despite the thick heat outside. The air inside the building seemed heavier, stiller. The wide lobby was dimly lit, and the fluorescent lights flickered, casting strange, shifting shadows across the walls. As we made our way up to the 13th floor, the faint hum of the elevator only added to the tension. Khaja had been living here for a while, so he seemed unfazed, but for me, the entire place felt off.

Once we reached the corridor, I noticed how unnervingly quiet it was. The kind of quiet that wasn't peaceful, but unnaturally still, like the building itself was holding its breath. The only sounds came from the muted hum of air conditioners and the occasional distant thud of doors closing on other floors. But beyond that, nothing. It was as if the building was too old, too tired to make noise.

I shook it off feeling it was nothing more than my imagination. After all, this was just another apartment complex, right? A place where people live their lives, unnoticed and uninterested with other. But even as I tried to dismiss my unease, there was a persisting sense that something was watching, something I couldn't see but could feel. The long hallway leading to Khaja's flat stretched out in front of me, darker at the far end where the lights seemed to flicker more often.

I could feel it! Something wasn't right.

When we finally reached Khaja's door, the neighboring flat caught my glance for a moment, I thought I saw a figure standing at the end, was it just a shadow? It disappeared quickly as I noticed it. I felt as if, it could have been my mind playing tricks on me, but it unsettled me all the same.

Khaja opened the door, laughing about something, and I forced myself to smile. Though I stepped inside his flat, I couldn't shudder at the feeling that ABK township was different from any. It wasn't just an apartment building. It felt like something more than it pictures, something that wasn't meant to be understood.

And as an add-on to the mysterious outlook the sounds lifted the life to terror.

At first, they were just faint whispers.

They were easy to ignore, especially in a place like ABK township where the walls were thin, and sounds bled through like water soaking into paper. In the beginning, I brushed it off as the usual noises of apartment life—neighbors talking, kids playing, the shuffle of footsteps. But soon, it was clear that this was unlike. The sounds weren't random; they were constant, patterned, almost rhythmic.

Every time I visited Khaja, the noise was alive, faint but persistent, seeping through the walls of his flat from the neighbouring apartment. It started late at night, just after midnight, as soon as the building had settled into its eerie silence, that's when I started hearing them—soft voices, muffled but unmistakable. They were too faint to make out, but I could hear them well enough to know they were arguing.

And then there were the children's voices.

It was strange, to hear them laugh or cry at such odd hours. I didn't think much of it until Khaja mentioned that it wasn't just me, everyone on the 13th floor had noticed and experienced them. Sometimes, the kids would be sobbing, sometimes shouting, as if they were being scolded or punished. The arguments between the adults would get louder, and more aggressive, and then again, they would quiet down, leaving the pale cry behind.

It was unnerving. We all assumed the family next door was just dysfunctional, maybe going through tough times. People never minded other than their own business in apartments like these. After all, it wasn't our place to ask questions. But over time, the sounds become harder to ignore.

There were nights when the children would cry for long hours, drawn-out wails that made your skin crawl. Khaja mentioned it casually, the way people talk about things that annoy them but seem too trivial to fix. He told me that his parents had complained about it to the building management more than once, but nothing changed. Other tenants had heard it too, and they were just as disturbed as we are by the constant arguments and crying. But no one ever saw the children. Not even once.

"Sometimes, I think those kids never leave the flat," Khaja said to me on an evening, laughing as if he was only half-joking. "I've never seen them, have you?"

I hadn't. But now that he'd mentioned it, I realized something strange: the couple rarely came out. On rare occasions when I visited Khaja during the day, the flat next door always seemed closed, curtains drawn, door shut, and no sign of life beyond the thin walls. The only proof that anyone lived there was the haunting noises that crept through the walls like a whispered secret.

Soon, it became more than just any background annoyance. The noises started to get under my skin. There was something unsettling about hearing the same argument on loop, the same child's cry, as if it was playing on repeat. It didn't help, the flat seemed eerily quiet during the day, almost like it was sleeping, only to come alive when the rest of the world went to bed.

That's when I began to wonder: Who were the people living next door? And why did it feel like their presence was spilling out into the building, haunting it, like the ghosts of life whom no one could see but everyone could hear?

Little did I know, this was just the beginning.

The day they left; the building fell silent.

It was the kind of silence that felt unnatural, as if something had been abruptly severed, leaving a void in its place. For two years, the noise had been constant—arguments, cries of children, the sounds of life being unfolded behind those walls. And then, without any warning, it all stopped.

I remember that morning it is still clear in my head. Khaja and I had just finished our breakfast when a familiar sound, the sound of a moving truck pulling into the parking lot caught our attention.

We went to the corridor and saw the couple from next door packing their things into the truck, the husband directing the movers while the wife stood quietly off to the side, watching.

Just like that. They were leaving."I heard they're moving to Dubai,"

Khaja said almost casually, as if it explained everything. "The guy works there. I guess they've finally had enough of this place."

But something didn't sit right with me. I had seen this couple only a handful of times, only from a distance, always looking worn and tired, as if the weight of something far bigger than an argument or children's tantrums was crushing them. And now, seeing them leave so quietly, with no sign of the kids, it struck me odd.

As the last count of the furniture was loaded into the truck, I noticed the watchman standing nearby, with a confused look on his face. He hesitated for a moment before approaching the husband."Sir, where are the children?"

He asked, his voice low but clear enough for Khaja and me to hear from the corridor.

The husband stopped for a moment, exchanged a glance with his wife, and then turned back to the watchman with a smile that didn't quite reach his eyes. "Children? "What children?"

The question hung in the air like a cloud of smoke, thick and suffocating. I felt my heart skip a beat, and I looked at Khaja, who was staring down at the scene below, his face pale with disbelief.

The watchman blinked, clearly taken aback. "Your kids... the ones we've been hearing for the last two years."

The husband's smile didn't falter. It grew colder. "We don't have any children. We've been trying for years, but... well, it hasn't happened yet."

He gave a small, dismissive shrug, as though the whole conversation was absurd.

I could feel the nerves creeping up my spine. How could that be? We had all heard the children—their laughter, their cries, the arguments late into the night. How could there have been no children?

The watchman stood there, his face with a mixture of confusion and unease, but he said nothing more. The couple finished loading their things and left without any other word, leaving behind nothing but an empty flat and the surviving shock of their denial.

The building felt different after that. The serene was oppressive and unnatural. It was as if the flat next door had been holding onto something, and now that it was gone, a strange emptiness took its place. There were no more late-night arguments, no more cries of the children echoing through the walls. The entire 13th floor seemed to breathe a collective sigh of relief—and yet, no one could shake the feeling that something wasn't right.

The other tenants were just as baffled as Khaja and me. Everyone had heard the children. For two years, those cries had been as much a part of the building as the walls themselves. But now, it was though as those sounds had never existed. The couple's denial didn't just confuse us, it unsettled us in a way that words couldn't explain.

How could we have imagined it? All of us?

I couldn't let it go. Khaja tried to laugh it off, calling it one of those strange things people eventually forget. But I couldn't. My mind kept circling back to that flat, to the voices I knew I had heard, and the children I was sure had lived there.

I couldn't shake the feeling that the couple had left behind more than just an empty flat. They had left behind a mystery—one that I was determined to unravel.

Fear started transforming into something else—an obsession.

After the couple left, everything about ABK township seemed different, even though nothing had visibly changed. The hallway outside Khaja's flat was just as it always had been long, narrow, lined with the same dim lights that flickered every now and then. But now, every time I visited, I found myself drawn to the door of the flat next door. The silence that came from behind that door was heavier than the noise that used to seep through it. It was as if the walls themselves were holding back secrets too terrible to speak.

Khaja had tried shrugging the whole thing off as a strange fluke. But I knew it wasn't that simple. The couple's denial, the years of arguments, the tears shredding through the wall, it all stayed with me, replaying in my mind like a broken record. There was something we had all missed, something lurking beneath the surface that no one had bothered to look for.

That's when I realized my fear had changed.

What had once terrified me—the unknown, the inexplicable—was now driving me. Instead of shrinking away from the unanswered questions, I found myself leaning on them. My fear was replaced by a relentless need to understand. How could the couple have no children? We heard their voices for two years, only for them to vanish without a trace the moment the couple left.

Late at night, when the rest of the building was asleep, I would lie awake in my room, running through every possibility in my mind.

Ghosts?

Delusions?

Could it really be that all of us—Khaja, his family, and the other tenants- had imagined the sounds? Or was there something far darker at play?

I needed the answers. But there was no one left to ask.

At first, I thought it would be easy to let it go, to move on and forget, just as Khaja had. But the more I tried to push it aside, the more it pulled me back in. Every visit to ABK township carried a gnawing sense of unease, an invisible force drawing my attention to that empty flat. Every whisper in the hallway, every creak of the floorboards, felt like a message—something waiting to be uncovered.

Eventually, I realized I couldn't leave it alone.

I had to know what really happened in that house. I had to find out why those voices had haunted the building for two years if it was only to disappear without a trace. Most of all, I had to find the strange, hollow look in the couple's eyes as they left—as if they were leaving behind something far more sinister than a few pieces of furniture.

The fear of the unknown had consumed me once, but now I was chasing it. I wasn't afraid anymore. I was determined.

I didn't know it at the time, but this would be the beginning of a journey that would lead me down through a dark and twisted path. A path with no destination marked, the uncovered, would be more terrifying than any ghost or shadow I had ever imagined.

Somewhere deep down, I knew that behind every fear, there was an undetailed explanation. But this one? This one would change everything.

Author Biography

Hello, I'm Advaita Bhushan, born into an Indian Army family. Having traveled across the States of India gave me the privilege of meeting and interacting with people from diverse backgrounds—different ethnicities, castes, religions, and cultures. These experiences have deeply grounded me, shaping my understanding of the world and fostering a sense of empathy toward others.

I consider myself an experimentalist, driven by an innate curiosity that navigates my path through life. This curiosity propels me forward, always seeking new destinations and understanding. Like many, I had my own fears before a life-changing incident during my post-graduation days, which gave me a new perspective on fear. That incident made me realize that fear is nothing more than an unexplained fact. Once that fact is recognized, the fear dissolves.

This book is for the one who is struggling with fear—anyone who feels trapped by their own anxiety or irrational thoughts. As Seneca wisely said,

"*We suffer more in imagination than in reality.*" Often, we construct illogical and irrational narratives in our minds, which can lead to unnecessary suffering and alarming panic. Through this book, I hope to help *you* the reader. I would like to convey to you that, the greatest threat isn't external—it's our own mind.

The tagline of this book, *"In Exile"* reflects the following central idea: Our most formidable challenge often lies within breaking free from the mental barriers we've constructed, daring to step beyond the familiar comfort zone. It's only then, by venturing into the unknown, that we uncover the light concealed within the darkness.

The plot of this book is based on a true event that happened in my life during my post-graduation. I hope that my journey and experience will not only resonate with you but will also inspire you anchor the turning point in your life and help you to become a more rational, fearless being.

With all of you being ready to sail, let's begin the voyage without further delay.

"We suffer more often in imagination than in reality."
-Seneca

CHAPTER I

Meet and Greet.

"The whodunnit realm"

Being a Young and ambitious person, I have always found myself entertained by learning and being updated with knowledge and skills, never letting myself down was the first mantra that I always practiced. There is a saying "The friends we get during our education will last forever." Indeed, it's a blessing to have a friend who lasts long, a person with whom you can have a glass to cheers, a person who can drive along with you through rocks and valleys, a person who can pick your call no matter the time is, and I feel blessed to have that person and he is KHAJA, the humble, grounded, innocent, honest and a soul you can rely on. He can make you laugh even when you are stuck within your web of thoughts, he does be at your side in the deepest dark.

I met Khaja at the end of under graduation, he was cherishing, and full of joy, and soon we met, and we got into a bro bond. As Khaja's parents were local residents of Vishakhapatnam, we decided to continue our education at a renowned university located there.

As I wanted to be close to nature, I found my place near the beach view, and Khaja stayed with his family at ABK TOWNSHIP.

We often used to hang, out and work on similar projects that motivated us to achieve our ambition of a successful career. One day, As I was heading out of town for a couple of days, with Assignments and Submissions in my head, I thought to hand over my work to Khaja as he could take care of the work in the university during my absence. *"Bro! are you home?"*

I messaged him, and I received a reply from him within 5 minutes of my text, saying...! *"Yes man, sup?"*

With the confirmation of his being at home, I packed the documents and files that I had to give him, grabbed the keys to my royal Enfield, and started driving towards ABK township.

The nearer I got to the venture, the cool breeze with sunset accompanied me.

ABK township was a strange place, even at first sight.

It stood tall and narrow, like a concrete monolith in the middle of the bustling city. From a distance, it looked like any other apartment building—functional, plain, unremarkable. But as I approached, something about it felt off. It wasn't just the building's aging façade, with its cracked plaster and faded paint. It was the air around it, the way the shadows seemed to cling to its edges, the way it loomed over the nearby streets like an uninvited guest at a party.

I had been to plenty of apartments in my life, but none of them had given me that sense of unease before I even stepped inside. ABK township wasn't just a building. It felt like something more. Something that had its own presence, its own weight in the world.

Khaja had invited me over many times before, but I had never really paid attention to the building itself. I was always focused on our plans, on catching up, or on whatever latest thing we were laughing about. But today, as I drove the narrow path leading to the entrance, I couldn't help but notice the subtle chill that settled in my bones. The kind of chill that had nothing to do with the weather.

The entrance itself wasn't much—just a set of glass doors with fingerprints smeared across the surface and a dimly lit lobby beyond. The usual apartment building fare. But as I parked my bike, and as I started stepped the lift, that feeling deepened. The air was still, too still for such a large building. It was evening and people should have been coming and going, but the lobby was empty, the elevator idle. The only sound was the faint hum of electricity overhead, the fluorescent lights flickering slightly as if they too were unsettled.

I pressed the button for the elevator to come down, watching as the numbers blinked down slowly from the top floor. While I waited, I looked around, taking in the quiet. I'd always prided myself on being rational, and grounded. I wasn't the type to get spooked by ordinary things. But something about ABK township made me feel... uneasy. Like the air was heavier, thick with something I couldn't see or name.

The elevator doors slid open with a soft ding, and I stepped inside, pressing the button for the 13th floor. As the doors closed, sealing me into the small metal box, I couldn't shake the feeling that this building was watching me, tracking every move I made. It was a ridiculous thought, but it sat in the back of my mind, refusing to let go.

When the elevator finally opened on the 13th floor, the hallway stretched out in front of me, long and narrow, lined with identical doors. It looked the same as any other apartment floor I'd ever been on, but the silence that greeted me when I stepped out was different. It wasn't the comfortable quiet of an empty place. It was the kind of silence that pressed against you, that made your footsteps sound too loud, too intrusive.

I stood there for a moment, staring down the hallway at the row of doors. There were no sounds coming from any of the apartments, no voices, no televisions, no music. Just stillness.

It was only when I heard Khaja's voice, light and casual, calling out from his open door that I snapped out of it. *"Come on, man! I'm making tea!"*

he shouted.

I shook off the strange feeling that had settled over me and walked toward his flat. But even as I stepped inside, greeted by Khaja's usual easy grin, I couldn't help but glance back at the hallway one more time.

Something about this place felt wrong. And I had no idea why.

Khaja had always been the type of person who could find humor in almost anything. It didn't matter what was going on around him—he'd crack a joke, laugh it off, and move on. He had this energy that made everyone around him feel at ease, even in the most uncomfortable situations. It was one of the reasons we became such close friends during our MBA program. Where I was prone to overthinking, Khaja was the kind of guy who simply lived—unbothered, carefree, always ready for the next adventure.

But something about his life here, on the 13th floor of ABK township, was different.

As I stepped into his flat, I was welcomed by the warm smell of freshly brewed tea, Khaja welcomed me with a wide grin. He was still the same Khaja I knew—relaxed and smiling—but there was a slight edge to his energy. I couldn't quite put my finger on it. *"Bro, you've got to try this masala tea I've been perfecting,"*

Khaja said, heading back to the kitchen, leaving the door wide open behind me.

I followed him into the flat, my eyes scanning the room. His apartment was cozy, not large, but filled with the usual essentials: a couch, a small dining table, and a TV mounted on the wall. It felt like home, but there was something off about the atmosphere. Maybe it was just me—still shaken by the unsettling silence in the hallway—but I couldn't help but feel a slight sense of tension. Not in the apartment itself, but in the air around it.

Dropping my bag on the couch, I joined him in the kitchen, watching as he poured tea into two cups. As Khaja's parents were away visiting relatives, explained why the place felt a little emptier than usual. *"So, how's life in this place?"* I asked casually, trying to mask my discomfort with small talk.

Khaja leaned against the counter, stirring his tea with a slow, deliberate motion. *"It's alright, can't complain. You know how it is—city life, apartment living. Everyone keeps to themselves."* with a shrug he said.

I nodded, taking a sip of the tea. It was good—spicy, with just the right amount of sweetness—but I wasn't really paying attention to the flavor. My mind was still on the building itself, the strange silence, the way the air felt heavier than it should. *"You get along with the neighbors?"*

I asked, keeping my tone light, though my curiosity was growing.

Khaja chuckled, shaking his head. *"To be honest, not really. People here don't talk much. I only had a few conversations with them, and even then, it's just the usual stuff— 'Hello,' 'How are you?' That kind of thing."*

He paused, his eyes drifting toward the door, then added, *"Especially the ones next door. They're... well, let's just say they're not the friendliest."*

My interest piqued. *"What do you mean?"*

Khaja set his cup down, leaning forward slightly, his voice lowering as if he were about to share a secret. *"It's weird, man. The couple next door they've got kids, but I've never actually seen them. I hear them all the time, though. Crying, arguing... it's like clockwork. Every night, like some kind of routine. But they never leave the flat. I've never seen the kids outside. Not once."*

I could hear my breath. The image of the long, silent hallway flashed in my mind the identical doors, the eerie stillness. And now this, **kids who were always heard but never seen?** *"Maybe they just don't go out much,"*

I offered, though the words felt hollow even as I said them.

Khaja shrugged again, but this time there was something else in his expression—a flicker of unease that I hadn't seen in him before. *"Maybe. Or maybe there's something else going on. Who knows? People in this building aren't exactly the talkative type."*

He laughed, trying to lighten the mood, but I could tell that it bothered him more than he was letting on.

I leaned back in my chair, sipping the tea slowly, letting the silence settle between us. The more I thought about it, the stranger it seemed. Khaja had always been the kind of person who made friends easily, yet here he was, living in a place where the people around him felt more like shadows than neighbors. There was something off about this building, something I couldn't shake. *"Have you ever tried talking to them?"*

I asked, half-joking, half-serious.

Khaja shook his head quickly.

"Nah, man. They're not the type you talk to. I don't think they're interested in making friends. The wife barely comes out, and when she does, she's like a ghost. Pale, quiet, always looking down. I think she might be going through something... or maybe they both are."

I frowned, glancing at the door. *"And the kids? You really never see them?"*

"Never."

Khaja's answer was immediate.

"But we hear them. Every night. It's not just me, my parents, and the people across the hall, they've all heard it. But no one's ever mentioned seeing them outside. Not once."

The silence that followed his words felt heavier than before, like a presence in the room that neither of us wanted to acknowledge.

I tried to brush it off, just like Khaja had. But the more I thought about it, the more unsettling it became. A family that never showed their faces, children who were only heard, and distant, cold neighbors who seemed content to stay hidden behind their doors.

Something about ABK township wasn't right. And I had a feeling that whatever was happening in that building was running deeper than either of us could imagine.

The hallway was so still, that we could clearly hear the sound of a pin drop on the 13th floor.

After the tea, I handed the bag of documents to Khaja and we decided to step out for a walk. As we left his flat, the first thing that struck me was the silence. It wasn't just the way any apartment complex would usually be, where the soft hum of distant conversations and the occasional clatter of footsteps echo from behind closed doors. **No,** this was different. It was the kind of silence that made your own movements feel too loud, and intrusive, like the building itself was absorbing every sound and turning it into nothingness.

I glanced down the hallway. It stretched out endlessly in front of me, bathed in the dim yellow glow of flickering lights. The narrow corridor seemed to go on forever, lined with identical doors on either side—each one closed tight like the secrets they held were too precious to let out.

But it was the stillness that gnawed at me.

The air felt thick, almost suffocating, as if the sound itself had been swallowed by the building. I strained my ears for any hint of life—a voice, at least TV sound, even the soft clatter of dishes. But there was nothing. No signs of anyone behind those doors, no indication that this floor was home to anyone at all. It felt as if we were the only ones there, walking through a space abandoned by the world. *"Is it always this quiet?"* I asked, my voice sounding louder than I intended in the empty hallway.

Khaja shrugged casually, locking his door. *"Yeah, pretty much. Like I said, people here keep to themselves. It's weird, but after a while, you get used to it."*

Get used to it? I wasn't sure how anyone could get used to this kind of silence. It felt unnatural like the entire floor was holding its breath, waiting for something to happen. I stuffed my hands into my pockets, trying to shake off the discomfort, but it clung to me like a second skin.

We started walking down the hallway, our footsteps echoing off the walls. Each step felt heavier than the last, the sound bouncing back at us in the emptiness. The floor creaked beneath our weight, and for a moment, I swear I heard something—a faint whisper, almost imperceptible, coming from one of the apartments. But when I paused and turned my head to listen, it was gone.

*"Did you hear that?"*I asked, stopping mid-step.

Khaja raised an eyebrow.*"Hear what?"*

I hesitated. It had been so faint, maybe I was imagining things. *"Nothing, it's probably just the building settling."*

I muttered, shaking my head.

But as we continued down the hallway, the odd sensation that we weren't truly alone lingered in the back of my mind. There was something about this place that seemed off, something lurking just beneath the surface of normalcy. I couldn't explain it, but I felt it in my bones—like an itch you can't scratch, a sense of being watched even when no one's there.

We passed by the flat next door to Khaja's, flat 03, the one with the family no one ever saw. I found myself glancing at the door, half-expecting it to swing open, to reveal some clue about the lives behind it. But the door remained closed, as always, and the hallway remained silent as a tomb.

Khaja seemed unfazed by the whole thing, moving with the ease of someone who had learned to ignore what they couldn't explain. Looking at me being anxious, he tried comforting me by saying, *"You'll get used to it."* He repeated.

"Get used to what?" I questioned immediately, Khaja being very calm and composed, with a comforting tone said *"The quiet, the people, just how things are here."*

"Maybe," I muttered, though I wasn't convinced. I couldn't shake the feeling that this silence was more than just a quirk of the building. The quiet felt as if, it was hiding things, that concealed what shouldn't be obvious. I glanced around again, with the hope of seeing the door crack open or hear a voice break the oppressive stillness.

But there was nothing.

We reached the elevator that was at the end of the hall, and as Khaja pressed the button, the soft ding echoed unnaturally in the stillness. We stood there for a moment, waiting, and in that silence, I thought I heard something again—a faint rustling sound, like the shifting of fabric or the scuff of feet behind a door. I glanced at Khaja to see if he had heard it too, but he seemed oblivious, scrolling through his phone with one hand and the other hand in his pocket.

"Are you sure you didn't hear that?" I asked, my voice being low.

Khaja looked up, confused. *"Hear what?"*

I shook my head, frustrated by how uneasy I felt. *"It's like... like there's something moving. I swear I heard it."*

Khaja let out a small laugh. *"You're overthinking, man. This place can mess with your head if you let it. Don't worry. It's probably just the neighbors, though they're quiet most of the time."*

The elevator arrived with a soft whirr, and we stepped inside. As the doors closed behind us, sealing off the hallway, I couldn't help but take one last glance down the corridor. The flickering lights cast long, distorted shadows, making the empty space look even more sinister. I was half-expecting to see something lurking in the darkness, something watching from behind one of those closed doors.

But the hallway remained as it was—silent, still, waiting.

I turned back toward Khaja as the elevator began its descent, but the unsettling quiet of the 13th floor stayed with me, like a whisper I couldn't quite hear.

Khaja walked with me towards my bike, and assured me, *"Don't think a lot, just enjoy your travel, be safe."*

I knew I was heading out of the place, but it all felt like I was still there, stuck behind.

As the days went by and I visited Khaja more frequently, that sound became harder to ignore. Whenever I was at Khaja's place, it may be afternoon or late at night—it seemed like the same repetitive noises would drift from the neighboring flat. At first, I tried not to think too much of it. After all, in apartments like these, noise was part of the deal. You can hear your neighbors' lives through the walls, like echoes of stories you were never meant to know.

But this sound was different.

It wasn't the usual hum of everyday life. It wasn't the soft clatter of dishes or the muffled buzz of a TV. Instead, it was always the same—a low, indistinct murmur, like someone speaking just below the level where you could make out the words. Occasionally, there were the sharp, clipped sounds of an argument, the rise and fall of voices caught in some endless dispute. And more often, there were children's voices, crying—sometimes softly, sometimes louder, as if they were being scolded or punished.

It never seemed to stop.

No matter how late I stayed at Khaja's, whether we were working on projects or just hanging out, the voices from the neighboring flat would always be there, bleeding through the walls like a distant memory. Sometimes, I found myself pausing mid-conversation, my ears straining to catch more details, but the words were always too muffled, too distorted to make sense of. It was just noise—an ever-present background hum that seemed to exist solely to remind me that something was going on next door, just out of reach.

"Do you hear that?" I asked Khaja one night, as the faint sound of a child's cry filtered through the wall again.

Khaja didn't even look up from his phone. *"Yeah, man. It's like that all the time."*

"But don't you wonder what's going on over there?" I pressed. *"I mean, it's strange, right?*

Hearing them argue like that, the kids crying... Have you ever actually seen them?"

Khaja sighed as if he'd been through this conversation before. *"I told you, I've never seen them. But it's probably just a regular family, going through their stuff. Every place has its loud neighbors."*

He spoke with the kind of indifference that came from living in a place too long, where the everyday oddities faded into background noise. But I couldn't let it go. There was something about the consistency of the sounds, the way they followed the same pattern night after night. Cry, Arguments, Silence, and Crying again. It was very predictable, and regular, like it was on a loop.

"You've never even seen the kids?" I asked again being more curious than ever.

Khaja shook his head. While scrolling through his phone *"Nope."*

Keeping his phone aside he said, *"Yeah, it is weird, but I don't think about it much. Maybe they're just really private. Or maybe they're just not the kind of family that lets their kids play outside."*

His explanation didn't satisfy me. I did live the apartment life before, and kids were always part of the scenery—running down hallways, playing outside, making noise in the common areas. But here! It was as if the kids didn't exist beyond the thin walls that separated us from them.

As the days turned into weeks, I became more aware of the pattern of sounds. The arguments seemed to happen at the same time every night, just after midnight, as if it was part of some unseen schedule.

The children's cries were always short-lived, as though they were quickly hushed, leaving an eerie silence in their wake. There was a rhythm to it, the more I noticed it, the more my skin crawled.

One evening, Khaja and I were sitting on the couch, the TV being on in the background, when I heard it again—the sound of something being dropped next door, followed by an adult's voice rising in frustration.

A child's whimper came next, soft and pleading.

I froze, my attention immediately drawn to the wall separating us from the neighboring flat.

Khaja, as usual, didn't seem fazed. drowning out the noise, he turned up the volume on the TV, but I couldn't let it go.

I kept listening, my heartbeat quickening as the muffled argument continued, the voices were sharp and angry. There was something about how the voices carried that felt wrong—too harsh, cold.

"I'm telling you," I muttered, half to myself, *"something isn't right over there."*

Khaja gave me a sideways glance, his expression with a mix of amusement and concern.*"Man, you've been spending too much time here. It's just a family being loud. It happens."*

But I wasn't convinced anymore. There was a weight to the sounds, something that hung in the air long after the argument died down, like a lingering shadow that refused to fade. Every time I heard it, I felt a growing sense of dread, **as if the walls themselves were trying to tell me something, warning me to pay attention.**

"Have you ever thought about...maybe, asking them if everything's okay?" I asked though I knew how strange it sounded.

Khaja laughed, shaking his head. *"What would I even say? Hey, I hear you arguing all the time. Just wanted to check if you're alright?' it's not my business."*

He had a point, but the nagging feeling in my gut wouldn't go away. It wasn't just the arguments or the crying—it was the silence that followed, the way it settled over the building like a shroud.

Each time the noise stopped, the quiet felt heavier, more oppressive, as if it was trying to bury whatever just had happened.

I couldn't shake the feeling that something was wrong in that flat. And as much as Khaja tried to brush it off, I knew that soon or later, I would have to find out what it was.

It didn't bother Khaja much, as it bothered me.

No matter how many times I asked about it, Khaja would always shrug off the strange sounds from the neighboring flat. To him, it was just another part of apartment life—something you dealt with, but never questioned deeply. The walls were thin, people argued, kids cried, and that was it. No big deal. But the more I spent at ABK township, the more noises intensively started to get under my skin. They didn't feel like the usual background of city life. They felt wrong.

One evening, after another long day at work, we were sitting on the balcony outside Khaja's living room. The sunset was casting long shadows across the city, and a warm breeze rustled the leaves of the trees below. It should've been peaceful. But even then, the muffled sounds from next door reached us through the open window, faint but constant.

"How do you live with that?" I asked, breaking the silence between us. I gestured toward the wall, where once again, the faint crying of children could be heard.

Khaja sipped his tea, his expression calm as ever. *"Start getting used to it, man. After a while, it just fades into the background. Honestly, I don't even notice it anymore."*

I stared at him, incredulous. *"You don't notice that? Every time I'm here, it's the same thing. Crying, arguing, slamming doors. How can you ignore it?"*

Khaja laughed, shaking his head. *"Dude, people argue. Families have problems. It's none of our business. Do you think that's weird? You should hear the guy on the floor below us. He's always on the phone yelling about some business deal. Sounds like a real nightmare, but I don't let it bother me."*

I leaned back in my chair, frustrated by how easily he dismissed it.

"But it's not just the arguing. It's the fact that no one has ever seen them. I mean, you've never even seen the kids, right? And yet, they're crying all the time."

Khaja shrugged again, his eyes wandering to the horizon.

"Yeah, I guess. But maybe they're just private. Some people don't like being out in the open. I don't know, man. It's not like we're best friends with our neighbors."

His carefree attitude only fuelled my growing unease. I wanted to let it go, to brush it off like he did, but I was unable to let the feeling slide that something wasn't right. It wasn't just about noisy neighbors anymore—it was the pattern, the routine that followed as a ritual, every night, the same clockwork. The voices seemed to stop so abruptly, leaving an almost unnatural quiet in their wake.

"Doesn't it ever get to you?" I asked, almost hesitant. *"The way it's always the same? Like... like it's stuck on repeat?"*

Khaja turned looking at me, his expression softening.

"I know it's weird,"

he admitted.

"But what can I do? March over there and ask them to keep their arguments quieter. It's just apartment life, man. People have their issues, and unless it's causing real trouble, I figure it's not our place to interfere."

Listening to him, I sighed, knowing he had a point. It wasn't like we could knock on their door and demand answers. And yet, the unease gnawed at me, refusing to let go. I couldn't stop thinking about the children being in tears so regularly, so familiar now that they had become almost a part of the building itself. It was like they were trapped in some endless cycle, echoing through the walls, **unheard by anyone but us.**

"Have you ever wondered what goes on in there?" I asked, more to myself than to Khaja.

He gave me a curious glance, then smiled. *"To be honest, Not really. I figure everyone has their problems. Some people are just louder about it than others."*

I wanted to push the subject further, to tell him that it wasn't just the noise that was bothering me, but the sense of something darker. But I knew how Khaja was!

Once he made up his mind to ignore something, it was as good as forgotten.

He wasn't the type to dwell on things he couldn't control. I envied that about him—his ability to compartmentalize, to let things roll off his back.

But I couldn't do the same.

The longer I stayed at ABK township, the more those sounds burrowed into my mind. They weren't just noise anymore—they were a question, a mystery I couldn't ignore. Every time I heard those weak, muffled crying, I felt the same creeping sense of dread. It wasn't just a family having a bad day. It was something more. Something hidden.

And as much as Khaja tried to brush it off, I couldn't help but wonder if, deep down, it bothered him too.

One night, as we sat in his living room playing games, I noticed him glance toward the wall when the familiar sounds started up again, the low murmured voices, the sharp tone of an argument, and the inevitable crying that followed. His reaction was subtle and barely a flicker of attention—but it was there. A moment of recognition, of acknowledgment, before he quickly turned back to the screen, pretending not to notice.

It was small, but it was enough to make me realize that Khaja wasn't as unaffected as he seemed. Maybe he didn't want to admit it, maybe he thought it didn't matter, but the truth was there, in the way his eyes remained on that wall for just a second too long.

"Come on, man," he said, grabbing the joystick and flipping through games, *"Let's not think about it. It's just noise."*

But I couldn't stop thinking about it. Putting on my shoes, I got my bag and waved *goodbye* to Khaja. I knew that the next time I came back; I'd be doing more than just visiting Khaja. I was going to start digging. I was going to find out who lived in that apartment next door. and I was going to figure out what was really going on behind those closed doors.

I took one last look at the wall separating us from the mysterious flat, feeling a tremble running down my spine. Whatever secrets were being hidden behind that wall, I had a feeling that they weren't the kind of secrets someone was supposed to uncover.

And I was going to do it anyway.

CHAPTER II

The Unsettling Sounds.

"Hush the tranquillity"

"It always started at the same time."

One day, I happened to stay back over at Khaja's place after a late night of work, being too tired to head home. We had been up talking about everything and nothing, the TV droning in the background while the soft glow of streetlights filtered through the blinds. Khaja had gone to bed, but I stayed awake, restless, lying on the couch in the living room. I couldn't shake the feeling that had been gnawing at me for weeks now, the sense that something was wrong in that apartment next door.

And then, right on cue, it began—the familiar sound of a child's cry. At first, it was soft, almost imperceptible, like a whimper. But it quickly escalated into something sharper, more distressed. I sat up, listening, my pulse quickening. The cry grew louder, more insistent, and then came the voices—the muffled arguments, the rise and fall of angry tone. I couldn't make out the words, but I could hear the tension,

the frustration and the fear.

I swung my legs over the side of the couch and stood up, my bare feet pressing onto the cold tile floor. The TV was still on, casting flickering shadows around the room, but I muted it, straining to hear more clearly. The argument was louder now, extremely aggressive, and the child's sobbing seemed to echo through the walls. It felt as though the sounds were vibrating through the very air, pressing against my skin.

I glanced at Khaja's bedroom door, hesitating if I should wake him.

But I knew it was pointless. He'd just brush it off like he always did and would tell me it was nothing, just the neighbors having a rough night. I wasn't interested to hear them all again. I needed to understand what was happening.

The cry continued, relentless. I slowly walked toward the wall that separated Khaja's flat from the neighboring one, my heart pounding in my chest. The sounds were so clear now, as though they were coming from the same room. The argument was scaling up, voices being overlapped, and then... silence. On a sudden note, the painful tears stopped, it made me freeze in place. The sudden quiet felt like a vacuum, sucking the air out of the room.

I pressed my ear to the wall, holding my breath. Nothing. Absolute silence.

For a moment, I wondered if maybe it was over—maybe the argument had stopped, and the child had finally fallen asleep. But just as I was about to step back, I heard it, a low, muffled thud, followed by a sharp intake of breath. Then, the crying started again, but this time it was different. It wasn't the sound of a child throwing a tantrum. It was the sound of fear. Raw, desperate fear.

It felt as if the time stopped. I stepped away from the wall, my hands shaking slightly. What was I supposed to do?

I couldn't just stand there and listen to this. But what could I say?

Khaja had already made it clear that he didn't want to get involved, and a part of me knew he was right. What would I even say if I go over there?

"Hey, I hear you yelling at your kid, mind keeping it down?"

It sounded absurd.

But something about tonight was different. The crying, the argument, it was too much intense. It didn't feel like a regular family fight. It felt like something was wrong. Deeply, disturbingly wrong.

I turned and glanced toward Khaja's bedroom again. The door was shut, and there was no sound from inside—he was probably fast asleep. I could feel my pulse pounding in my ears, the weight of the silence pressing down on me. I knew I wouldn't be able to sleep, not like this. Not with those sounds still ringing in my mind.

I took a deep breath and walked toward the door.

My hand hovered over the doorknob of our flat, hesitating.

What was I planning to do?

Go over there and confront them?

Knock on their door and demand answers?

I knew how insane it sounded, but my gut feeling wouldn't let go. I had to do something. I couldn't just ignore it anymore.

I slowly unlocked the door, pulling it open as quietly as I could. The hallway outside was bathed in the same dim, fluttering light's that seemed to be perpetually stuck in ABK township. It was as silent as death.

No sounds from the other flats, no movement, nothing. The air felt thick and heavy like the entire building was holding its breath, waiting for something to happen.

I stepped out into the hallway, the door closing softly behind me. My footsteps felt too loud against the cold floor, echoing unnaturally in the silence. I stood there for a moment, staring at the door to the neighboring flat. The same door I had walked past so many times, always closed, always silent. But now, the quiet felt ominous, like something was hiding just behind it, waiting for me to make the first move.

My heart pounding in my chest, I approached the door. I stopped just a few feet away, my hand hovering in the air, unsure whether to knock. I tried hearing again, pressing my ear to the cold wood. The crying had stopped, but I could hear something—a faint rustling as if someone was moving quietly inside.

My mind raced with thousands of thoughts, each one more unsettling than the last.

What was happening in there?

Why did it feel so wrong?

I stood there, frozen, debating whether to knock or retreat back into Khaja's flat. But just as I made up my mind to step away, I heard it, a soft, barely audible whisper.

It wasn't coming from behind the door, I felt as if It was coming from right next to me.

I spun around, my breath catching in my throat. The hallway was empty. There was no one there, no one behind me. But I had heard it. A voice, just for a second, as clear as day. And then... nothing.

I stood there for what felt like an eternity, my impulses racing, trying to make sense of what had just happened. The hallway was silent again, but I could still feel the presence of something, hanging around just out of reach, hidden in the shadows.

Without thinking, I took a step back, away from the door. My hands were sweating, and the air around me felt colder than it should have been. I didn't know what I had just heard, but I knew one thing for certain:

Whatever was happening in that apartment was more than just a family argument. And it wasn't something I could ignore anymore.

Something that I was failing at letting it go.

I had retreated back into Khaja's flat, locking the door behind me and trying to convince myself it was nothing, the feeling of dread lingered. I sat back down on the couch, but the unease was still there, gnawing at the edges of my mind. My heart hadn't quite settled, and every creak, every distant hum in the building felt like an extension of the strange energy I had encountered in the hallway.

I stared at the TV, but the screen was just a blur. My thoughts kept drifting back to the door next to Khaja's flat, to the whisper I heard in the hallway—so soft, so real, yet so out of place. It had only lasted a second, but that second felt eternal. It was enough to plant a seed of doubt, a question I couldn't shake: ***Was someone, or something, in that apartment trying to communicate with me?***

I glanced toward Khaja's closed bedroom door again, half-expecting him to emerge and tell me I was being ridiculous, that I was letting my imagination get the best of me. But he didn't come out. He was asleep, blissfully unaware of the growing storm of confusion and fear building inside my mind. He didn't hear what I heard. He didn't feel the oppressive weight of the silence that followed the disturbances.

I looked at the clock. It was past 2 a.m. The crying had stopped hours ago, but the memory of it still echoed in my ears. I stood up, pacing the living room, trying to make sense of it all.

What was it about that apartment?

Why had no one seen the kids?

Why did the voices always seem to follow the same pattern, the same cycle of arguments and sobbing?

I replayed everything in my mind—the crying, the muffled arguments, the strange rustling sounds, the way the noises would stop so abruptly, as though someone had flipped a switch. And then, of course, there was the whisper in the hallway. That was the part that really stuck with me, the part that refused to fade. It had felt so close, so real like someone had leaned in just behind me and spoken softly in my ear.

But no one had been there.

I wanted to wake up Khaja and tell him what I had experienced, but I already knew how the conversation would go. He'd laugh it off and would tell me I was overthinking. And maybe he was right. Maybe I was letting my mind get carried away, letting the late hour and the sinister atmosphere of the building mess with my head. But there was something deep inside me constantly telling me that, this wasn't just my imagination. Something real was happening here—something I couldn't explain.

I sat back down on the couch and stared at the wall separating Khaja's flat from the one next door. My curiosity was in full bloom now, overtaking any sense of logic I had tried to cling to. The more I thought about it, the more I realized that I couldn't just leave it alone. I needed to know what was happening in that apartment. I needed to understand why the sounds never changed, and why no one ever saw the children. Why do the arguments follow such a strange, unbroken pattern?

I leaned forward, resting my elbows on my knees, my mind racing with possibilities. Could it be something as simple as a dysfunctional family?

A couple struggling with parenting, with the frustrations of life in close quarters?

Maybe. But then why the secrecy?

Why had no one in the building ever seen the kids?

And what about the whisper I had heard? Was it just in my head, or had something—someone—really been trying to get my attention?

I didn't have answers, but I knew one thing for certain: I wasn't going to let this go. I couldn't. I had to find out what was going on, even if it meant pushing Khaja out of his comfortable denial and dragging him into the mess with me.

The sound of footsteps from the hallway interrupted my thoughts. I froze, my eyes snapping toward the front door. The footsteps were soft, barely audible, but distinct—someone was walking down the hallway outside.

My heart pounded in my chest as I listened, straining to make out the direction they were coming from.

They grew louder, moving closer to Khaja's door. For a moment, I thought whoever it was might stop, knock even, but the footsteps continued, passing by the flat and fading into the distance. I stood up and walked over to the door, peeking through the peephole. The hallway outside was empty, just as it had been every time I had looked before. Whoever had walked by was gone.

I stood there for a long moment, my mind racing. The footsteps, the whispers, the crying—it all started to blur together in my mind, twisting into a tangled web of fear and curiosity. I couldn't shake the feeling that something was deeply wrong in ABK township, something more than just noisy neighbors.

That night was long and still in my head,

The next morning Khaja looked at my eyes being red, with all the concern he asked,

"You didn't sleep last night?"

I was still zoned out, I just nodded.

Khaja tried comforting me with his words,

"It may be because of the new place?" I was listening to him, but I was in a state of being unable to answer, and I expressed what all happened last night, listening to me he said,

"Man, it can be your imagination, stop worrying.'

I wasn't imagining.

I couldn't be.

He left for his jog and I tried resting for a while.

Every night, just after midnight, the noises would begin again, almost like clockwork. I had been staying at Khaja's flat more often, partially because of work, but mostly because I couldn't push off the sense that something was deeply wrong in the apartment next door. And every night, without fail, the cycle repeated itself.

The crying came first. Always soft at the start, like a child trying to muffle their sobs so they wouldn't be heard. I would lie there on the couch, staring at the ceiling, waiting for it to build. I knew it would.

After the cry the arguments followed by muffled voices, rising and falling like a tide, words lost behind the thin walls but the tone unmistakable. It was always angry, always tense. It felt like something was about to snap every time I heard it.

The arguments were laid down by the silence. That was the part that got me the most, the way everything would stop so abruptly, like as if someone hit pause on a recording. The silence was heavy, and oppressive, pressing down on the flat and making the air feel thicker, and harder to breathe. It was the kind of silence that wasn't natural. It was too complete, too sudden as if the building had stopped to listen.

I could never hear anything during the day. ABK township was noisy enough, with tenants going about their lives, and the hum of the city outside. But once night fell, everything seemed to change. The building would settle into an unnatural and quiet, and the noises from the neighboring flat would rise out of that quiet, creeping into Khaja's flat as if something was alive.

The first few times I heard it, I told myself that they were just a coincidence like *Kids cry, families argue, and apartment walls are notoriously thin.* But by the third or fourth night, I couldn't ignore the regularity of it. Midnight.

Every single time.

I remember lying there one night, exhausted but unable to sleep, waiting for the cry to start again. It was 12:04 a.m. when I checked my phone. It was like, the walls were noting the time, like the disturbances were with some kind of twisted schedule.

Khaja had already gone to bed. He had become so used to the noise that it didn't seem to bother him anymore. But to me, it was impossible to tune it out. Every time I thought it was over, it would start again—louder, closer, more insistent.

I sat up, swinging my legs over the side of the couch. The TV was still on, casting a faint glow across the room, but I had muted it, unwilling to let any more noise add to the chaos in my mind. My eyes drifted to the wall, the one separating us from the mischievous neighboring flat. The crying was louder tonight, more desperate.

I knew what would come next. The argument. Those angry voices. I waited for it, my hands clenched in my lap, my pulse quickening with every second that passed. And then, right on time, the argument started. I couldn't make out the words—just the rising and falling cadence of anger, frustration, and things else that I couldn't quite place. Fear, maybe.

I checked my phone again. 12:07 a.m. It always follows the same pattern. Always the same. Always predictable. And that predictability made it worse. It was like the apartment next door was trapped in an endless loop, repeating the same cycle night after night, without any resolution. Just a wheel of crying, arguing, and silence ending with no result.

I found myself wondering what kind of family could live like this.

What kind of parents could subject their kids to this every night?

And why had no one else noticed? Why hadn't anyone said anything?

The worst part wasn't just the sounds to themselves—it was the fact that they seemed to exist only at night when the rest of the world was asleep when no one else could hear them but **me**. It was as if the walls had chosen me as their audience, forcing me to listen to a performance that I couldn't escape.

I stood up and walked to the wall, pressing my ear against the cold plaster. The crying was louder now, punctuated by the sharp rise of a woman's voice, scolding and yelling!

I strained to catch a single word, anything that would give me a clue about what was happening over there. But as always, the words were muffled, formless, lost in the barrier between us.

Still, I knew what I was hearing. I knew something was wrong. I just didn't yet know what they were.

I pulled myself away from the wall, feeling the shiver through. Every period of the moon, at the same clock. The same track. And, the same question haunted me:

*"**What exactly was going on behind that door?**"*

"You're overthinking this, man."

was the only phrase I had heard from Khaja at least a dozen times in the past few weeks. Every time I brought up the noises, every time I hinted that something was off in the neighboring flat, his response was the same as usual: a shrug, a dismissive wave of his hand, and that sentence—like it was enough to explain away everything.

But it wasn't enough. Not for me.

We were sitting in his living room again, the TV being on in the background, though neither of us was really watching it. I had tried to ignore the sounds from next door, tried to focus on the movie playing on the screen, but the low murmur of voices from the other side of the wall was seeping through again. This time, it wasn't just the child's crying. It was the adults—their muffled, angry voices filtering through the walls like the thrum of distant thunder. I had learned to recognize the tones, even if I couldn't understand the words.

"I'm serious, Khaja,"

I said with my frustration creeping into my voice.

"Doesn't it bother you? The way it's always the same? The crying, the arguing, every night like clockwork?"

Khaja barely glanced away from his phone.

"Bro, we've been through this. It's just a family going through stuff. Maybe the kids are going through a phase, or the parents are stressed. It's not our business."

I shot back, *"It's been weeks,"*

the irritation rising in my chest.

"No one cries like that for weeks. And have you ever seen them? The kids, I mean. I've never seen them outside. Not once."

Khaja finally looked up from his phone, his brow furrowing slightly.

"You're really worked up about this, huh?"

I admitted,

"Yes,"

the tension clear in my voice.

"Yes, I am. Because this isn't normal, Khaja. There's something wrong in that apartment, and we're just sitting here pretending it's not happening."

Khaja sighed leaning back on the couch, putting his phone aside he said.

"Look, I get that it's weird. But what do you want me to do? Go knock on their door and ask them to stop arguing. The situation is definitely not ours.

I pressed.

"But what if it's more than that?"

What if something's really wrong in there? We're hearing the same thing every night—the same pattern. It's too... structured. It doesn't feel like just any normal family argument."

Khaja rubbed his temples, clearly growing tired of the conversation.

"Man, I've lived in apartments all my life. This stuff happens. Families quarrel, and kids cry. You just don't get involved unless it's a real problem. And so far, it's just noise. That's it!"

His casual dismissal fuelled my frustration. It wasn't just noise—it was a pattern, a routine, something that had become so predictable that I couldn't believe no one else was noticing it. How could Khaja sit there, night after night, listening to the same sounds and not feel even a shred of concern?

I stood up, pacing the room, trying to let the tension out of my body.

"I just don't understand how you can ignore it. You're right here, every night. You hear it too."

I muttered.

Khaja shrugged again, his tone softening as he spoke.

"Yeah, I hear it. But what am I supposed to do? Go to the building management and tell them the neighbors are fighting. They'll just tell me it's not their problem. And honestly, it's not like they're smashing windows or anything. It's just arguing. I've heard worse."

I stopped pacing and turned to face him.

"It's more than just arguing. I can feel it."

Khaja looked up at me, the hint of a frown pulling at the corners of his mouth.

"You're letting it get to you. I think you're overthinking it, letting your imagination run wild."

I opened my mouth to protest, but I could see in his eyes that he wasn't going to budge. Khaja had already made up his mind that it was nothing more than a typical family issue, and no amount of convincing was going to change that. He wasn't wired to dwell on things the way I was. He had the ability to let things slide off his back, while I was stuck turning every little detail over in my mind, trying to make sense of it all.

Khaja continued *"I'm just saying, maybe you should stop focusing on it so much. The more you think about it, the weirder it'll seem. Let it go, man."*

Let it go?

How could I let it go when it was right there, every past 12 PM, a constant reminder that something wasn't right?

I took a deep breath, trying to calm the frustration that was wrapping me up inside me. Khaja wasn't going to help. That was clear. He had made up his mind that this was nothing, just noise, and I was making too much of it.

But it wasn't nothing. And I couldn't just sit by and pretend it was all nothing.

"Fine,"

I muttered, sinking back down onto the couch.

"Maybe you're right."

Listening to me, Khaja smiled, clearly relieved that the conversation was over. He picked up the remote and turned up the volume on the TV, drowning out the muffled voices from next door. But I wasn't done. Not by a long shot.

No matter how much Khaja tried to convince me, I knew what I was hearing. And the more he ignored it, the more determined I became to figure it out.

I didn't say anything else for the rest of the night. But as the argument next door faded into silence, I made a promise to myself:

if Khaja wasn't going to do anything about it, I would.

The cry wasn't just getting louder, it was getting deeper.

I had been noticing it for a few nights now, the cry from the neighboring flat seemed to intensify, at first, it had been faint, a distant sound that barely broke through the walls. But now, it was unmistakable, louder, more desperate, almost as if the child had gotten closer. Pressing up against the wall just like I had been, trying to reach out for something or someone.

The least I could say was It was unsettling. The louder the crying became, the more restless I grew. It wasn't just noise anymore, it felt... *like a prayer for help*. Each night, as I lay on Khaja's couch, the cry started getting earlier, lasted longer, and pierced through the thin walls like a jagged knife.

I couldn't escape it. Even when I wasn't at Khaja's place, the sound would replay in my head, creeping into my thoughts during the day, sticking around like an echo of something constantly pushing me that I should have done it, it used to feel like a calling. I would find myself in the middle of a conversation at work, distracted, my mind suddenly drifting back to the muffled sobs I had heard the night before.

The worst part was the desperation in it—the kind of crying that came deep within, the kind that wasn't just about being scolded or punished. It was a kind of fear I recognized, though I wasn't sure why. It got under my skin, and the more I heard it, the more I knew I couldn't ignore it anymore.

It turned louder now. Too loud to pretend it wasn't happening. Too loud to write it off as just another tantrum. The child was terrified, I could hear it in every sob, every breathless gasp for air.

One night, as the crying reached its peak, I sat up on the bed, staring at the wall that passed the flow of noises to us from the neighboring flat. My heart started to race, my palms sweating. I had been trying to sleep, but the sound kept pulling me back into a state of hyper-awareness.

I glanced at the clock ticking 11:58 p.m.

It was earlier than usual. Normally, the sobbing would start after midnight, part of that strange routine I had come to expect. But tonight, it had started earlier, louder, more insistent. My pulse quickened as the familiar sound of an argument followed the crying. The same pattern, but more intensed, more violent. It was as if the tension was in the building, the cycle spiraling out of control.

I tried to steady my breath, but my mind was racing. I couldn't just sit there and listen anymore. I needed to do something. Anything.

I stood up, pacing the room, my bare feet padding softly against the cold tile. The painful sound of the crying filled the small living space, making it feel even smaller as if the walls were closing in around me. I could hear the child now, clear as in day—every sob, every plea, every cry for mercy that was being ignored by the adults on the other side of the wall.

My hands clenched into fists by my sides.

I wanted to scream, to pound on the wall, to shout at them to stop. But I didn't. I couldn't.

I wasn't even sure what I was afraid of, but the fear was there, palpable, hanging in the air like smoke. I wanted to believe Khaja's explanation—that it was just a family with problems, that it was none of our business—but the louder the crying became, the less I believed him.

Because this wasn't just a family problem. It was something darker, something I didn't yet understand fully.

Pressing my ear to the wall, I tried to make out more of the argument, trying to pick up on the words being exchanged between the adults. But as always, the words were lost in the muffled echoes of anger. I couldn't make any sense of it. All I knew was that the child's scream was getting louder, and more desperate, and the argument's growing more heated.

And then, suddenly, it stopped.

The silence was so abrupt that I almost stumbled back from the wall. One minute, the flat next door was filled with the sounds of a child's sobbing and an argument teetering on the edge of violence.

The next, there was nothing.

I stood there, frozen, my ear still pressed against the wall, straining to hear anything—any small sound that would break the oppressive quiet. But there was nothing. Just the faint hum of the refrigerator from Khaja's kitchen, the distant buzz of the city outside.

For the first time, I realized I was holding my breath. I tried to let it out slowly, trying to calm my nerves. But the silence wasn't reassuring. It was heavy, and thick, as if the entire building was holding its breath along with me, waiting for something to happen.

I stepped back from the wall, my mind scrambling.

What had just happened? Why had the crying stopped so suddenly?

And why does this silence feel so wrong?

I wanted to wake Khaja and tell him that this wasn't any normal, that we needed to work something out. Knowing what he would be saying I struggled to be myself, maybe it was just my mind playing tricks on me. Maybe the family had finally calmed down, and the child had fallen asleep.

But deep down, I knew that it wasn't the phase. The crying had stopped too abruptly, and completely. It wasn't the sound of a child who had been soothed or who had cried themselves to sleep. It was the sound of being silenced forcefully for long.

I stood there staring at the wall marking the time, waiting for the noise to start again. But it didn't. The flat next door remained as if nothing had ever happened. **Similar to the quiet of death**

I didn't sleep that night. I couldn't. Because the crying continues to ring in my ears, louder than ever. And I couldn't shake the feeling that whatever had happened next door was far worse than anything I had imagined.

I had to do something. - I spoke to myself

The tearing throat, the raising voices, and the never-ending arguments seated night to night.

They were getting worse, louder, and more desperate. Each night, I found myself growing more and more agitated, more convinced that whatever was happening behind those walls, was far more than just a family squabble. It was something darker, something dangerous. But it wasn't just the noise anymore—it was the silence that followed. The sudden, unnatural quiet that seemed to swallow everything, as if the entire world stopped to listen, and then it... fell silent in a snap of an eye.

The unexpected turning started to drive me insane.

I tried to push it out of my mind, to convince myself that it wasn't my problem. Khaja had done a good job by telling me to let it go, to leave it alone.

But, how could I?

The noise was alive, pressing against my thoughts like a weight I couldn't lift. And no matter how hard I tried to ignore it, it kept pulling me back.

The following night, the noise started earlier than usual, just after 11:30 p.m. The suffering cry was louder than ever and echoed through Khaja's flat as if the source was being right beside me. It wasn't the normal sobbing. It was worse—frantic, breathless. I could hear the child gasping for air between the sobs, pleading in muffled words that were unable to form into a sentence.

I could feel my pulse quickening, I stood in the living room, listening. It wasn't just an argument anymore. The panic in the child's voice, the desperation—it was too much. Things happening next door, sensed Something bad.

The argument started up again, but this time, it wasn't a back-and-forth exchange. The voices were sharper, angrier, cutting through the walls like blades. The woman's voice—always a little too harsh, had taken on a sharper edge, her words rapid and filled with venom. The man's voice came next, lower, more controlled, but intense. The child's cry grew louder, drowning out the argument until it became the only sound in the room.

I couldn't take it anymore.

Without thinking, I grabbed the keys to the flat from the table and walked out of the flat, the door clicking shut behind me with a quiet finality. I stood in the hallway, bathed in the dim, flickering light that always seemed to make ABK township feel like a different place at night. The crying was even clearer out here, no longer muffled by Khaja's walls. I could hear the sobs, the gasps, the stifled words, all too real, too close.

I turned toward the neighboring flat, my heart pounding in my chest. The door was just a few steps away, plain and unassuming, like any other door in this building. But behind it, I could feel the tension, the fear, the violence brewing. I stood there, my hand hovering over the door, unsure of what to do.

Should I knock?

Should I call out?

What if they answered? What would I even say?

Even before I could make a decision, the weeping stopped.

Just like that, as if someone had flipped a switch, the flat fell silent. The sudden quiet hit me like a punch to the gut, making me freeze in place. One moment, the air was filled with the desperate sobs of a child. The next, there was nothing.

I stood there, staring at the door, being unable to believe it.

what had just happened?

Why had the crying stopped so suddenly? I took a step closer, pressing my ear to the door, straining to hear anything—any movement, any sign of life. But there was only silence.

My hand hovered over the door again, this time closer to knocking. I could feel the cold metal beneath my fingertips, my knuckles just inches from making contact. But was stopped by something.

It was the silence.

It wasn't the comforting kind of silence you'd expect after a child has finally calmed down. It was thick, too absolute, like the entire building was trying to hold its breath. I knew that knocking wouldn't break that silence—it would only make it even worse. Because whatever was happening behind that door, it definitely didn't want to be disturbed.

With a heavy heart, I stepped back, my hand was shivering, though I wasn't sure why.

Why had I come out here being driven with every intention of knocking, of confronting whoever was inside, of asking what was going on? But now, with the silence pressing in on me, I couldn't do it. A deep insight warned me that it wasn't safe, that knocking on that door wouldn't bring the answers I was looking for. It would only bring more questions.

I took another step back, my back pressing against the opposite wall. The hallway was still empty with the flickering lights projecting long shadows that danced across the floor. It felt like the entire building was watching me, waiting to see what I would do next.

But I couldn't do anything.

It felt like hours standing there, staring at the door, my mind spinning with possibilities. What had stopped the crying abruptly?

Why had the argument fallen silent?

And most importantly, why did I feel like I was standing on the edge of something I couldn't understand?

I didn't knock. I couldn't.

After what felt like an endlessness, I turned and walked back to Khaja's flat, my footsteps loudening in the empty hallway. The door closed behind me with a soft click, sealing me off from whatever was happening next door.

I sank onto the couch, my heart still racing, my hands trembling. The silence from the neighboring flat was louder than any of the noise that we had ever heard, filling the room with a tension I couldn't escape. I sat there, staring at the wall, waiting for the crying to start again.

But it didn't.

That night, the crying didn't return.

And for the first time, I wasn't sure if that made me feel better or worse.

It had been a few days since my failed attempt to confront the neighbors. Since that night, the noises had quieted down, almost as if they knew I had tried to interfere.

The crying hadn't returned, but the silence that replaced it was worse. The oppressive, unnatural quiet that followed me through every hallway, down every stairwell of ABK township, had grown heavier. Even Khaja noticed it, though he never mentioned it directly.

The strange tension that had built between us since I started questioning the sounds that were still there, hanging over our conversations like an unspoken warning.

But it wasn't just Khaja. The entire building seemed different. The tenants, the few I ever saw, moved through the hallways quickly, avoiding eye contact, their footsteps unnaturally quiet. The place felt abandoned, though I knew it wasn't.

It was that feeling of being watched, of something lurking just beneath the surface—that led me to ask the watchman about the neighbors. I didn't expect much but just a casual conversation, maybe a little insight into who they were. But his reaction was anything but casual.

I had caught him the security guard, by the lobby late one evening as I was coming back from work. He was sitting behind the desk, reading a newspaper, his eyes tired and his posture slouched.

There was nothing unusual about him—he was the same older man I'd seen a hundred times before, a permanent fixture in the building. But tonight, when I approached him, something in his demeanor changed. The moment I mentioned the family on the 13th floor, his expression shifted. His easy, tired posture stiffened, and his eyes flickered with something that I couldn't quite place, The fear, maybe. Or was it something else?

I asked him, trying to keep my tone light.

"What do you know about the family living next to my friend's flat on the 13th floor?"

The watchman's gaze darted toward the elevator, then back to me, his lips pressed into a thin line. He didn't answer right away, and the silence that followed felt long, and deliberate.

"I'm not sure what you're talking about,"

He finally said, but the lie was clear in his voice. His eyes gave him away. He knew something.

"The family next door,"

I pressed.

"They have kids, right?

We hear them all the time—crying, arguing. I was just wondering if you've ever noticed anything... strange?"

The watchman's jaw tightened. He looked down at his newspaper, then back up at me, his face unreadable.

"You should leave it alone,"

he said quietly, his voice barely above a whisper.

I frowned, caught off guard by the sudden seriousness in his tone.

"What do you mean?"

He glanced around the empty lobby, his eyes darting to the shadows in the corners as if making sure no one else was listening.

"The people on the 13th floor... they've been here a long time. Longer than most of the tenants."

I leaned in closer, my curiosity piqued.

"What do you mean? Have you seen them? Do you know what's going on in there?"

The watchman shook his head quickly, almost too quickly.

"I don't ask questions. It's not my job to interfere. People move in and out all the time, and I keep to myself. But..."

He hesitated, his eyes shifting toward the elevator again.

"That family... they've always been different. And you're not the first person to notice the noises."

My stomach twisted.

"What do you mean I'm not the first?"

The watchman sighed, his shoulders slumping as if he had been carrying a burden too heavy to bear, and said, if you want to know any more details, meet me at the basement.

"Basement?"

I questioned,

To my surprise he said,

"There's a reason we're meeting down here."

The watchman's words echoed in my mind as I descended the narrow staircase into the basement of ABK township. The air felt different down here—heavier, colder. Each step I took sent a hollow echo reverberating through the dimly lit stairwell as if the building itself was warning me to turn back. But I couldn't. I had to know what he meant, what secrets he was hiding. And more than that, I had to understand the strange, suffocating presence that seemed to hover over the 13th floor.

The stairs seemed to stretch on longer than I remembered, each step taking me deeper into a world that felt more and more removed from the ordinary. The air grew colder as I went, and I could smell something faint but unsettling—a mix of dust and dampness like a place long forgotten.

When I finally reached the bottom, the basement stretched out before me, dimly lit by a few flickering overhead lights. The space was vast, with rows of old storage units and forgotten boxes, their contents long abandoned by tenants who had come and gone. It was the kind of place no one came unless they had to.

And tonight, I had to.

In the far corner, the watchman stood waiting, his silhouette outlined against the shadows that loomed around him. He looked smaller down here, hunched as if the weight of whatever he was about to tell me had shrunk him. His face was partially hidden beneath the brim of his cap, but even from a distance, I could sense his unease.

I walked over slowly, the soft scuff of my shoes on the concrete floor breaking the thick silence. The closer I got to him, the stronger the feeling that something was deeply wrong in this building settled over me. The walls seemed to close in, their cracked surfaces and exposed pipes barely holding back something darker, something that had been hidden here for years.

"You came,"

he said, his voice low and gravelly as if he'd been whispering secrets in the dark for far too long. His eyes flickered toward me, filled with a nervous energy that immediately made me question if I should be here at all.

"*I had to,*" I replied, trying to keep my voice steady. "*You said you had answers.*"

He nodded slowly, glancing around the basement as if to make sure we were truly alone.

"*There's a reason we're meeting down here,*"

he repeated his voice barely above a whisper.

"*Upstairs... it watches. It listens. But down here, it's quieter. Safer.*"

I frowned, unsure what he meant. "*What listens? What watches?*"

The watchman's eyes shifted to the ceiling for just a moment, before returning to mine. "*The building. Or... something in it. Whatever's been here, it knows when people start asking questions.*"

A cold shiver ran down my spine. I'd expected strange answers, but this was more than I'd bargained for. "*What are you talking about?*"

I asked, my voice lowering instinctively to match his. "*What is it that knows?*"

He let out a long sigh, like someone who'd been holding their breath for too long.

"*I don't know what it is. No one does. But I've been here long enough to see it. To feel it. It's like the building's alive, but not in the way you'd expect. It reacts when people notice the flat. The one next to your friend's place. It doesn't like attention.*"

I stared at him, my mind racing.

"*The flat?*"

I said, the words almost catching in my throat.

"*You mean the family next door?*"

The watchman nodded slowly, his face shadowed beneath the dim light.

"*They've been here longer than anyone else,*"

he said quietly.

"*But no one really sees them. You've noticed that, haven't you? The noises, the arguments, the crying... but have you ever actually seen them?*"

I swallowed hard, memories of the past weeks flooding back to me. He was right. I hadn't. I'd heard them almost every night—the child's desperate sobs, the adults' muffled arguments—but I'd never seen them. Not once.

"No,"

I admitted.

"I haven't."

The watchman's expression darkened, as if he had expected my answer but still dreaded hearing it.*"You're not the first to notice,"*

he said.

"But those who do... well, they either leave or they disappear."

"Disappear?"

I repeated, my voice dropping lower. The word sent a jolt of fear through me.

"What do you mean disappear?"

He hesitated for a moment as if weighing whether or not to tell me the full truth. *"Tenants who've lived on the 13th floor,"*

he said slowly,

"they hear the noises, just like you. They ask questions, just like you. But after a while, they either move out suddenly—no goodbyes, no forwarding addresses—or... they vanish. Their apartments are left empty, untouched as if they never lived there."

I felt my heart pounding in my chest. This was worse than I'd imagined. *"And you don't know why?"*

The watchman shook his head, his hands trembling slightly. *"I don't know what it is. But whatever's in that flat, it's been here a long time. It doesn't like being disturbed. And it doesn't like people asking questions."*

I opened my mouth to speak, but the words wouldn't come. My mind was reeling with the implications of what he was saying. People vanishing, the flat reacting to attention, the building itself somehow... alive? It sounded impossible, but I couldn't shake the growing dread in my gut. I had heard the noises. I had felt the wrongness in the air. There was something here—something hidden beneath the surface.

"You have to be careful," the watchman warned, his voice hushed. *"Now that you've noticed, now that you've started looking... it's watching you too. You need to stop. You need to leave before it gets worse."*

I stared at him, my pulse racing. *"What happens if I don't?"*

His eyes locked onto mine, filled with a fear that made my skin crawl. *"Then it'll find you."* *"You weren't the first one to ask."*

The watchman's words hung in the cold air of the basement, sending a chill down my spine. The dim, flickering light overhead cast long shadows that danced across the damp walls, making the space feel even more oppressive than it already was. His tone carried the weight of countless secrets—secrets that had festered in this building for years, maybe decades.

I stepped closer to him, the hairs on the back of my neck standing up. "What do you mean? Who else asked about the family?"

The watchman shifted uncomfortably, his eyes flicking toward the stairwell as if he expected someone—or something—to descend at any moment. *"Tenants,"* he said softly, almost as if he didn't want to say the words aloud. *"People who used to live on the 13th floor. They heard the noises too, just like you."*

He leaned back against the wall, letting out a heavy sigh, the kind that comes from carrying too much for too long. *"The thing is,"* he continued, *"no one stays there for long. The ones who do start noticing things... they always leave. And some of them? Well, they disappear."*

My stomach twisted. *"Disappear? What do you mean?"*

His eyes narrowed, and for a moment, he looked like a man haunted by what he had seen—by what he knew. *"The ones who stay too long, the ones who dig too deep... they vanish. Their apartments are left untouched, their things still inside. But they're gone. It's like they were erased from the building entirely."*

I stared at him, the implications of his words sinking in. *"And no one does anything? No investigations? No police?"*

He shook his head, his expression dark. *"When people ask questions, they get stonewalled. Management brushes it off and says the tenants just moved out. They're good at covering things up. I've seen it happen. The police don't even bother. It's like everyone's agreed to pretend it never happened."*

The weight of his words pressed down on me, but I couldn't let go of the nagging questions forming in my mind. *"What do you think happened to them? The ones who disappeared?"*

The watchman was silent for a long moment as if considering how much to tell me. When he finally spoke, his voice was low and grim. *"I don't know. I've been here for over fifteen years, and I've seen people come and go. The ones who disappeared... I never saw them leave. And it's not just people moving out without notice. It's like they're swallowed by this place. And once they're gone, the building doesn't remember them."*

The building doesn't remember them. The words sent a shiver through me, their meaning chilling in its vagueness. I tried to wrap my head around what he was saying, but nothing made sense. How could a building make people disappear? How could it erase them from existence?

"And the family next door," I pressed. *"The one making the noises. What do you know about them?"*

The watchman hesitated, his eyes flickering with something close to fear. *"They've been here longer than anyone else,"* he said quietly. *"Longer than any tenant, longer than me. But no one knows much about them. No one's ever seen the kids, at least not in person. We hear them, sure, but no one ever sees them outside, playing in the halls, nothing."*

"How is that possible?" I asked, trying to keep my voice steady. *"How can they live here for years and no one ever sees them?"*

He shrugged, his face a mask of resignation. *"I don't know. I've tried to figure it out myself, but every time I get close, something stops me. It's like the building itself pushes back. Whenever people ask too many questions, the sounds get worse. More intense."*

I swallowed hard, my mind racing. *"Do you think they're real? The family, I mean. Do you think they actually live there, or... or is it something else?"*

The watchman's face darkened, and for a moment, I saw real fear in his eyes. *"I've thought about that a lot. I don't know if they're real in the way you and I are. But they're there. I hear them. You hear them. The others who used to live here... they all heard them too."*

He paused, looking down at the cold, damp floor beneath us. *"But there's something wrong with them. Something is not quite... right. I've heard the arguments, the crying, just like you have. But no matter what, the family never seems to change. It's always the same. The same voices, the same sounds. Night after night, like they're stuck in some kind of loop."*

A chill ran through me. I thought back to all the nights I had heard the crying, the shouting, and the eerie silence that followed. He was right—it was always the same. The same pattern, the same tone, the same desperation. I had never really noticed it before, but now that he had pointed it out, I couldn't unhear it.

"Do you think it's haunting?" I asked, my voice barely above a whisper. It felt ridiculous to even say the words, but in this basement, with the air so cold and the watchman's fear so real, it didn't seem that far-fetched.

The watchman shook his head slowly. *"I don't know if it's a haunting, or something else. But whatever it is, it's been here a long time. It's tied to this place. The family, the noises—they're not just tenants. They're part of the building. And once you start noticing them, once you start paying attention... it's hard to stop."*

I felt a knot tightening in my stomach. The pieces were starting to come together, but the picture they were forming was dark, distorted, and filled with shadows I didn't want to face. *"Why are you telling me this?"* I asked, my voice tense. "If it's so dangerous to ask questions, why are you helping me?"

The watchman looked up at me, his eyes filled with a tired resignation. *"Because I've seen too many people disappear,"* he said softly. *"Too many people who didn't get the chance to understand what they were dealing with. You've already started looking for answers. You're in too deep now. But maybe, if you know the truth, you'll stand a chance."*

A shiver ran down my spine. *"A chance for what?"*

"To get out," he said. *"Before it's too late."*

"They've been here longer than anyone else."

The watchman's words echoed in the dim basement, the flickering light above casting uneasy shadows across his face. His statement felt more like an accusation, heavy with the weight of something I didn't fully understand yet. How could a family live in an apartment for so long without anyone really knowing them? And how could they remain so hidden, so elusive, yet so present through the noises that never ceased?

I shifted on my feet, feeling a creeping chill that had nothing to do with the cold, damp air of the basement. *"You're saying the family has been in that flat for years... but no one's ever seen them?"* I asked, trying to keep my voice steady despite the tension gnawing at me.

The watchman nodded, his eyes distant as if he were recalling a long history of strange events. *"They've been here longer than any tenant. Longer than me, even. And in all that time, I've never seen them. Not once."*

"But we hear them," I insisted, my voice tinged with confusion. *"We hear the child crying, the arguments, the sounds—they're so clear. How can they be there, making that much noise, and no one's ever seen them,"*

the watchman ran a hand through his thinning hair, his face darkening with frustration.

"That's the part I've never been able to figure out. No one has. People hear them all the time—crying, shouting, the same arguments over and over. But when you go up there, when you knock on the door... there's no answer. There's no one."

I felt a shiver run through me as I remembered the night I had stood outside the door to the neighboring flat, my hand poised to knock. The crying had stopped so suddenly, leaving an eerie silence that had pressed down on me like a weight. I hadn't knocked, but something told me even if I had, no one would have answered.

"I don't understand," I said quietly, more to myself than to the watchman. *"How can they be so... invisible?"*

The watchman's gaze met mine, his expression grim. *"That's the thing. They're not invisible. They're there. But it's like they exist in the shadows, just out of reach. I've had tenants come to me before, saying they heard the noises too, asking me to check on the family. So I've gone up there. I've knocked on that door more times than I can count. And every single time... nothing. No answer. No sound. Like the flat's empty."*

He paused, his brow furrowing as if he was remembering something unsettling. *"And then, after I leave, after I walk back down the hall, the noises start up again. As if they were waiting for me to leave."*

A knot tightened in my stomach. The idea that the family—or whatever they were—seemed to know when they were being watched or investigated sent a wave of unease through me. *"But... the other tenants, the ones who asked questions, the ones who disappeared... they heard the noises too?"*

The watchman nodded, his face shadowed in the dim light. *"They all did. That's why they started asking questions, why they tried to figure out what was going on. But every time someone got too close to the truth... they left. Or worse."*

I swallowed hard, my throat suddenly dry. *"Worse?"*

His eyes flickered with something close to fear. *"They disappeared. Just like I told you. One day, they'd be there, asking me about the family, about the noises. The next day, their flat would be empty. No sign of them. Their stuff was still there, untouched, but they'd be gone. It's like the building took them. And no one ever talks about it. No one ever asks."*

My heart pounded in my chest. This was worse than I had imagined. The family next door wasn't just strange—they were something else entirely, something tied to the building in a way I couldn't begin to understand.

"But why?" I asked, the question spilling out of me before I could stop it. *"Why does the building... or the family... react like that? What do they want?"*

The watchman's expression grew even more somber, his eyes darting toward the stairwell as if expecting something to emerge from the shadows. *"I don't know,"* he admitted quietly. *"All I know is that once you start noticing them, once you start paying attention, they notice you back. And they don't like it."*

I felt a chill run down my spine. *"What happens when they notice you?"*

His silence was answer enough.

I took a step back, the weight of everything I'd learned pressing down on me like a heavy fog. This wasn't just a matter of curious neighbors or strange noises. The family in the flat next door wasn't living a normal life—they were part of something far more disturbing. Something that felt ancient, as if it had always been there, lurking just out of sight, waiting for people like me to dig too deep.

And now that I had started digging, I couldn't stop. Even as the watchman warned me to leave it alone, I knew I wouldn't. I couldn't. The pull of the mystery was too strong, the need for answers too consuming.

But there was a question still lingering in the back of my mind, one that terrified me more than any of the others.

"If no one's ever seen them," I asked slowly, *"how do we know they're even... alive?"*

The watchman's face paled, and for a moment, I thought he might not answer. But then, in a voice barely above a whisper, he said, *"That's the thing. We don't."*

My heart skipped a beat, the implications of his words sending a jolt of fear through me. I had assumed the family was just strange, maybe even dangerous. But the idea that they might not even be alive—that they were something else entirely—sent my mind spiraling into a darkness I hadn't expected.

I opened my mouth to ask another question, but the watchman raised a hand, stopping me. *"You need to be careful,"* he said, his voice urgent. *"Whatever they are, they don't want you to find out. The more you dig, the closer you get, the worse it gets. You've already drawn their attention. You can't unsee them now."*

I felt my pulse quicken, the weight of his words settling in. *"What do I do?"*

The watchman hesitated, his eyes filled with something close to pity. "You need to stop, Walk away while still can. Leave the building if you have to. Because once you're too deep... they won't let you go."

I stood there, my mind spinning with fear and questions, but I knew one thing for sure: I was already too deep.

The watchman's gaze fell again. He didn't respond for a long moment. Then, finally, he said, *"I don't know. But I've learned one thing in this building and sometimes it's better not to know. **The less you see, the safer you are.**"*

His words felt like a warning, one I wasn't sure I wanted to heed. I couldn't shake the feeling that I was standing on the edge of something much darker than I had anticipated. Whatever was happening in that flat, it wasn't just a family argument. It was something more—something that no one wanted to talk about.

I thanked the watchman and walked back upstairs, reaching the elevator, my mind spinning with everything he had said. As the elevator doors closed, the weight of the silence in the building pressed down on me again, heavier than before. I rode the elevator up in silence, my thoughts racing.

When I stepped out onto the 13th floor, the familiar tension gripped me again. The hallway was empty, but it felt alive with an unseen presence like the walls themselves were holding secrets too dark to share. I hesitated outside Khaja's flat, glancing toward the door of the neighboring apartment, my hand trembling at my side. The watchman's words echoed in my mind: **You should leave it alone.**

I knew I couldn't. Whatever was happening on the other side of that door wasn't going to stop. The more I learned, the more I realized that I was already in too deep.

There were always stories about this place.

After my conversation with the watchman, I couldn't get his words out of my head. He had hinted at something far darker than I had ever imagined, but he had been careful to keep most of the details vague, almost as if he was afraid of saying too much. The more he avoided the specifics, the more my curiosity grew. If other tenants had moved out abruptly because of the noises, then something was seriously wrong.

That night, I lay awake in Khaja's flat, my mind buzzing with questions. The building had started to feel different, not just unsettling but alarming. As if the walls were hiding something far worse than just an unhappy family. The watchman had confirmed that I wasn't the first to be disturbed by the sounds, and that fact clung to me like a shadow.

What had driven people away?

What exactly was going on behind those doors?

With all the questions grooving in my head, the **clock ticked 13:03** a that very moment I decided firmly that I needed answers.

CHAPTER III

The Sudden Departure.

"It happened when no one expected it."

For weeks, the relentless sounds of arguments, children crying, and the strained, frustrated voice of the woman in the neighboring flat had filled the halls of ABK township. It had become part of the rhythm of life on the 13th floor—a constant hum of disturbance that every tenant had learned to live with, however grudgingly. But now, something was different.

The change was subtle at first. One morning, I woke up and realized that the familiar sounds that had once irritated and frustrated me were gone. The air in the building felt different, lighter but unnervingly still. It wasn't just silence, it was the kind of silence that hangs heavy in the air, a silence that makes you feel as though something is waiting just beneath the surface, ready to break through at any moment.

I shrugged it off at first. Perhaps it was just a temporary lull—an unusually quiet morning in a household that was otherwise turbulent. But as the hours passed, the silence persisted, stretching on into the afternoon and beyond. I didn't realize how much I had grown used to the noise until it was no longer there.

"Do you hear that?" I asked Khaja when I met him in the hallway later that day.

He frowned. *"Hear what?"*

"Exactly,"

I expressed and spoke.

"It's too quiet."

Khaja raised an eyebrow, glancing toward the door of the neighboring flat. *"Yeah, you're right. I hadn't noticed, but now that you mention it... it's been quiet for a while."*

We stood there, both of us staring at the door as if expecting it to burst open, as if the woman would come storming out, yelling at her unseen children, breaking the stillness that had descended over the building. But nothing happened. The door remained shut, and the silence lingered.

It was unsettling.

As the day wore on, I couldn't shake the feeling that something was wrong. The usual tension on the 13th floor, the constant background noise that had always been there, was now replaced by a void, and that emptiness felt more ominous than the chaos it had replaced.

I saw the watchman in the lobby that evening and asked him if he had seen anything unusual.

"Nah," he said, shaking his head. *"I haven't heard a peep from that flat*

all day. Maybe they finally learned to keep it down."

I wasn't convinced.

"Have you seen them today?"

The watchman frowned, considering.

"Now that you mention it... no, I haven't. But that's not unusual right? They don't come out much. You know it right?"

He shrugged, but there was a flicker of something in his eyes, a hint of unease that mirrored my own.

I went back to Khaja's place later that night, but the quiet followed me. The building felt different, almost like it was holding its breath. It was too still. Too empty. I tried to shake off the feeling, tried to convince myself that it was just a rare moment of peace, but deep down, I knew something had changed.

The strange thing was, I didn't realize how much the noise had become a part of my life until it was gone. There was an absence, a void that was more unsettling than the disturbances that had once annoyed me. It was as if the silence itself was alive, pressing in on me, whispering that something wasn't right.

And yet, for all my unease, I couldn't quite put my finger on what was wrong.

Not yet.

The Unbelievable stillness held my sleep, I thought to jog it off, and putting on my track, I opened the door, making sure to cause no sound, that could wake up Khaja, and as I stepped into the hallway, I found the building's atmosphere even more unnerving. There was still no sound from the flat next door, but now, something else had changed. The hallway felt different—emptier somehow. The same quiet that had begun the day before it completely stretched into this morning. As I walked down the hallway, the mysterious flat being closed, as usual, was never an addon to my glance. As I descended the floors and entered into the parking, I noticed the security guard being rushed and wandering around a mover truck, I was surprised by the thought, who would be shifting at this time? I thought to conversate with the watchman when I came back and headed on my jog.

As I came back, I ran into the watchman in the lobby. He looked more tense than usual; his brow furrowed as he checked something on his phone.

"Everything okay?" I started the conversation, feeling that same nervous energy bubbling up in my chest.

He looked up, surprised to see me.

"Oh... yeah, I guess." He hesitated, glancing over his shoulder toward the front of the building. To break the moment of silence around us, I asked,

"Have you seen them today?"

He being startled, gazed at me and asked,

"Have you noticed a truck? The mover's truck in the early hours of today's morning?"

What was he saying? I was asking something and despite of answering it, he was questioning me something else. I took a moment to understand what he was trying to talk about and I replied.

"Yes, I did notice, anyone moving in or someone moving out?"

Even before I could ask more questions, his answer made me take a step back.

"It's just... I think they're gone."

Without any pause, I asked. *"Who?"*

He said,

"The couple,"

Lowering his voice as if someone might overhear us.

"The ones in the flat next to your friend. They left early this morning."

My mind raced as I processed his words.

"They moved out? Just like that?"

The watchman nodded, but there was something off in his expression, a tightness around his eyes.

"Yeah, real early. A truck showed up at dawn. I wondered who would it be?"

Listening to his words, my blood ran cold, i eagerly asked, *"and?"*

Being in distress, the security guard replied.

"I came back from my rounds and the truck was already loading up the stuff.
When I asked the movers, who is shifting? The movers said we are shifting the goods of the family who lives on the 13th floor."

His eyes were clearly addressing the depth of the conversation. As I couldn't hold myself any longer, I questioned *"And?"*

The security guard continued,
"I asked, which family is moving out, They said, the one who is living in 03 flat on the 13th floor."

With an intense tone, I expressed,
"They are our neighbors, right?"

The security guard nodded and extended his conversation
"The movers said they were done and leaving soon."

Taking a moment to understand, I needed more information and I asked,
"Have you seen them?"

Hearing the depth of my vitality, the security guard replied.

"I have seen the couple, looking strange equivalent to their behavior..."

The whole thing felt wrong, like a puzzle where the pieces didn't quite fit together. If they had moved, why had they done it in such a hurry, and more importantly, where were the children?

Even before he finished his words I questioned,
"Did you see the kids?"

Security guard froze for a moment, with his eyes warning the extensity of what he was about to say, with his hands shivered, he finally spoke out.
"They don't have kids."

That knot of unease tightened in my stomach. It didn't make sense. The crying, the shouting, the arguments—they had been the background noise of the building for years. And now, suddenly, the family was gone without a trace, without anyone even seeing them leave, and denying about their kids.
"I asked them about the kids, but..."

He looked shaken as he recounted the moment, he confronted the couple during their departure. He shifted uncomfortably as we stood near the elevator, his voice dropping to a whisper even though there was no one else around to hear us.

"I tried to ask them; you know?"

He said, his eyes flicking toward the door of the now-empty flat.

"When I saw the movers leaving, I walked over and asked the man about the kids. I said, 'What about your children? Where are they?' I'd heard them like everyone else—crying, laughing, running around. But when I asked..."

He trailed off, glancing nervously down the track the vehicles left. I could see the tension in his face like he was trying to make sense of something that simply didn't add up.

"What did he say?" I pressed, my heart racing with anticipation.

The watchman swallowed hard; his voice quiet but tinged with disbelief.

"He looked at me—looking right into my eyes—he said, 'We don't have any children.' "

My breath caught in my throat, a chill spreading down my spine. I expressed *"What?"*

The watchman said, "Exactly,"

nodding as if he still couldn't believe it himself.

"The man said, 'We've been trying for years, but no luck. We don't have any kids.' And then he just... walked away."

I stared at him, the weight of his words sinking in. The couple had been living in the building for years. Everyone—every single person on the 13th floor—had heard the sounds. The crying, the scolding, the children's voice echoing through the walls. It had become a part of our daily life in the building. And now, this man was claiming he had no children?

"Are you sure that's what he said?" I asked, even though I already knew the answer. The look in the watchman's eyes told me everything I needed to know.

"I'm sure," he said firmly, his voice almost a whisper. *"I asked him twice. I thought maybe I misheard him or he didn't understand me. But*

no. Both times he said, 'We don't have any children.'"

My mind was spinning, trying to reconcile what I was hearing with what I knew. How could this be possible? For years, we had heard those voices—night after night, the same cry, the same argument—and yet now, we were being told that the children didn't exist.

"What about the woman? I asked, trying to piece together any shred of logic. *"Did she say anything?"*

The watchman shook his head, his face grim.

"No, she didn't say a word. She just stood there, staring off into the distance, like she wasn't even listening. Like she was... somewhere else."

The mental image of the woman, detached and silent, jerked through me. I remembered seeing her once or twice passing, always with a distracted look on her face, as if she was caught up in a world of her own. But now, knowing what it did, that image seemed more sinister. There had always been something off about her, something I couldn't quite put my finger on. But this... this was something else.

"And you didn't see any children leave?" I asked, even though I already knew the answer.

"No,"

The watchman confirmed saying, *"No kids, no toys, nothing. Just the two of them and a few suitcases."* shaking his head slowly.

I stood there, trying to wrap my mind around it, but the more I thought about it, the more impossible it seemed. There had to be an explanation. Maybe they had lied for some reason—maybe they were hiding something, trying to protect their children. But then why leave portraying as if they never exist?

And why had no one seen or heard the children as they moved out?

"There's something wrong,"

I muttered, more to myself than to the watchman.

"Something's not adding up."

He nodded, his face pale and tense.

"I've been thinking the same thing. I've been working here for years, and I've never seen anything like this. People come and go, sure, but not like this. Not in the middle of the night, without a trace. And those

kids… where did they go?"

A heavy silence fell between us, the weight of the unanswered questions pressing down on both of us. Just as we git deepen into our conversation, the secretary of the building gave a voice to the watchman asking him to

"Check the vacated flat on the 13th floor and make sure it is locked properly."

The watchman replied to the secretary "Okay, sir."

As I had to head back to the 13th floor, I said, *"Uncle, let's go together.'*

Closing the door of the security office, both of us headed towards the lift.

We were waiting for the lift, and with thousands of questions running in my head, I tried to stay calm. We entered the lift, and along with the lift ascending the floors, my spirit of inquiry was boosted.

Breaking the silence in the lift,

"There's something else," the watchman added, his voice dropping even lower.

"I asked the movers where the couple are leaving to, and they didn't seem to know much. Just said they were heading out of the country."

"Out of the country?" I repeated, the words sounding strange as I tried to process them.

"Yeah, something about moving to Dubai or some other place. They didn't seem like they were coming back anytime soon. Maybe never." the watchman replied.

My mind spun as I tried to wrap my head around this. The couple had been a fixture in the building for years. And now, out of nowhere, they were gone, with so much, not even a goodbye or even a glimpse of them leaving. The idea that they had just quietly packed up and left in the early hours of the morning, without a word, didn't sit right with me.

The whole conversation with the watchman made my intuition grow even stronger.

As we stepped out of the lift, I noticed that the door to the couple's flat was slightly ajar. The movers must have left it open after they finished, and now it hung there, swinging ever so slightly in the building's stale air.

I peeked in standing outside, with my heart pounding in my chest.

The flat was empty. Completely empty. No furniture, no boxes, nothing left behind. It was as if the couple had never lived there at all. But that wasn't what disturbed me the most.

There were no signs of children. No toys, no clothes, nothing to suggest that kids had ever been in that flat. It was pristine, sterile, almost too clean, as if it had been wiped of any trace of life.

It was as though the children we had all heard—their voices, their painful tears—had never existed in the first place.

Conversation with the watchman was stuck in a loop, being repeatedly played in my mind, and I was unable to get out of it.

The watchman glanced back at the empty flat, the door still ajar, and shook his head. *"I don't know what's going on in there, but whatever it is... it's not normal."*

I nodded slowly, my mind racing with possibilities, none of them comforting. I knew that the truth, whatever it was—it indeed was far darker than we could imagine. The couple's denial, the absence of any sign of children, the strange way they had disappeared into the night without a word—it all pointed to something deeper, something we hadn't even begun to understand.

The watchman shifted uneasily beside me.

"Listen," he said, his voice low and cautious. *"You should be careful. I don't know what's going on here, but you don't want to get too involved. Trust me."*

I looked at him, his face filled with quiet concern, but I knew it was already too late. I was involved. The mystery had sunk its claws into me, and there was no walking away now. Not until I knew the truth.

"I'll be careful," I lied, already knowing that I wouldn't stop digging.

As I turned to walk away, the watchman called after me one last time.

"Just remember what I said—don't go looking for answers you don't want to find."

But the problem was, I did want to find them.

The whole floor was talking about it.

I thanked the watchman and headed back to the flat. Though I came into Khaja's, my soul was still stuck behind, It felt as if I got myself inserted within the obscurity of the couple. I saw Khaja was still taking his nap, not bothered by what was happening around him.

By the time evening rolled around, and as I came back from the college, word of the couple's strange departure had spread in the air, throughout the building floor like wildfire. Conversations echoed in the hallway, and tenants gathered in small clusters, whispering and speculating about what had happened. The once-familiar routine of the building had been disrupted, and the unsettling silence that had replaced the constant noise from the flat seemed to hang over everyone like a dark cloud.

I found myself standing near the elevator, waiting for the lift to board, overhearing snippets of conversations from other residents.

"Did you hear they just left without saying a word?"

one woman whispered to her neighbor; her voice filled with disbelief.

"And what about those kids?"

The neighbor replied, her eyes wide.

"We all heard them, didn't we? How could they just vanish?"

There was confusion and unease in every voice. It was clear that I wasn't the only one who found the couple's abrupt departure unsettling. People were talking, but no one had any real answer. Theories bounced from one conversation to the next, each one stranger than the last.

"They must have been hiding something,"

A man insisted.

"Maybe they were in trouble. It wouldn't surprise me if they were running from something. Or maybe they were never really right in the head,"

another tenant offered, shaking his head. *"I mean, who argues that much? It's not normal."*

The conversations felt like an echo of my own swirling thoughts, many questions with no clear answers. As I listened to the voices around me, I couldn't help but feel that the residents of the building were just as trapped in this mystery as I was. Each tenant had their own theory, but none of it seemed to come close to explaining what had really happened.

I entered the flat, trying to pull myself out, as the clock turned around, I waited for Khaja, so that, I could tell him, what all had happened.

I caught Khaja later that evening as he came home from work. He was heading toward his room, with his headphones around his neck, and I stopped him.

"Hey," I called him from the kitchen, and he turned, raising an eyebrow at the intensity in my voice. *"Have you heard about the couple?"*

Khaja nodded slowly, his expression neutral. *"Yeah. The whole building is buzzing. They're gone, right?"*

I sighed, leaning on the couch. *"It's more than that. They left without anyone seeing them. And the weirdest part, when the watchman asked about the kids, they said they didn't have any."*

Khaja's eyes widened slightly, but instead of shock, I saw a flicker of unease. Leaning back onto the wall, He crossed his arms, shifting his weight from one foot to the other.

"That's... odd. But are you sure the watchman got it right? Maybe they were talking about something else."

"No," I replied, shaking my head. *"He asked them directly about the children we've been hearing for years. They said they didn't have any. And there's no sign of the kids. It's like they were never there."*

Khaja frowned, his face tightening with concern, but I could tell he wasn't fully convinced.

*"Maybe they were lying. Maybe they didn't want people asking questions. Or..."*He paused, lowering his voice as though he didn't want to say it out loud.

"Maybe something's wrong with them. You know, mentally."
That thought had crossed my mind too, but it still didn't explain the knot behind the missing children or the strange way they had vanished.
"Even if they were mentally unstable, why would they leave like that? Why deny having kids when everyone in the building heard them?"
Khaja glanced down the hall as if expecting someone to appear and answer our questions.
"I don't know, man. But if they're gone, maybe it's better we leave it alone. People like that... you don't want to get too involved with them. It's probably nothing more than a weird domestic situation. They left, so maybe it's over."

I could hear the hesitancy in his voice. He wanted to believe it was over, that there was nothing more to worry about. But deep down, I knew he was just as unsettled as I was.
"Do you really believe that?" I asked, studying his face. *"Do you really think it's over?"*

He shrugged, looking away.
"I want to believe it's just a simple explanation. But..."
He paused, glancing back at me.
"There's something about this whole thing that doesn't sit right with me. The way they left. The kids. The noise. It's all... wrong."

I nodded and felt relieved that I wasn't the only one feeling that way. *"Exactly. It doesn't make sense."*
Khaja sighed, running a hand through his hair.

"What are you thinking, then? Are you going to try to figure this out?"

I could feel the pull of curiosity tugging at me again.

"I can't just let it go, Khaja. There's something bigger going on here, and I need to know what it is. People don't just leave like that. Kids don't just disappear."

He gave me a wary look as if he knew what was coming next.
"And how are you going to figure it out? What's the plan?"

I didn't have an answer for him, not yet. But I knew that I wasn't ready to walk away. Not until I had answers. *"I'll start with the flat.*

Maybe there's something left behind. Something that explains what was really going on."

Khaja hesitated, then nodded slowly. *"Alright. But be careful, man. I don't want to find you wrapped up in something you can't handle."*

I gave him a small yet tight smile. *"Don't worry. I'm just looking for answers."*

Listening to me, he headed back to his room and as we ended our conversation, we headed back to our remaining day but even as I said the words, I could feel the weight of the mystery growing heavier, pulling me deeper into something I might not be able to escape from.

For the first time in years, the building was silent.

The days that followed the couple's departure were drenched in an unnatural stillness. It was as if the walls of ABK township, which had once echoed with the constant cries and arguments from the flat next door, were now holding their breath. No one dared talk about it openly anymore, but the absence of noise was suffocating in its own right.

The strangest thing wasn't just the lack of crying or shouting—it was the complete void that had taken its place. Even the creaks of the building, the low hum of distant conversations, and the sound of footsteps in the hallway seemed to fade into a stifling silence that pressed down on everyone who lived there.

I found myself walking the hallways more than usual, lingering outside the door to the now-abandoned flat. Each time, my hand hovered near the door, as if I could knock and bring the noise back, return the building to some sense of normalcy. But I never knocked. Something held me back. Maybe it was the gnawing fear of what I might find—or not find—if the door opened.

Khaja kept his distance more and more. I would catch him avoiding the hallway where the flat was, and every time I brought up the couple, he would shrug, offering a half-hearted attempt to dismiss the mystery.

He would say,*"They're gone, man, Let it go.".* His voice quiet but firm, as if he was trying to convince himself more than me.

But I couldn't let it go. The silence was worse than the noise that we had ever been through. The arguments and crying had been annoying, but they had been real. Tangible. Something you could complain about, roll your eyes at, and move on with your day. But this silence, it felt like the building itself was holding onto a secret, and that secret was threatening to swallow everything whole.

One night, as I lay on my bed, I realized just how the absence of sound had affected me. I couldn't sleep. The quiet was too loud. Every small noise I made—shifting in bed, breathing, the rustling of the sheets—sounded deafening in the stillness. I missed the distant hum of life, the soft murmurs of the world around me. But now, there was nothing. Just the heavy, oppressive silence.

The entire building felt like it had been hollowed out. The tenants were quieter, their conversations hushed. The watchman, usually chatty, now gave brief and unsure nods when I passed by him as if even he was afraid to speak too loudly after the couple's disappearance.

I kept wondering about the children. Their voices they were so vivid, so persistent for years—were now nothing more than a memory that seemed to remain in the back of my mind, haunting me more even in their absence. It was as if they had been erased, not just from the building but from everyone's minds.

No one talked about them anymore, as if they were trying to forget the sounds they had heard for so long. But I couldn't forget. I couldn't shake the feeling that something terrible had happened, something far worse than anyone in the building was willing to acknowledge.

One night, the darkness sounded deeper than usual, The clock ticked past 12, and it felt as if the kids, were right behind me, their soft giggles, with no snap, turned into painful screams, it felt as if they were trying to grab my notice. It felt so real. It felt as if I was being imprisoned in a vacuum, I was suffocating to breathe, and my body started sweating...

"no, no, no... this can't happen, no... "
I was trying to scream and protect myself from something that I was unable to reach out at. I started hearing the footsteps, they were following towards me, and I could sense human hands on my cheeks. I started hearing.
"look at me, look at me..."

I flashed into my senses, and I saw it was Khaja, trying to wake me up from my dream.
"Are you okay? What happened? What are you dreaming about?"
Khaja was concerned and I could clearly see him being panicked.
"Nothing, I.. I.. I was just lost."
I have never even thought I was dreaming, all the cries and arguments felt very actual.
"You sure, that you are okay?"
Khaja's voice reflected how worried he was about me.
With a tiny smile on my face, I assured him that I was totally fine, and listening to me he said,
"I know you are stuck with the neighbors, but be safe okay.?" Saying it, he left the room.

But the tranquillity made me feel traumatized. I was unable to sleep that night. I sat on the couch, being unable to bear it anymore. I opened the door, stepped out into the hallway, and started heading towards the neighbor's door, the hallway looked so still, I stood before the door, it felt as if someone was behind the door, waiting for my arrival as if they were wanting me to burst in, The lock case that was placed right on the top corner just beside the door, with all the keys hanging, I couldn't resist my divination anymore, I followed my instinct and grabbed the key through which I can unlock that door, and as soon as I tried to insert the key, I felt as if someone or something stopped me, with a cool breeze spreading a vibration throughout my body, I hanged the keys back at their place and I headed back with grief in my heart weighing more than actual.

The next day I ran into Mrs. Varma an elderly woman who lived on the same floor. She had always been a quiet resident, keeping to herself and only occasionally exchanging pleasantries with the other tenants. But this time, she stopped me, her wrinkled hand reaching out to touch my arm gently.

"They left, didn't they?"

she asked, her voice low and strained, her eyes shadowed with something I couldn't quite place.

I nodded slowly. *"Yes. a few days ago, early in the morning. They're gone."*

She looked over her shoulder, almost as if expecting someone to be listening. When she turned back to me, her eyes were filled with something close to fear and said, *"That's good. It's better that way."*

I frowned, taken aback by her sudden statement. *"What do you mean?"*

She sighed heavily, leaning in closer.

"This place... it was never right after they moved in. The noises... it wasn't just the children, you know. There were other sounds too. Things I couldn't explain. Things that shouldn't have been there."

Her voice wavered, and I could see the unease in her eyes.

*"What kind of sounds?"*I asked, my curiosity piqued.

She hesitated, as though speaking the words would somehow make them real again.

"I would hear things late at night," she said her voice barely above a whisper. *"Not just the crying or the arguments, but... movement. Like footsteps, but not from the apartment. From the walls. The floors. As if something was walking between the spaces, where there shouldn't have been anyone."*

A cold shiver ran down my spine, and i asked *"Did you tell anyone?"*

She shook her head, her expression grim.

"No one would have believed me. They would have said I was just an old woman hearing things. But I know what I heard. And I'm telling you, it's good that they're gone. The building feels... different now. Quieter. But I don't think that means it's over."

"What do you mean?" I asked, my voice a little too eager.

She didn't answer right away, instead glancing nervously down the hallway again. Finally, she said,

"There's something wrong with this place. There always has been. And

the couple... they were part of it. But it's not just them. This building holds secrets, boy. Be careful what you're looking for, or you might not like what you find."

With that, she turned and shuffled away, leaving me standing in the silent corridor, the weight of her words sinking into me like ice. Being in the unended maze, I was confused, how did, Mrs. Varma, know I was trying to find the answers?

I ran towards her immediately stopping her I asked, *"Mrs. Varma, how do you know I was trying to find out things?"*

Looking at my hustled breath, she replied *"I saw you trying to open the door last night."*

She also added,

"It is not just me who knew about it, even the building itself knew it, that you are looking for the answers"

The silence was suffocating now. And for the first time, I wondered if it was better to leave it undisturbed.

"We couldn't just let it go."

Despite Khaja's warnings and the unsettling silence that had settled over the building, I couldn't stop thinking about the couple and their sudden, inexplicable departure. The absence of any sign of their children haunted me, along with the strange denial from the man that they had ever existed. The conversations with the watchman and Mrs. Varma kept replaying in my mind, fuelling a need to uncover the truth.

I knuckled up, this journey is not going to stop anymore.

Echoes of the Past.

"It exists even when it doesn't subsist."

The building felt different now, like a vacuum where life had once existed.

After the couple left, ABK township was quieter than it had ever been. The constant cries, the arguments, and the daily disturbances that had become so ingrained in the life of the building were gone, leaving behind a heavy, unsettling silence. It wasn't the peaceful kind of quiet people craved—it was the kind that made you more aware of everything else. It was a silence that weighed on you, pressing down until you couldn't breathe.

I couldn't shake the feeling that something was missing, something more than just the noise. The silence was wrong. It wasn't natural. It was as if the building itself had emptied out, as though the life that had filled it had been sucked away with the departure of the couple. Yet despite the quiet, there was a tension that continued in the air, as if everyone was holding their breath, waiting for something to happen.

For days, I found myself walking through the halls, expecting to hear the familiar sounds of the children's cries or the harsh voice of the woman scolding them. But it was always silent. The only sound was the soft echo of my footsteps on the tile floors, and even that felt too loud. The walls seemed to absorb everything as if the building itself was swallowing up any trace of life left in it.

Khaja noticed the shift too. One evening, as we sat in his flat, he commented on how unnerving it all was.

"It's weird, right?" he said, his voice quiet as though he didn't want to disturb the silence. *"It's like the whole building is... empty."*

I nodded, staring out the window at the darkening sky.*"I can't stop thinking about it. The quiet is... too much."*

Listening to me, he leaned back in his chair, rubbed his eyes, and replied, *"Maybe we were habituated to the noise. I mean, it was terrible, but at least it was something. Now, it's like the place is dead."*

That was exactly how it felt—**dead.** Not just quiet, but void of life. It was as if the couple had taken the life with them when they left, something more than just their belongings. The emptiness weighed on me in ways I couldn't explain. I found myself replaying the memories of the noise, the arguments, and the crying in my head. It was as though the absence of those sounds had given them more power over me.

I muttered, almost to myself.*"I can still hear them,"*

Khaja gave me a strange look.*"What do you mean?"*

Expressing my inner thoughts I said, *"The kids. The noise. It's like it's still there in my head, even though the flat is empty."*

Khaja shifted uncomfortably, glancing toward the door as though expecting something to come through it. *"You need to stop thinking about it, man. They're gone. It's over."*

But it didn't feel over. The silence wasn't a settling resolution—it developed a beginning. A new, unsettling chapter that left me with more questions than before. The flat next door was empty, but the memories of what had happened there staggered. I couldn't shake the feeling that the quiet was more dangerous than the noise had ever been.

I spoke, *"I don't know,"* with my basic tone. *"It feels like there is something still over here. Like the silence isn't just silence anymore."*

Khaja sighed, with his frustration beginning to unveil.

"You're letting this get to you. They're gone. The noise is gone. Isn't that what we wanted?"

Was it? The peace that we had all longed for now felt like a note pressing down on me, suffocating in its stillness. The echoes of the past filled the entire space, making it impossible to forget what had been there before.

The children's cries, the arguments, they were louder in my memory than they had ever been in real.

"I need some air." I stood up, unable to sit still any longer.

Khaja didn't stop me, the concern was rolling through his eyes. *"Just... don't overthink this. It is done."*

But it wasn't done. I knew it wasn't. There was something about the silence, something lurking beneath it, waiting for the right moment to make itself known. The building might have been quiet now, but the past still echoed through it, louder than ever.

"The questions crawled, even if no one wanted to ask them."

The days after the couple's sudden departure stretched on the silence, making it grow more oppressive with each passing hour. But it wasn't just the lack of hail that bothered me, it was the way everyone seemed to avoid talking about what had happened.

As if ignoring it would make the strangeness of it disappear all at once.

Even when I passed neighbors in the hallway or caught snippets of conversations in the elevator, there was a peculiar shift. The usual small talk about the weather, groceries, or repairs now felt forced, as though everyone was purposefully steering away from the subject that hung like a shadow over the building—the couple and their mysterious departure.

Khaja, was the one who was adamant about moving on. He insisted that we should stop thinking about it, that we were making it a bigger deal than it needed to be. But every time I tried to forget; the weight of the unanswered questions would pull me right back.

I found him sitting on his couch one evening, headphones plugged on and his laptop open, working on some project for school. I had barely walked in the door when I blurted out, *"Something's still off, Khaja. I can't shake it."*

Looking at my steps ascending, He paused, pulling off his headphones and raising an eyebrow. *"You look drenched in those thoughts, You're still on this?"*

I dropped into the chair opposite him, frustration wrecking at me. *"I can't help it. Man, It's not just the noise. There's something odd about the way they left, the way everyone's avoiding the topic. Don't you think it's weird?"*

Khaja sighed, closing his laptop. *"Certainly, it is Weird, and I am not denying it, but it's not worth obsessing over! They left, man. People leave. Maybe they had their reasons."*

"But what about the kids?" I asked, my voice sore and quieter now, almost as if I was afraid to say it out loud. *Everyone heard them. And now... it's like no one wants to admit that they have ever existed. Even when I bring it up with other tenants, they brush it off. It's just like they don't want to talk about it."*

Khaja leaned forward, rubbing the back of his neck. *"Look! people don't like weird stuff, alright? It freaks them out. And yeah, the whole thing with the kids is strange, but people want to move on. I don't blame them."*

I pressed. *"But don't you want to know? Don't you want to understand why they lied about having kids? What happened to them?"*

Khaja's expression tightened, and for a moment, I thought I saw a flicker of uncertainty in his eyes. But he shook his head, standing firm in his decision. Khaja said, *"What's the point, man? You're not going to find any answers. And even if you do, what good is it going to do? They're gone. The noise is gone. Maybe it's better this way."*

I couldn't understand his apathy. How could he just let it go when so many things didn't add up?

It felt like trying to piece together a puzzle when half the pieces were still missing.

The more I thought about it, the more I realized, that no one else seemed interested in finding those missing pieces which were connoting the silence, with the unanswered questions, and all of this felt as if I was on tiptoe.

I left Khaja's flat feeling more unsettled than ever.

The weight of the mystery clung to me, a constant presence in the back of my mind. Even in the moments when I tried to distract myself, it was always there nagging me, pulling me back.

The next day, I ran into Mrs. Varma in the hallway again. Based on our previous conversation, I had a hope that she could help me dig more and track down the darkling path.

"Good morning," she greeted me with a tight smile, her wrinkled hands clutching a grocery bag.

"Good morning, Mrs. Varma," I replied, hesitating for a moment before deciding to ask her about what had been bothering me. *"Can I ask you something?"*

She nodded, her kind eyes peering at me through her thick glasses. *"Of course, dear. Is it about the couple again?"*

I knew she advised me not to dig, but I couldn't stop, I was hesitant, but I couldn't give up, she had been living here since before Khaja's family shifted here.

"Mrs. Varma, I am sorry, but I couldn't resist myself anymore, but the couple that lived next door," I began cautiously, *"Do you still...?"*

Her smile faltered slightly, and her grip on the grocery bag tightened. She seemed uncomfortable, as though she knew exactly what I was asking but didn't want to engage with it.

"Oh, well," she started, her voice a bit strained, *"I try not to pay attention to these things, you know? Few lives are scratched with their troubles. That can sometimes make us feel their scars even with their absence"*

"But you heard them, the echoes and the painful kneeling the kinds paid, right?" I pressed, feeling a strange urgency to get an answer.

Mrs. Varma glanced down the hallway as if making sure no one was listening.

"Yes," she said quietly, her voice barely above a whisper. *"I heard them, and I still hear them. We all did, and we all will. It is hard not to."*

I was listening to her, it felt as if each part of my body was paying attention to her, I was trying hard to know more and I shoved, *"Don't you think it's strange that they said they don't have children? That no one saw them leave?"*

Her lips tightened, and for a moment, she looked like she was about to tell me something. But then she shook her head. *"Dear, some things are best left alone, People have their reasons, and it's not shielding for us to dig too deeply. Sometimes, the past is better left where it belongs."*

I stared at her, my mind racing. It was the same response I had gotten from nearly everyone else—vague, dismissive, as if acknowledging the oddness would somehow make it worse. I could see the fear in her eyes, the fear of stirring something that was better left untouched.

"Are you sure there's nothing more?" I asked, my voice soft but insistent.

Mrs. Varma hesitated, then gave me a sad smile.

"We all have our ghosts," she whispered. *"Maybe it's better we don't go looking for theirs."*

With that, she shuffled off down the hallway, taking her path, leaving me standing there with a hundred more questions that had no answers.

And staring at the hallway, it felt like, **Sometimes, it felt like the walls were listening.**

The oppressive silence continued to press down on ABK township and started to grow heavier with each passing day.

But now, it wasn't just the quiet that bothered me, nor it was the way the silence seemed to twist and warp. It was the whole; it was as if the building itself was hiding something within its walls.

At first, I told myself I was imagining. The faint noises, I thought I heard—whispers, footsteps, and the occasional soft sound of a child's laugh—had to be my mind playing tricks on me, right?

After all, I had spent weeks haunted by the noises that used to come from the flat next door.

It made sense that my brain, desperate to fill the silence, was conjuring those echoes from memory.

But the more I listened, the more I realized something was wrong. It wasn't just my imagination. The sounds were there, faint but unmistakable, coming from places they shouldn't have. The first time I noticed it, I was standing in the hallway, just outside my door. The air was still, and everything was quiet. But then, just as I was about to head back inside, I heard it—a soft, muffled sound, like the rustle of clothes or someone moving slowly across the floor.

I froze, my hand hovering over the doorknob. The sound was coming from the empty flat. My heart began to pound as I leaned closer to the wall, straining to hear.

It was faint, but unmistakable. Footsteps. Slow, deliberate, and moving within the empty space next door.

For a moment, I stood there, paralyzed, unsure whether to knock on the door or run back inside. But the footsteps stopped just as suddenly as they had started, leaving me standing there in silence, my pulse racing.

I tried to tell myself it was nothing, that it was just the building settling, or maybe someone from another flat making noise that carried through the walls. But it didn't feel right.

It felt... intentional, like someone—or something—was moving just out of sight, just beyond the boundaries of my understanding.

The next few days were worse. Every time I walked through the hallways, I could feel the presence of something just behind the walls. Sometimes, it was a faint laugh, like the sound of a child playing in the distance. Other times, it was a soft whisper, so quiet I couldn't make out the words, but enough to separate my body and bones.

I often found myself lost outside the door of the couple's old flat, drawn to it as though it held the answers I was searching for. The empty, darkened windows seemed to watch me as I stood there, listening for any sign of life within.

The footsteps.

The whispers.

The laughter.

They echoed through the walls, just on the edge of perception, taunting me with their presence.

Khaja was no help. Whenever I told him about the noises, he waved it off, brushing aside my concerns with his usual skepticism.

"You're hearing things, man?" he said one afternoon when I brought it up again. *"The place is empty. It's probably just the pipes, or maybe the sound is carrying from another apartment."*

I wanted to believe him, but deep down, I knew it wasn't that simple. I could feel it—there was something in that flat, something left behind when the couple disappeared. **The building hadn't yet forgotten. The walls hadn't forgotten.**

One night, as I was lying in bed, the feeling of unease became unbearable. I had tried to sleep, but every time I closed my eyes, I felt as though I was being watched. My room was dark, the air thick with the weight of the silence that seemed to press in on me from all sides. And then, just as I was drifting off, I heard it again.

A whisper.

It was so faint I almost convinced myself it wasn't real. But as I lay there, perfectly still, the whisper grew louder.

It was coming from the walls, which were just behind my head. I couldn't make out the words, but the sound was unmistakable, the voice of a child, soft and urgent, as fit as if it was trying to tell me something.

I sat up, my heart hammering in my chest. The whisper faded as soon as I moved, disappearing into the stillness of the night. But it left behind a cold fear that gripped me tightly.

I wasn't imagining it. I wasn't just hearing things.

The walls were alive with their voices. The flat next door wasn't as empty as it seemed, but it felt still alive.

I got out of bed and walked to the window, hoping the cool air from outside would calm me down.

But as I stared out into the quiet streets below, I couldn't stand the feeling that something was wrong.

The noises weren't just sounds—they were memories!

Memories that were still messing through the walls of ABK township, waiting to be acknowledged.

The next day, I confronted Khaja again. *"I'm telling you, it's not just in my head. The walls... they're holding onto something. It's like the building is evoking the past."*

Khaja raised an eyebrow, clearly unconvinced. *"The building? You think the building is haunted?"*

"I don't know," I said, my frustration growing. *"But something's happening. I hear them—the kids, their laughter, their whispers. The footsteps. It's not just my imagination."*

He sighed, rubbing his temples. *"You've been thinking about this too much. You're hearing things because you want to hear them. Let it go, man."*

But I couldn't. The whispers, the footsteps—they weren't going to let me go. Not until I figured out what they were trying to tell me.

"The absence of noise started to feel like a presence of its own."

The searing quiet inside ABK township wasn't confined to the building alone.

Over the following days, I started to notice something more disturbing—the neighborhood itself seemed to have fallen under the same eerie silence.

The sounds of everyday life that had once filled the streets around the apartment complex were now muted, almost as if the silence from the 13th floor had spilled out and was spreading further into the world outside.

The hum of traffic that usually thrummed in the distance was now distant and thin, barely audible even during rush hour.

I noticed fewer people out on the streets, and those I did see moved quickly, as though they too were trying to escape the strange quiet that had settled over the area.

The usual lively atmosphere of children playing, dogs barking, and the general chaos of city life had somehow evaporated.

One morning, I stood at my window, looking out over the neighborhood. It was odd still.

The trees barely swayed in the soft breeze, and the few cars that passed by seemed to move more slowly, their engines making little noise as they went. It was like watching a film with the sound turned down—everything was happening, but it felt distant, disconnected from reality.

I mentioned it to Khaja later that day, hoping he would notice the change as well. We were sitting in a small café just down the street from ABK township, the same café we had visited countless times before.

But even here, something was off.

The usual clinking of plates, the hum of conversation, the soft background music—it was all subdued, as though someone had turned the volume down on the entire world.

"Do you hear that?" I asked, leaning forward.

Khaja gave me a look, his brow furrowed. *"Hear what?"*

I said, *"Exactly,"* In a muted tone. *"There's nothing. It's too quiet. Even the café feels dead."*

He sighed, stirring his coffee with a little more force than necessary. *"You're letting this whole thing get to you. Not everything is connected to that couple and their flat. Sometimes things are just... quiet."*

I shook my head, my frustration building. *"It's not just quiet, Khaja. It's like everything has changed. The neighborhood doesn't feel the same anymore. The people, the sounds—everything's different."*

Khaja stared at me for a long moment, his eyes searching mine. I could tell he was starting to get irritated with my constant need to talk about this, but I couldn't stop. The weight of the silence, both inside and outside the building, was suffocating, and I needed him to see it too.

"You're seeing patterns where there aren't any," he said finally, setting his spoon down with a clink. *"Look, I get it. That flat creeped us all out. The couple was weird, the whole thing was strange. But not everything is a big mystery. The world's not out to get you."*

I clenched my jaw, holding back the urge to argue further.

But the more I thought about it, the more convinced I became that something was wrong.

The silence followed me beyond the walls of ABK township, creeping into the streets, the shops, and the very air around us.

It was like a presence, something intangible yet all-encompassing, pressing down on me wherever I went.

We finished our coffee in relative silence, and when we stepped back outside, the feeling only intensified.

The streets, which should have been bustling with activity, were haunting empty. The distant sounds of traffic were muffled, and the pedestrians moved with a strange sense of purpose, avoiding eye contact, speaking in hushed tones if they spoke at all.

Even the birds seemed quieter. The usual chatter of sparrows and pigeons was subdued, their songs muted as if they too had fallen under the spell of the growing quiet.

I couldn't shake the feeling that the world was holding its breath, ***waiting for things to happen. Something terrible.***

I looked over at Khaja, who seemed oblivious to the change in atmosphere.

"You really don't feel it?" I asked, unable to hide the concern in my voice.

He shrugged, shoving his hands into his pockets. *"Nope. It's just another day, man."*

But it wasn't. I knew it wasn't.

Back at the apartment, the sensation grew worse.

Every time I entered the building, I felt like I was walking into a void, a place that had been drained of life.

The silence was thick, almost tangible, and it followed me wherever I went.

Even the tenants who used to fill the hallways with their chatter and noise seemed to have withdrawn into themselves.

I barely saw anyone anymore, and when I did, they hurried past me, their faces blank and their footsteps unnaturally quiet.

One evening, I stood in the hallway outside the flat where the couple had lived, listening for anything—any sound, any sign of life. But there was nothing.

The air was thick with stillness, and I couldn't shake the feeling that I was being watched.

Not by a person, but by the building itself. As though it had grown aware of my presence, aware of my curiosity, and was waiting for me to push further.

It wasn't just about the couple anymore. The silence had taken a life of its own, creeping into every corner of my existence.

It wasn't just inside ABK township—it expanded into the streets, into the proximity. **And I couldn't escape it.**

"The past wasn't gone it was still here, being present, living in the shadows."

The days stretched into weeks, but the silence inside ABK township—and throughout the neighborhood, never lifted. If anything, that made progress was, that it became more oppressive, weighing down on me like a heavy blanket that I couldn't carry off.

The absence of noise wasn't just unsettling anymore; it was suffocating, almost as if the silence had taken on a life of its own. And with every passing day, I became more convinced that the answers I sought lay buried in the echoes of the past.

I couldn't stop thinking about the couple, about their strange departure, and the children who never seemed to exist.

Their absence felt wrong, like a gaping wound that refused to heal.

Every time I closed my eyes, I could hear the faint traces of their lives—the crying, the arguments, the laughter of the children—echoing in the back of my mind, as though the building itself was refusing to forget them.

But it wasn't just the sounds that I remembered.

There were times when the flat next door, empty and lifeless, seemed to be calling out to me.

I would walk past it, hear the faintest noise—a whisper, a breath of air—and feel compelled to stop, to listen. It was as though the walls were holding onto something, a secret that refused to be silenced.

Khaja had given up trying to convince me to let it go. We still talked, but the conversations had become strained, and I knew he was worried about me. I could see it in his eyes every time I brought up the couple, or the sounds, or the suffocating silence that seemed to follow me everywhere I went.

"You're obsessed," That was the only answer he gave.

One evening he told me.*"This is getting unhealthy, man. You need to let it go."*

I knew he was right, at least logically. But the truth was, I couldn't. The mystery had its claws stuck in me, and the more I tried to walk away, the deeper it pulled me in.

I couldn't forget the voice of the children being alive, couldn't forget the way the couple had denied their very existence. Something terrible had happened in that flat, and I knew the answers were still there, hidden in the silence.

One night, I found myself standing outside the door of the couple's old flat again, unable to resist the pull. The hallway was empty, bathed in the dim glow of the overhead lights. The stillness was absolute, but as I stood there, listening, I could hear it—the faintest sound, like a whisper from the past. It was so quiet that I could have convinced myself it wasn't real, but I knew better by now.

I pressed my ear to the door, my heart pounding in my chest. There it was again—soft, almost imperceptible.

A child's voice, barely more than a breath. I couldn't make out the words, but the sound was enough to send a chill racing down my spine.

The flat was supposed to be empty. But it wasn't.

I pulled back, staring at the door, my pulse racing. This wasn't just a memory playing tricks on me.

This was real.

There was something in that flat, something that hadn't left with the couple. And I knew, in that moment, that I had to find out what it was.

I knocked on the door, my hand trembling slightly. The sound echoed down the empty hallway, but there was no response. I knocked again, harder this time, my knuckles rapping against the wood. Still nothing.

The air around me seemed to thicken, the silence pressing down on me from all sides. I could feel the weight of it, suffocating and inescapable, as though the building itself was alive and watching me.

Without thinking, I reached for the doorknob, expecting it to be locked. But to my surprise, it wasn't. The knob turned easily in my hand, and with a soft creak, the door swung open, revealing the dark, empty flat beyond.

I hesitated, the hairs on the back of my neck standing on end.

The air inside the flat was cold, colder than it should have been.

It smelled faintly of dust and something else—something metallic, like old blood.

I stepped inside, my footsteps echoing in the stillness. The flat looked just as it had when I peeked in from the outside—empty, lifeless. But the feeling of unease was stronger now, almost palpable, as though the walls themselves were holding their breath, waiting for me to uncover whatever secret they had been hiding.

I moved further into the flat, my heart pounding in my chest. The whispers had stopped, but I could still feel them, hanging in the air like a ghostly presence. Every step I took felt heavier than the last, the silence pressing in on me like a physical weight.

I reached the small bedroom, I assumed it was the place where the children were supposed to have sleep, though there had never been any sign of them. The room was dark, the faint glow from the hallway barely illuminating the corners. I stood in the doorway, staring into the empty space, my mind racing with questions I couldn't answer.

And then, in the stillness, I heard it again. A soft, breathy laugh—faint, but unmistakable. It came from the corner of the room, just beyond the reach of the light.

I froze, my breath catching in my throat. The laugh was followed by a soft whisper, like the voice of a child, barely audible. My blood ran cold as I realized the voice wasn't coming from outside the room.

It was coming from inside.

I took a step back, my heart racing, but something in me wouldn't let me leave. I had come this far, and I knew there was no turning back now. Whatever was in that flat, whatever had been left behind, I had to face it.

I stepped into the room, my pulse pounding in my ears, and as I did, the whispers grew louder, more insistent. The past wasn't gone. It was still here, lingering in the shadows, waiting for someone to uncover it.

And I knew, in that moment, that the echoes of the past would haunt me until I figured out the mystery.

CHAPTER V

The Mental Hospital Visit.

It wasn't over. Not by a long shot.

A few days had passed since my last strange encounter with the flat next door, but I couldn't get it out of my head.

The whispers.

The laughter.

The unsettling silence—it all haunted me. But there was something more deeply churning me, that truly pushed me over the edge. One rainy morning, while standing in the lobby waiting for my cab, I overheard two tenants talking in hushed voices. Their conversation was about the couple who had once lived next door to us.

"They're at the mental hospital,"

One of them whispered, I immediately looked up from my phone, her eyes being wide with a mix of shock and pity.

"Both of them?"

The other tenant asked out of curiosity,

It felt as if, they knew I was trying to hear their conversation, and the tenant who spoke about them being at mental hospital, replied

"Yes, both are in mental hospital now, they got admitted just after they left from here.

Can you believe it?

Both of the tenants left the place as soon as they spoke them out, I was puzzled, clustered in my head, with my phone vibrating with a notification of my cab arrival, I got back on my feet, Boarding the cab, I conveyed the OTP to the driver, with the cab being commenced towards the drop location, I was still stuck with those words,

The words were so deep that I was able to see my veins popping out of my body, as I absorbed the words. ***The couple had gone straight from ABK township to a mental institution?*** I didn't know why, but I had to find out more. There was something deeply wrong about this whole situation. The children, the silence, the couple's denial of their existence—it was all connected. And now they were locked away in a mental hospital.

I knew I needed to see for myself.

Later that evening, I told Khaja about what I'd overheard. We sat in my living room, the lights dim, the heavy silence of ABK township hanging between us. Khaja wasn't as convinced as I was.

"This is getting out of hand, man,"

he said, shaking his head.

"We shouldn't be digging into this. They're gone, right?

They're in a hospital now. Maybe that's where they need to be. Why should we get involved?"

Khaja voiced, it sounded more like, as if he was questioning, listening to him, I leaned forward, my fingers gripping the edge of the coffee table.

"But don't you see?

This isn't just about them being gone. There's something more.

Why were we hearing children's voices from our neighbouring flat, when they didn't have kids?

And now they're in a mental hospital. It's connected, Khaja.

I know it is."

Khaja sighed, rubbing his face.

"You're obsessed.

Look, people can be... weird. Maybe they're just sick. Maybe they're just mentally ill. But it doesn't mean we need to go prying into it."

I could see the care in his eyes, but I couldn't let it go. The more I thought about it, the more the need for answers gnawed at me. This wasn't just curiosity anymore—it was a compulsion. Something was pulling me toward the truth, and I knew I wouldn't be able to rest until I had it.

I said quietly,

"I need to know,"

With a firm voice I uttered,

"I'm going to see them."

Khaja stared at me for a long moment, his eyes narrowing.

"You're serious?"

With a soft nod, I said,

"I'm going to the hospital."

He exhaled sharply, leaning back in his chair.

"You're crazy, you know that?"

I know, I am pushing myself, looking at the frazzle expression on Khaja's face, I said

"Maybe. But I must do this."

For a moment, Khaja didn't say anything. He seemed to be weighing his options, trying to decide whether to support me or pull away. Finally, he sighed again, but this time there was a resignation in his voice.

"Fine,"

he muttered.

"But I'm coming with you. Someone's got to keep you from doing anything stupid."

I always felt assured with Khaja being around, listening to him a thin smile arrived on my face, looking at his wristwatch, Khaja said,

"let us go in the morning, it is already dark now."

The following day, Khaja and I grabbed our car keys, and headed down to the parking. We noticed the watchman being unusual and nervous, his eyes were trying to convey something which is being resisted by his body moments, heading towards the watchman I asked Khaja to bring the car out, and I reached the watchman at his cabin, and asked him,

"Uncle, can you give us the information about the neighbours who used to stay next to our flat?"

He was startled for a moment, I thought he was lost in his thoughts, and I called him again,

"Uncle,"

He slowly looked into my eyes; they were flushed with deep thoughts. He grabbed the file that consists of the details of all the residents and the tenants living in the building and he took a paper and wrote their names, folding it slowly, he glanced out, as if he was making sure, no one was watching us, he gave me the folded paper, and with a dense voice,

"Be careful, the path you are stepping towards, is deeper than to its visibility."

It felt like he was warning me, I just nodded, putting the paper he gave me into my pockets, and I headed out with all the words delivered by the watchman being on loop in my head, stepping into our car, I shut the door. Khaja and I glanced at each other and made our way to the hospital.

The sky unfolded its colors, it was over us casting a dull, Gray light over the streets as we drove. Neither of us spoke much during the ride, the silence between us was heavy enough, that filled with unspoken tension. Khaja was still reluctant, his hands gripping the steering wheel tighter than usual, while I stared out the window, trying to prepare myself for whatever we might find.

The mental hospital was located on the outskirts of the city, as soon as we were getting near to it, I can see a grim-looking building surrounded by high iron gates. It loomed before us, its concrete walls stained by years of neglect, and the windows were small and barred, adding to the sense that this place was more of a prison than a hospital. The moment we pulled up, I felt a A shiver went down my spine. Something about the building itself seemed to exude dread.

Khaja parked the car, but neither of us moved right away. He looked over at me, his jaw tight.

"Are you sure about this?"

he asked, his voice quieter than usual.

I nodded, feeling the weight of my decision settle in my chest.

"I need to see them. I need to know what's going on."

Replying to him, we got out of the car and walked toward the entrance, the gravel crunching under our feet. As we approached, my heart was thumping loudly in my chest.

a mix of fear and anticipation building inside me. The hospital's entrance was as unwelcoming as the rest of the building—cold, Gray, and sterile. A heavy metal door stood at the top of a short flight of steps, and a small sign above it read St. Mark's Psychiatric Facility.

As we entered the lobby, the atmosphere shifted. The air inside was stale, thick with the scent of antiseptic, and the fluorescent lights cast a harsh, unnatural glow over everything.

The waiting room was sparse, with plastic chairs lined up against the walls and a few faded posters about mental health hanging limply from peeling paint. A nurse sat behind a glass window at the far end of the room, her eyes fixed on a computer screen.

Everything about this place screamed neglect. It felt wrong, like a place where people were forgotten, not healed.

I swallowed hard, trying to push down the growing sense of unease that threatened to bubble up.

"We shouldn't be here,"

Khaja muttered under his breath as we approached the nurse's desk.

I ignored him, stepping up to the window. The nurse glanced up, her eyes cold and indifferent.

"Can I help you?"

she asked, her voice monotone.

I hesitated for a moment, unsure of how to approach this.

"We're here to visit two patients."

Saying it I picked out the paper that consists the details of the couple, which was given by the watchman and I gave it to the nurse

She tapped at her keyboard, glancing at the screen.

"Ward 4. Down the hall, second door on the right."

Her eyes shifted back to the screen, as if we were already forgotten.

No further questions.

No interest.

Just another day in a forgotten place.

Listening to her, we made our way down the long hallway, the fluorescent lights flickering overhead. The walls were lined with faded tiles, and the occasional murmur of patients or the shuffle of nurses' feet echoed through the hall. It was as if the very building was suffocating under the weight of the people inside it.

I could feel Khaja's growing discomfort beside me.

His silence spoke volumes, and I could tell that every step he was making brought him more and more uneasy. But I couldn't turn back now. I had to know.

We reached Ward 4, a heavy door with a small rectangular window, covered with bars. I glanced through the window, my chest heaving with my heart inside. The ward was dimly lit, with a few sparse beds lined up against the walls. Most of the patients were either sitting or lying down, staring blankly ahead, their faces gaunt and tired. It was a place where time seemed to have no meaning, where people went to disappear.

"There they are,"

I whispered, pointing to the far corner of the room from the outside of the ward.

The couple was sitting together on a narrow bed, the woman lying back with her eyes closed, her lips moving as if she was talking to herself. The man sat beside her, motionless, his eyes fixed on the floor.

He looked even more distant than I had imagined—like a shell of a person, hollowed out and empty.

A shiver went down my spine as I watched them. They were nothing like the noisy, disturbing presence they had been at ABK township. Now, they were silent, broken, and disturbingly out of place.

"What do we do now?"

Khaja whispered, his voice low and tense.

I had no idea.

A Part of me had hoped that seeing them would bring some clarity, some understanding of what had been happening in that flat. But standing there, looking at them, I only felt more confused. More afraid.

There was something deeply wrong with them, and I knew this visit wasn't going to give me the closure I'd hoped for. If anything, it was only going to drag me deeper into the mystery.

"We talk to them, We need to know what happened."

I said, though my voice lacked confidence.

Khaja didn't respond, but I could feel his reluctance as I reached for the handle and pushed open the door.

I couldn't believe what I was seeing.

The door to Ward 4 creaked as I pushed it open, the sound cutting through the heavy silence of the room. As we stepped inside, the dim lighting and stale air seemed to thicken, wrapping around us like a suffocating fog. The sight of the couple being together in the far corner shivered down my back. They looked even more out of place than I had imagined.

The woman was laying back on the narrow bed, her eyes half-closed, but her lips moved in constant motion, muttering to herself. Her voice was low, almost a whisper, but the way her mouth moved, it was as though she was talking to someone—or something—unseen.

The man sat beside her, still and silent, his eyes fixed on the floor. He didn't acknowledge us as we approached, he didn't even flinch. It was as though he was lost in another world, detached from everything around him.

I stopped a few feet away from the bed, my heart thumping fiercely inside me. Khaja stood beside me, his unease palpable, but I was transfixed by the woman's behaviour. Her muttering grew louder as we drew closer, and I realized that her voice wasn't consistent—it was changing, shifting in pitch and tone, as if she was having a conversation with herself.

"I told you to stay here,"

she whispered, her voice soft and motherly.

"You have to be quiet now."

Then, in a higher pitch, almost childlike, she responded to herself,

"I'm sorry, Mommy. I didn't mean to."

My blood ran cold. The voice was identical to the sounds I had heard through the walls of the flat for all those years. The soft scolding, the gentle replies—she was recreating the same scene, repeatedly, as if the voices of the children hadn't been real at all, but some twisted projection of her mind.

I stood frozen; my eyes locked on her as she continued her unsettling conversation with herself. She switched effortlessly between the motherly voice and the childish responses, her expression changing subtly with each shift. It was as if she had become both the parent and the child, trapped in some kind of loop, repeating the same dialogue endlessly.

"She... she's mimicking the voices,"

I whispered to Khaja, my voice shaking.

"This is what we heard. This is what we thought were the children."

Khaja, for once, seemed shocked to respond. He stared at the woman, his face pale.

I could tell he was horrified, but I couldn't tear my gaze away from her. Every word she spoke, every shift in tone, was a direct echo of the voices that had haunted ABK township for years.

"Mommy, I'm scared,"

She whispered again, her voice soft and trembling, like that of a frightened child. Then, without pause, she answered herself in the same soothing, motherly voice,

"It's okay, baby. I'm here. I'll always protect you."

It was unbearable to watch, and yet, I couldn't move. My mind raced, trying to process what I was seeing. The children we had heard—they had never been real. They had been a figment of this woman's fractured mind, an illusion she had created to fill some void in her life. And the worst part was that it made sense. The lies, the denial of their existence—it was all because those children had never truly existed.

The woman's voice grew softer again, trailing off into unintelligible murmurs. Her eyes fluttered shut, as though she was drifting back into some half-conscious state. But her lips kept moving, still trapped in the same cycle of conversation, locked in her own twisted reality.

I took a step closer, trying to understand, trying to wrap my mind around what I was witnessing.

"How... how long has she been like this?"

I muttered, mostly to myself, but Khaja heard me.

"She's... she's not well,"

Khaja whispered, his voice filled with both fear and pity.

This isn't just madness. It's... something else. But I wasn't sure what it was. The sight of her lying there, mimicking those voices—it was more than just illness. It felt like something darker, something that had been festering for years, hidden behind the walls of their flat. I had come looking for answers, but now I wasn't sure I wanted to know the truth.

The woman's muttering faded into silence, and she lay still, her eyes closed. For a moment, the room felt frozen, as if time itself had stopped. Khaja and I stood there, motionless, the weight of what we had just witnessed pressing down on us like a physical force.

And then, just when I thought it was over, her eyes snapped open.

She didn't look at us. Her gaze was unfocused, distant, but her lips began to move again, slowly at first, then faster, as if she was trying to catch up with her own thoughts. But this time, her voice was different. It wasn't the gentle, motherly tone from before. It was harsh, urgent, and filled with a kind of manic energy.

"They're gone,"

she whispered, her voice shaking.

"They're gone, and it's my fault. I didn't mean to. I didn't mean to..."

I froze, my heart racing. This wasn't part of the cycle. This was something new, something she hadn't said before.

Khaja took a step back, his face pale.

"What is she talking about?"

I whispered,

"I don't know,"

my eyes locked on the woman as she continued to mutter, her words tumbling out faster and faster.

"I didn't mean to,"

she repeated, her voice growing more frantic.

"They were supposed to stay. They were supposed to stay with me..."

Her voice cracked, and for the first time, I saw tears well up in her eyes. She wasn't mimicking anyone now. She was speaking in her own voice—raw, broken, and filled with despair.

I didn't know what to say. I didn't know how to react. All I could do was stand there, watching as the woman's mind unravelled before my eyes, revealing the dark, twisted reality that had been hidden beneath the surface all along.

As the woman's frantic whispers trailed off into a broken silence, I felt my attention shift to the man sitting next to her. And the men,

He didn't say a word. He didn't even look at us. He had been so still, so quiet this entire time that it was easy to forget he was even there. He hadn't moved once. Not a flinch, not a blink. Nothing.

I looked at him now, trying to get a read on him, but there was something deeply unsettling about his stillness. His face was blank, drained of expression, his eyes unfocused and empty. He stared at the floor, as if the world around him no longer existed. His wife was breaking down beside him, caught in the tangle of her own fractured mind, and yet he sat there, as though he were frozen in time.

Khaja must have noticed the same thing, because he nudged me lightly, his voice low.

"What's wrong with him?"

I shook my head, unsure. There was a hollowness to him that I couldn't quite explain. It was like he had shut down, completely disconnected from reality. The man who had once been at the centre of so much noise, so much chaos, now sat in eerie silence, locked inside his own mind.

"We need to talk to him,"

I whispered, more to myself than to Khaja.

If anyone had answers, it was him. He was the only one left who might be able to tell us what had really happened. But looking at him now, I wasn't sure if he was even capable of speech. There was something broken inside him—something far beyond repair.

I took a tentative step closer to the bed on which the couple were sitting, my heart racing through my chest.

"Sir,"

I said quietly, my voice careful.

"Can you hear me?"

No response.

I swallowed hard and tried again.

"Sir, we need to ask you something. About your apartment. About the children..."

His eyes flickered slightly, and for a moment, I thought he might respond.

But he didn't. His gaze remained locked on the floor, as if the words I was speaking weren't reaching him at all.

I glanced back at Khaja, who stood a few steps behind me, his arms crossed tightly over his chest. He looked just as uneasy as I felt.

"Maybe he can't hear us,"

Khaja muttered.

"Maybe he's... too far gone."

But I wasn't ready to give up. I stepped closer, my voice firmer now.

"We heard them, you know. The children. We all heard them."

At that, something changed. The man's eyes shifted—just for a second—toward me. It was a small movement, barely noticeable, but I caught it. He had heard me.

I took another step, my heart racing with a mix of fear and hope.

"You don't have to pretend anymore. We know something happened. We just want to understand."

His gaze flickered again, this time rising slightly off the floor, but still, he said nothing. His hands, which had been resting limply on his lap, twitched ever so slightly. I could see it now—the tension in his body, the way his muscles tightened under his skin, as if he were holding something back.

"Please,"

I urged, my voice soft but insistent.

"We just want to know the truth."

For a long moment, there was nothing. The silence stretched on, thick and suffocating. And then, just as I was about to step back, he moved. It was a small movement, barely more than a shift in his posture, but it sent a ripple of unease through me.

His hand lifted, trembling slightly, and for a moment I thought he might reach out, might say something. But instead, he raised his hand to his mouth, pressing his fingers against his lips in a gesture that was almost reflexive—like someone trying to stop themselves from speaking.

And then he whispered, barely audible,

"It wasn't supposed to happen."

Listening to him I froze, the words hitting me like a punch to the gut. Khaja took a sharp breath beside me, and I could feel the tension radiating off him.

"What wasn't supposed to happen?"

I asked, my voice shaking.

The man's fingers trembled against his lips, his eyes still unfocused.

"The children,"

he muttered.

"They were supposed to stay quiet. We didn't... we didn't mean for it to go so far."

My spine tingled with an icy shock. His words were disjointed, almost incoherent, but I could feel the weight of them. There was something dark, something terrible lurking just beneath the surface of his broken mind.

"We?"

I pressed, my voice tight.

"Who is 'we'?

What happened to the children?"

But as soon as the question left my mouth, the man's hand dropped from his lips, and he fell silent again. His gaze returned to the floor, and the brief flicker of life that had passed through him was gone, replaced once more by that hollow, vacant expression.

I stood there, frozen in place, the weight of his words hanging heavy in the air. I had come here looking for answers, but all I had found was more confusion, more darkness. Whatever had happened in that flat, whatever had driven this couple to the brink of madness, was still out of reach, hidden behind a wall of silence and broken memories.

Khaja tugged at my sleeve, his voice tight with fear.

"We should go."

I didn't want to leave. Not yet. But I could see the truth in Khaja's eyes—there was nothing more we could get from them. The woman was lost in her own mind, and the man, whatever role he had played in this nightmare, was too far gone to explain it.

I nodded slowly, stepping back from the bed.

"Yeah. Let's go."

As we turned to leave, I cast one last glance at the couple. The woman had fallen silent again, her eyes fluttering shut as she mumbled to herself. The man sat motionless, his face blank, his eyes distant. They were both trapped—trapped in whatever horror had taken place in that flat.

And I knew, as we walked out of the ward, that the mystery was far from over.

It was not the end. It was merely the beginning.

As Khaja and I left the ward, the cold air of the hospital hallway hit me like a wave, but it did nothing to shake the unease that had settled deep in my chest. The sounds of the woman's mimicking voices still echoed in my ears, and the man's cryptic words,

It wasn't supposed to happen—kept replaying in my mind.

We walked in silence down the long, sterile corridor, our footsteps the only sound cutting through the stillness. Khaja, his face pale and his hands jammed into his pockets, looked more shaken than I had ever seen him. He had been reluctant from the start, but now I could see that this visit had affected him more than he wanted to admit.

When we finally reached the hospital's exit, he stopped, turning to face me.

"This is too much,"

he said, his voice tight.

"We shouldn't have come here. They're broken, man.

They're not going to give us any answers. You saw them—they're lost."

I looked at him, his words barely registering. My mind was still racing, trying to piece together what we had seen and heard. The children's voices, the woman's disturbing mimicry, the husband's quiet, haunted confession—it all pointed to something darker than I had anticipated. Something terrible had happened in that flat, something they had both been part of.

"They know something,"
I said quietly, my voice firm.
"We're missing a piece of the puzzle, but they know something about those children."
Khaja shook his head, running a hand through his hair.
"And what does it matter?
You heard the guy, he's barely there. Whatever he knows, he's not going to tell us. And the woman—"
He trailed off, shivering at the memory of her eerie behaviour.
"She's gone, man. There's nothing more to find here."
I insisted
"But there is,"
the conviction in my voice stronger now.
"The children— after listening to them I feel like they were never real. It was all in her head. That's why they denied having kids. But something happened that pushed them over the edge, and we're not getting the full story."
Khaja stared at me, his eyes wide with disbelief.
"So, what now?
You're just going to keep digging until you find out what?
What if it's something we don't want to know?"
I didn't have an answer for him. All I knew was that the mystery wasn't over. The couple's collapse into madness wasn't the end of the story. It was only the beginning. I had to figure out what had really happened in that flat, and why they had tried so hard to hide the truth.
"There's more to this,"
I said, my voice low but resolute.
"The voices, the kids—they might have been part of her delusion, but that doesn't explain everything. The way the husband reacted—there's something he's not telling us. They're hiding something bigger."
Khaja took a step back, his face hardening.
"I can't do this anymore, man. I thought this was just some weird, creepy mystery, but it's way more than that.
These people—they're seriously messed up. This isn't a game."

I could hear the fear in his voice, and part of me understood. This had gone far beyond what we had initially imagined. It wasn't just about strange noises or unsettling neighbours anymore. It was about something darker, something that had twisted this couple's minds and left them trapped in a nightmare of their own making.

But I couldn't stop now. I was too deep. The mystery had its hooks in me, and I knew I wouldn't be able to rest until I had uncovered the truth.

"I'm not asking you to keep going with me,"

I said softly.

"If you want to step back, I get it. But I can't let this go. Not now."

Khaja looked at me for a long time, his expression unreadable. I could see the conflict in his eyes—part of him wanted to walk away, to leave this entire nightmare behind. But another part of him, the part that had been with me through all of this, understood why I had to keep going.

Finally, he sighed, shaking his head.

"You're going to get yourself in trouble, you know that?"

I managed a small, grim smile.

"Probably."

He rubbed his temples, muttering under his breath.

"Alright, but you're on your own from here. I can't do this anymore. It's too much."

I nodded, feeling a strange mix of relief and sadness.

Khaja had been my partner through all of this, but I knew he couldn't follow me any further. The road ahead was too dark, too dangerous.

"I get it,"

I said.

"Thanks for sticking with me this far."

He didn't respond, just gave me a long, hard look before we started our car. Through the journey it was just silence that is being communicated among us. As soon as we reached the apartment complex, Khaja parked the car, stepping out,

"Just... don't do anything stupid,"

he said over his shoulder as he moved toward the parking lot.

I watched him go, feeling the weight of his absence settle over me like a cold shadow. For the first time since this whole thing began, I realized I was truly on my own.

But I wasn't afraid. The fear that had gripped me for so long now had turned into something else—an obsession, a drive to uncover the truth, no matter how dark or terrifying it might be. The couple's madness, their strange behaviour, the mystery of the children's voices—it was all leading to something, and I was determined to find out what.

As I turned and walked back toward my bike, I couldn't shake the feeling that this wasn't the last time I would see that couple. Inserting the key, I took of my bike, I started heading towards the old library to dig more information.

Their story wasn't over, and neither was mine.

CHAPTER VI

The Deepening Mystery.

I knew I couldn't stop now. The more I uncovered, the darker it became.

Visit made by us to the mental hospital felt as if deepened the eerie silence of ABK township seemed louder than ever. As I headed towards the old library, I couldn't shake the image of the couple from my mind—her twisted mimicry of children's voices, his cryptic words about something that wasn't supposed to happen. It gnawed at me, pulling me deeper into a web of unanswered questions. There had to be something more. Something that connected all of this.

As soon as I reached the library, I knew this closed book would take the good number of days, and I began spending my days combing through every scrap of information I could find about the building, it wasn't easy—they had been careful to leave few traces behind. But I wasn't about to give up.

I decided to do some research. I knew the building had been around for years, one of those old apartment complexes that had seen countless people come and go. There must have been to be something about its history that would explain the strangeness. I started by searching online, digging through old forums and tenant reviews of ABK township. I dug through old newspapers, local archives, and even neighborhood gossip forums, hoping to find a thread to pull.

At first, it was just the usual complaints—poor maintenance, noisy neighbors, high rent. But then, buried in the depths of an old forum, My blood ran cold as I came upon a post.

It was from a former tenant, dated over five years ago. The post was short, but it caught my attention right away:

"Lived on the 13th floor for 6 months. Heard strange things at night—crying, banging, voices. My neighbors were weird, never saw them. Moved out after things got too creepy. Don't recommend staying there for long. The place feels haunted."

The post was filled with vague descriptions of unsettling noises and strange encounters, but it was enough to confirm that the watchman and Mrs. Varma had hinted that **the 13th floor had a reputation. And it wasn't a good one.**

I dug deeper, searching for any mention of the 13th floor, and soon I found more posts. Former tenants shared eerily similar stories—noises at night, strange occurrences, and an overwhelming sense of unease. Some of them mentioned the family in the flat next door, though none of them had ever seen the children. The stories were all the same: people heard the crying, and the arguing, but no one ever saw the family come and go. They lived in the building like ghosts, invisible yet ever-present, haunting the lives of those who lived around them.

One post in particular sent a shiver down my spine:

"There's something wrong with that apartment. People don't stay on the 13th floor for long. They move in, hear the noises, then they leave. My family stayed there for three months before we had to go. The crying... it never stops. We asked the building management about it, but they said there was no record of anyone living in that flat for years. Whatever's going on there, it's not normal."

No record of anyone living there?

I read the sentence over and over, trying to make sense of it.

How could that be possible? We had heard them—arguing, crying, living their lives behind closed doors. But if what the post said was true, then something wasn't adding up.

I sat back in my chair, my thoughts racing. Could the flat next door really be empty? Even before these couples moved in.

If so, who—or what—was making all that noise?

I decided to dig even further, searching public records for any mention of the flat. It was tedious work, but eventually, I found something. The apartment had been sold several times over the years, with each owner staying only for a brief period before selling again. And there was something else—each sale was followed by a long period of vacancy, sometimes years. It was as if no one could live there for long, and when they left, the flat stayed empty, untouched.

As I perused the documents, my heart raced in my chest.

The most recent sale had been nearly two years ago, and according to the records, the flat had been vacant ever since. No one had registered to live there, and no utilities had been activated. As far as the official documents were concerned, the flat was uninhabited.

But I knew better. I had heard them, we all did, the family, the crying, the arguments—it was real. It had to be.

There was no way I had imagined all of it. But if the flat was supposed to be empty, what was really going on?

My mind spinning with possibilities. The building always had a strange vibe, but now it felt like more than just a bad atmosphere. It felt like something was wrong with the very foundation of the place like the walls themselves were soaked in secrets.

The posts from former tenants confirmed what the watchman had hinted at—there was a history of strange happenings in ABK township. But it didn't answer the most important question:

what was happening in that flat?

Was the family next door real?

Or were they something else entirely?

Are these couples the same tenants the posts were describing?

How can it be possible, that they have shifted here two years ago? With all the questions in my head, I felt like the more I searched, the more disturbing the details were.

In order to clear my mind, I started digging into the couple, who were admitted in the mental hospital now.

The first clue came from a brief news article I found buried deep in the local archives. It was dated ten years ago, from a small town not far from here. The couple had lived there briefly, and during their time in that town, there had been reports of strange disturbances—neighbors complained of hearing children crying late at night, though the couple had no children at that time. But that wasn't the worst part. There were also whispers about a missing child, a six-year-old boy who had disappeared without a trace.

No leads, no suspects. Just gone.

It was the same pattern, over and over. The couple moved frequently, never staying in one place for more than a few years. In each town or city, they had lived, there were always murmurs of something being off complaints from neighbors, reports of strange noises, and, in a few cases, disappearances of young children that had never been solved.

The more I read, the more unsettled I became.

How could this couple have lived in so many places, leaving behind a trail of unanswered questions and missing children, without anyone putting the pieces together?

I scrolled the notes furiously, trying to make sense of the pattern. It was almost as if they had been running—moving from place to place to avoid suspicion.

But suspicion of what?

And what had really happened to those missing children?

My obsession with finding the answers only grew stronger. I couldn't stop thinking about the woman's muttering in the hospital, her mimicry of the children's voices. It was like she had been living in some alternate reality, playing both the mother and the child. But there was something more beneath her madness, something darker. The man's cryptic words,

"It wasn't supposed to happen,"

echoed in my mind.

I was certain now that the couple's strange behavior was tied to the disappearances. There was no other explanation. But I couldn't prove it. Not yet.

It was late one evening, after hours of searching, when I stumbled across an old photograph on a community forum. It showed a group of children at a school event in one of the towns the couple had lived in.

I was about to ignore it when I observed something unsettling: standing off to the side, the man and woman were watching the children. They weren't interacting with anyone, just standing there, observing.

The caption mentioned that the event had taken place just a few days before a child had gone missing in that same town.

A knot of fear formed in my abdomen. This wasn't just a coincidence. They had been there—always lurking on the edges of these communities, always present when children disappeared.

I couldn't sleep that night.

Every time I closed my eyes, I saw the couple's vacant expressions, the woman's voice echoing in my mind.

The pieces of the puzzle were starting to come together, but the picture they formed was something far darker than I had imagined.

The next morning, I have decided.

I had to go deeper.

I had to find out what had really happened in those towns, and why the couple had been so desperate to run from their past.

There had to be someone who knew more—someone who had seen or heard something that could explain the connection between the couple and the missing children.

But I knew one thing for sure: whatever I uncovered; it was going to change everything.

It made me feel as if, *People did know something was wrong, but no one wanted to say it out loud.*

After digging through the couple's past and finding unsettling patterns of missing children, I knew that I needed to take my investigation closer to home. If there were hidden details about their lives in the apartment, someone in ABK township had to know something. People didn't just live next door to a strange couple for years without noticing things—no matter how much they tried to ignore it. And I knew **the problem was getting people to talk.**

Ever since the couple left, the building had grown quieter, as if the tenants were trying to forget the strange happenings of the past few years. Most avoided eye contact when I tried to bring up the couple or the noises. It was almost like an unspoken rule—no one talked about it. They had been disturbed by the strange sounds, the constant arguments, and the eerie presence of the children's voices, but now that the couple was gone, no one wanted to dwell on it. Everyone was trying to move on, as though forgetting was the only way to protect themselves from whatever darkness had touched the 13th floor.

But I wasn't letting it go. I couldn't.

I started knocking on doors, asking questions, hoping someone would open up. Most people were polite but vague shrugging off my inquiries with phrases like,

"Oh, I didn't really know them"

or

"I never got involved in their business."

It was frustrating but understandable. People didn't want to get caught up in something that felt too dark, or too mysterious.

Finally, on the third day of my persistent questioning, I knocked on the door of

Mr. Varun. He was one of the longest-standing tenants in ABK township, a retired schoolteacher who had lived on the 12th floor for nearly 20 years. If anyone knew something, it must be him.

Mr. Varun answered the door, his face lined with age and weariness, but his sharp eyes were as observant as ever. I had spoken to him in passing many times before, but never about anything serious. He was always kind, offering polite conversation, but he wasn't the type to meddle in others' affairs.

"Ah, it's you,"

he said, squinting at me as if he was trying to read my intentions.

"What brings you to my door at this hour?"

I hesitated for a moment, unsure of how to approach the subject. But I needed answers, and I had a feeling that Mr. Varun was my best chance of getting them.

"I've been looking into the couple who used to live next door, to us"

I said carefully.

"I... I think something was very wrong with them. I was wondering if you noticed anything strange about them—anything at all."

Mr. Varun's expression changed slightly, a flicker of unease crossing his face. He stepped back from the door and gestured for me to come inside.

"Come in, come in,"

he said, his voice quieter now.

"It's not a conversation to have in the hallway."

I followed him into his small but tidy apartment, the scent of old books and strong tea filling the air. He motioned for me to sit at the small table by the window, where a pot of tea was already set up. As I sat down, I noticed how quiet the room was, the kind of quiet that made you feel like even your thoughts were being overheard.

Mr. Varun poured himself a cup of tea, then sat down across from me, his hands trembling slightly as he held the cup.

"You're not the first to ask questions about them,"

he said after a long pause.

"But I'll tell you this—their story didn't start with them. There's been something wrong with this building for years, long before they moved in."

My spine tingled with cold.

"What do you mean?"

Mr. Varun sighed, leaning back in his chair.

"People in this building have always kept to themselves. It's the way things are in any apartment complex. But strange things have been happening here for a long time. People don't talk about it because it's easier to pretend it isn't happening.

Easier to live your life without wondering what's going on in the flat next door."

He took a sip of his tea, his eyes far away as if recalling distant memories, and continued

"I've lived here for nearly two decades, and I've seen tenants come and go. But the strange disturbances—those started years ago. Long before the couple, you're asking about.

At first, it was small things—odd sounds at night, footsteps when no one should be walking, whispers in empty hallways. People would complain, but the building management never found anything. No explanations. Just... noise."

I leaned in closer, feeling the tension rise in my chest.

"But it got worse, didn't it?"

He nodded slowly.

"Yes, it did. About five years ago, people started hearing children's voices—just like you did. We all heard them, but when we went to check, there were no children. People would report it, but again, nothing. It didn't make sense.

Then came the couple her, with her unsettling calmness, and him, always so quiet.

After they moved in, the disturbances got worse. More frequent. Louder. And then..."

He trailed off, his voice dropping to a whisper.

"The disappearances started."

I whispered back,

"Disappearances?" my pulse quickening.

Mr. Varun's hands trembled as he set his cup down.

"Two years ago, a young boy who lived in the building went missing. He was only seven, and one day, he just vanished. His parents were frantic, the whole building was turned upside down looking for him, but he was never found. The police came, of course, but they couldn't figure it out. No signs of a struggle, no evidence of foul play. Just... gone."

I stared at him, unable to speak.

The missing boy.

The children's voices.

It all made sense now.

The couple hadn't just been strange—they were tied to something far darker. And the building... the building itself was part of it.

Mr. Varun looked at me, his eyes filled with a quiet sadness.

"People think they can ignore it, pretend it isn't real. But something is wrong here, something has been wrong for a long time. And I fear it's only going to get worse."

Listening to him, I left Mr. Varun's apartment with my mind racing, and my heart pounding.

The mystery had deepened in ways I hadn't anticipated. The couple wasn't just part of this, they were part of something bigger, something that had been lurking in the shadows of ABK township for years.

And now I was caught in the middle of it.

"I knew I was missing something crucial, something that tied it all together."

The conversation with Mr. Varun left me reeling. I couldn't get rid of the feeling that there was something far darker and more profound than I had ever thought possible hiding beneath the surface.

It wasn't just about the couple anymore—**it was about the building itself.** But the more I tried to piece it together, the more elusive the truth seemed.

As I sat in my apartment later that night, my thoughts ran in circles. I had spread out all my notes, photographs, and clippings across the floor, trying to find some connection, some pattern that I hadn't seen before.

I was convinced there was a missing piece, something that could make everything click into place. But no matter how hard I looked, nothing seemed to fit.

The couple's strange behavior, the voices, the missing boy—it all pointed to something terrible, but I still didn't know what had triggered it.

Why had they denied having any children at all?

What had caused the disturbances to intensify after they moved in?

Why do we still hear the children's voices from that flat?

I sifted through the articles I had found about the couple's previous stay, re-reading the accounts of missing children and unexplained sounds in the other towns they had lived in.

There were the same unsettling trends,

Complaints from neighbors, strange noises, occasional disappearances. But the couple had always left before anyone could connect the dots.

It wasn't until I reviewed the timeline of their stay at ABK township that something clicked. The noises, the children's voices, the strange disturbances—they always seemed to follow a pattern. The couple had moved into the building just before the voices enhanced. And every time the voices grew louder, it was at the same time of day—late afternoon, just before dusk.

I pulled out my notebook, scribbling down the timeline. The first report of the children's voices had been made around 5:30 p.m., and every complaint from the tenants after that had been around the same time. That was when the crying, the laughter, and the arguments would echo through the walls. The couple had always been at home during those times, but no one had ever seen the children.

What if it wasn't a coincidence?

What if something triggered those voices every day?

What if the kids weren't just the woman's imagination?

I leaned back, staring at the timeline I had drawn. The pattern was clear, but the why still escaped me.

What was special about the time of day? What could have caused the voices to start, and why had they grown louder over time?

My thoughts spiraled, dragging me deeper into my own obsession.

I couldn't stop thinking about the woman's mimicry in the hospital, the way she had slipped so seamlessly between the voice of a mother and the voice of a child.

Was she mimicking the voices she heard?

or was she creating them herself?

And why had the man been so cryptic in his response— "It wasn't supposed to happen."

What wasn't supposed to happen?

I stood up and paced the room, my mind racing. I had to be missing something. Something crucial. The noises, the children, the disappearances—it all tied back to the couple. But there was something more, something that went deeper than just their twisted behavior. Something that had to do with the building itself.

I thought back to what Mr. Varun had told me—the strange noises had started long before the couple had moved in.

The whispers, the footsteps, the eerie disturbances had been part of ABK township for years. The couple had only intensified them.

But how? and why?

Suddenly, it hit me. The voices weren't just tied to the couple—they were tied to the building. And whatever had caused the disturbances had been lying dormant, waiting for something—or someone—to trigger it.

The couple hadn't brought the darkness with them. They had woken it up.

I grabbed my jacket and rushed out of my apartment, heading straight for the 13th floor of ABK township. My pulse quickened as I reached the hallway, the familiar sense of unease settling over me like a heavy blanket. I stopped outside the couple's old flat, staring at the door that had been the source of so much confusion and fear.

The hallway was quiet, too quiet, the kind of silence that felt wrong. I stood there, waiting, listening, but nothing happened. No voices, no whispers, no crying. Just silence.

But I knew it was there, lurking beneath the surface. I could feel it.

I glanced at my watch. It was 5:15 p.m. The voices always started around 5:30, according to the records. If I was right, if the disturbances followed a pattern, then something should happen soon.

I leaned against the wall, trying to calm my racing thoughts. The minutes ticked by the silence pressing in around me. I could hear the faint hum of the building, the distant sounds of traffic outside, but nothing else.

It soon ticked 5:25 p.m.

Breathing deeply, I waited and paid attention.

And then, just as the clock struck 5:30, I heard it.

A soft, barely audible whisper. At first, I thought I was imagining it, but then it grew louder, clearer. It was the sound of a child's voice, soft and trembling, coming from the direction of the flat.

"Mommy..."

I froze, my heart pounding in my chest. The voice was faint, distant, but unmistakable. It was the same voice I had heard all those months ago, the same voice that had echoed through the walls of ABK township.

"Mommy, I'm scared..."

The whisper sent a shudder down my spine. I strained to hear more as I put my ear to the door. The voice was growing louder, more insistent.

"Mommy, don't leave me..."

It wasn't real.

It couldn't be. But there it was, clear as day, coming from an empty flat.

I stepped back from the door, my mind racing. The pattern was real. The voices were tied to something beyond the couple's madness, something that had been part of the building long before they arrived.

And I had just found the missing piece.

The realization that the strange voices followed a pattern—a specific time each day—sent a jolt through me. But knowing when the voices occurred wasn't enough. I needed to understand why they were happening.

Why were they tied to this building, and more specifically, to this flat?

I had exhausted the archives I could access online and the knowledge of the tenants. And I knew There was one place I hadn't looked, one place that might hold the answers. And there were still the building's old records, the ones buried in the storeroom that is in the parking lot of the building, untouched for years. The building had been around for decades, and I was willing to bet that there were things buried in those files that the management wanted forgotten.

That night, after most of the residents had gone to bed, I made my way to the parking lot. This time the air down here was thick with dust, the smell of mildew clinging to every surface. A single dim bulb flickered overhead, casting long shadows along the narrow corridor. The old storage room, where the building's records were kept, sat at the end of the parking lot, hidden behind a rusty metal door that looked like it hadn't been opened in years.

I hesitated for a moment, feeling the weight of the silence pressing in on me. Something about this place felt wrong like the building itself didn't want me down here. But I shook off the feeling. I had come too far to turn back now.

The door creaked as I pushed the storeroom it open, to my surprise the storeroom was not completely locked, and it quickly opened with no effort, revealing rows of old filing cabinets and stacks of dusty boxes. The air was stale, thick with the scent of paper that had been left to rot. I grabbed a flashlight from my pocket, flicked it on, and began searching through the files. Most of them were mundane—old maintenance records, rent rolls, complaints from tenants about broken elevators, or noisy neighbors. But as I dug deeper, I found what I was looking for.

At the very back of the room, hidden behind a stack of old paperwork, I found a box labeled "Incident Reports—ABK township, 1980–2000."

My heart raced erratically. As I opened the box. The thick folders filled with yellowed papers—complaints, reports, letters. I began flipping through them, my hands trembling slightly.

The first few reports were nothing unusual complaints about faulty plumbing, noise disturbances, and minor repairs. But as I dug deeper, something that chilled my blood was discovered.

It was a report from 1993. A tenant had filed a formal complaint about hearing strange noises coming from the 13th floor. According to the report, the tenant claimed to have heard children crying late at night, even though no children lived on that floor at the time. The tenant mentioned that the voices seemed to come and go at specific times—mostly in the late afternoon, just before dusk.

I kept reading, my pulse quickening. Over the next few years, more reports appeared, all from different tenants who had lived on or near the 13th floor. Each one described hearing the same eerie sounds—children crying, voices whispering, footsteps in the hallways when no one was there. Some of the tenants mentioned feeling an overwhelming sense of dread whenever they were alone on the 13th floor as if they were being watched.

Then I found something even more disturbing.

In 1997, a six-year-old boy had gone missing from the building. His parents lived on the 12th floor, and one day, without any explanation, he disappeared. There were no signs of a struggle, no clues as to where he might have gone. The police had searched the building thoroughly, but the boy was never found.

I flipped through more reports, my hands shaking. In 2002, another child—this time a seven-year-old girl—had disappeared under similar circumstances. She had lived on the 11th floor with her mother, and one day she simply vanished. No one in the building had seen or heard anything unusual that day, but some of the tenants reported hearing children's voices in the hallways the night before she disappeared.

The reports continued. Over the years, more children had gone missing—always from the lower floors, and always without a trace. And each time, the voices had been heard in the days leading up to the disappearances.

My heart raced as I connected the dots. The couple wasn't the first to be the source of those voices, and they weren't the first to experience or cause strange disturbances in the building. The voices, the disappearances, the sense of being watched—it had been happening for decades. The couple had only been the latest victims of whatever haunted this place.

And the building management had covered it up. The reports I found had never been made public. The police investigations into the missing children had turned up nothing, and eventually, the cases had gone cold. But the management had known. They had known all along, and they had buried the truth.

I was unable to get rid of the impression that the building was somehow implicated.

The strange pattern, the way the voices always seemed to come from the 13th floor, the way the children had vanished without a trace—it all pointed to something beyond the couple's madness. Something far more sinister.

As I shut the last file, a chilly shiver went down my spine. I had come here looking for answers, and I had found them—but now I wasn't sure I wanted to know what they meant.

I stood in the silence of the parking lot, surrounded by the forgotten records of ABK township's dark history, and realized that I had uncovered something much bigger than I had ever anticipated. I closed the door of the stoor room, but the thoughts began sprinting through my mind.

The couple hadn't brought the evil with them—it had been here all along, lurking in the shadows of the building, waiting for someone to notice.

And now that I had, I couldn't turn back.

I wasn't sure if the building was watching me, or if I was losing my mind.

After uncovering the hidden files, I returned to Khaja's flat, my mind buzzing with everything I had just read. The weight of the building's dark history, the years of disappearances, the eerie reports of crying children—it was all too much to take in at once. The walls of ABK township felt like they were closing in on me, their silent presence growing heavier with every passing moment.

I couldn't stop thinking about the voices. The crying, the laughter—echoes of the past that seemed to haunt this place long before the couple ever lived here.

How had no one else noticed?

How had this been kept quiet for so long?

I sat at my kitchen table, staring at the timeline I had scribbled in my notebook. There were gaps, and pieces that still didn't fit, but the outline was there. ABK township wasn't just a building. It was a trap—a place where children vanished without explanation, where their voices lingered like ghosts, trapped in the walls. The couple had been victims of something far older and far darker than their own madness.

But what had awakened it?

I needed answers, but I wasn't sure where to look next. The files had given me a glimpse of the truth, but they hadn't explained why. Why were the children disappearing?

Why were their voices tied to the 13th floor? And why did it all seem to revolve around a specific time of day?

As the questions raced through my mind, I stood up and walked to the window. The sky was dark, and the city lights flickered in the distance, casting long shadows over the streets below. The building felt different tonight—heavier, almost as if it were watching me. I had spent so much time trying to uncover its secrets, and now it felt like the building was aware of my presence, aware that I was getting closer to the truth.

I glanced at the clock. It was just after 11 p.m., and the building was quiet. Too quiet.

The silence pressed in around me, thick and oppressive, broken only by the occasional creak of the old pipes in the walls. I couldn't shake the feeling that something was wrong, that something was watching me from the shadows.

I grabbed my flashlight and decided to take another walk through the halls. I needed to clear my head, to shake off the growing sense of dread that was clinging to me like a second skin. But as I stepped out into the hallway, the unease only grew stronger.

The hallway was empty, but the air was thick with tension. The flickering lights cast long, distorted shadows along the walls, and the silence was suffocating. It was the kind of silence that felt alive, like it was waiting for something to happen.

I walked slowly, my footsteps echoing softly in the quiet. As I approached the 13th floor, that familiar sense of dread washed over me. The same feeling I had every time I stood outside the couple's old flat—the feeling that something was watching me, waiting for me to make the wrong move.

I stopped outside the flat, staring at the door. The voices had gone silent since the couple left, but the memory of them still lingered in the back of my mind. I could almost hear them now, faint and distant, like an echo of the past.

My hand hovered over the doorknob, and for a brief moment, I considered opening it. But something stopped me. Something in the air, something I couldn't quite explain. It was as if the building itself was warning me to stay away, to leave whatever darkness lurked behind that door alone.

I took a step back, my heart pounding in my chest. The silence felt heavier now, pressing in from all sides. And then, just as I turned to leave, I heard it.

A soft whisper. So, faint I could barely make it out, but unmistakable.

"Help me..."

I froze, my blood running cold. The voice was coming from inside the flat. But that wasn't possible. The flat was empty. No one had lived there since the couple left.

"Help me..."

the voice whispered again, louder this time, more desperate.

My breath caught in my throat as I stood there, paralyzed. The voice was a child's, soft and trembling, just like the voices I had heard before. But it wasn't an echo.

This was real. It was happening now.

Even before I could open the lock, I saw a hand resting on my shoulder, I looked around, and it was Khaja.

114

CHAPTER VII

The woman's Recognition.

I thought trying to enter the couples flat would provide answers, but I hadn't expected Khaja at my back.

The silence between Khaja and me was palpable as we walked down the hallway, after me trying to encounter in the abandoned flat at this late night, we both knew we couldn't ignore the mystery any longer. Something terrible had happened in that apartment—something that went beyond mere madness—and the details which I found in the storeroom, strengthened my intuition to dig deeper.

As we entered the flat, Khaja stood in the living room, his eyes were ignited with anger, I have never seen him, being so furious, and he questioned,

"What do you think, you were trying to do?"

I didn't know, whether to answer at that moment, knowing that he was being loud due to concern, I stood still.

After a moment, I started explaining all the information that I gathered, and I started telling him about the dark pattern that still concealed behind these walls.

Khaja heard me with all the patience, looking at me being completely involved into the situation, he seated himself on the couch, and rubbing his face, he told,

"What are you going to do now?"

I knew he doesn't want himself to get involved into this, and I said,

"I am thing to visit the couple again."

Staring at the floor, he nodded his head, he stood up, and said,

"Let's go tomorrow morning, now get back to your room and sleep."

That's it, he didn't deny this time, I headed back to my bed and waited for the sun to rise.

We started our journey towards the mental hospital mid-morning. The closer we got to the hospital, the more I felt the unease in Khaja. He gripped the steering wheel tightly, his knuckles white, his jaw clenched. I knew he didn't want to be here. He had made it clear after our last visit that he didn't believe anything more could be gained from speaking to the couple again. And yet, he still travelled with me, because he was scared of me getting into trouble. To him, they were just two broken people lost in their own delusions, But I couldn't shake the feeling that there was more to the story—something deeper that we hadn't uncovered yet.

"We don't have to do this if you're not up for it,"

I said quietly, breaking the silence.

Khaja shot me a glance, his face tense.

"We're already on our way. No turning back now."

I nodded, though I could sense the hesitation in his voice. For the past few days, I had noticed a growing unease in him, as if he was afraid of what we might find. But this visit wasn't just about being curios anymore, it was about answers. There was something strange about the way the couple had denied having children, something unsettling about the spectral sounds that continued to haunt the 13th floor. The missing children, the hidden files in the building's store room, the dark history of ABK township—it all pointed back to the couple.

If the woman knew something, we needed to find out.

The mental hospital loomed ahead as we approached, its stark walls and small barred windows casting a sense of foreboding. The place gave the same orgone as the last time. We parked and made our way inside, the air thick with hopelessness, walking along the long, sterile corridor towards the ward where the couple was confined, the fluorescent lights overhead flickered.

Khaja walked a few steps behind me, his footsteps slow and reluctant. I could feel his hesitation growing with each step, but I didn't turn back. I couldn't.

When we reached the door to the woman's room, I paused, my hand hovering over the handle. A part of me was nervous, very nervous about what we might discover, worried about the effect this visit might

have on Khaja. But I couldn't let that stop me.

With a deep breath, I pushed opening the door.

The room was exactly as we had left it the last time. The woman laying on the narrow bed, her frail body curled up under the thin, white blanket. Her eyes were half-closed, her lips moving in that same, slow rhythm as before, muttering words that barely made sense. Her husband sat in the corner, as motionless as ever, his eyes vacant, staring at the floor as though he had already drifted away from this world.

For a moment, it seemed like nothing had changed. But then, as Khaja stepped into the room behind me. All of a sudden, The woman's muttering stopped.

At first, I didn't notice it, but the sudden silence felt like a weight pressing down on the room. I glanced over at her, and that's when I saw it. Her eyes, which had been glazed and unfocused moments before, were now wide open being fixed directly on Khaja.

I froze, my heart pounding in my chest. The way she was looking at him—intense, focused, almost as if she recognized him sent a chill down my chine.

Khaja stopped in his tracks, clearly unnerved by the sudden change in the woman's demeanour.

"What... what's going on?"

he muttered, taking a step back.

I didn't answer.

I couldn't. All I could do was stare as the woman slowly sat up in her bed, her eyes never leaving Khaja. Her lips moved, but this time, it wasn't the nonsensical mumbling we had heard before. She was saying something—something specific, something directed at him.

"You..."

She whispered, her voice low but clear.

"You were there."

Khaja's face went pale. When she saw Khaja, something in her face changed.

The air in the room felt different now—thicker, heavier, charged with a tension I couldn't quite explain. It was as though time had slowed, and the woman's every movement was being drawn out, each second feeling like it stretched for an eternity. Her eyes, which had been dull and unfocused just moments ago, now seemed sharp, alive with a strange intensity as they locked onto Khaja.

"You..."

she repeated, her voice trembling but growing stronger.

"You were there."

Khaja took an instinctive step back, the color draining from his face.

"What... what is she talking about?"

His voice wavered, and for the first time since we started this investigation, I saw fear in his eyes.

I wanted to answer him, but the truth was, I had no idea what was happening. I turned my gaze back to the woman, my heart pounding. She was no longer the shell of a person lost in her own madness.

Now, she seemed aware, almost lucid, her gaze fixed solely on Khaja, as if no one else existed in the room.

The room felt colder, the stillness of it pressing down on us. I could hear Khaja's breathing quicken beside me, but I couldn't take my eyes off the woman. She slowly raised a trembling hand and pointed directly at him.

"You... watched,"

she whispered, her voice filled with a strange mix of accusation and recognition.

"You were there when they cried... you were there when they went away."

I glanced at Khaja, waiting for him to respond, but he was frozen, his eyes wide with disbelief. His entire body had gone rigid, and his hands were shaking slightly, as if her words had hit something deep inside him—something he didn't understand or couldn't face.

"What are you talking about?"

I finally asked, trying to break the heavy silence that had settled in the room.

"What do you mean he was there?"

The woman's eyes flickered toward me briefly, but they quickly snapped back to Khaja, as if he was the only one who mattered.

"You saw them,"

she said, her voice trembling with emotion.

"You were there. You let it happen."

Khaja's face twisted with confusion and fear.

"No, no, that's not true!"

he shouted, his voice rising in panic.

"I've never seen you before in my life! I've never... I wasn't there!"

The woman shook her head slowly, a small, unsettling smile creeping across her face.

"You were,"

she whispered.

"I remember."

The room felt like it was closing in around us. The woman's words hung in the air, heavy with accusation, and I could see the way they were affecting Khaja. He was visibly shaken, his usual calm demeanour shattered by the weight of her recognition. His hands clenched into fists at his sides, his breath coming in short, uneven bursts.

I tried to reason with myself. This woman was mentally ill. She had been confined to this hospital for years. She had no real grasp on reality, no way of knowing what was true or what wasn't. But the way she looked at Khaja, the certainty in her voice—it was unnerving. It was like she truly believed what she was saying.

"I don't know what you're talking about,"

Khaja muttered, his voice quieter now, but filled with desperation.

"You've got the wrong person. I was never there. I don't even know you."

The woman's smile faded, and her expression darkened. Her hand dropped back to her side, and for a moment, she looked like she might start crying. But then she whispered something else, that made me breathe consciously.

"They're still with you."

The room went deathly silent, even though I didn't completely understand what she meant, the words hit me like a punch to the gut. I could see the confusion and terror on Khaja's face, his eyes darting wildly between me and the woman, as if searching for some kind of explanation that simply wasn't there.

"I... I wasn't there,"

Khaja stammered again, his voice barely above a whisper now.

"I don't know what she's talking about."

But the look in the woman's eyes told a different story. She believed every word she had said, and as she stared at Khaja, I couldn't shake the feeling that maybe... just maybe... there was some truth to her words. What did she mean by *they're still with you?*

What was she seeing in Khaja that we couldn't?

The tension in the room had become unbearable. Khaja took another step back, his hands shaking more visibly now.

"Let's go,"

he muttered under his breath, avoiding the woman's gaze.

"We need to leave."

I didn't argue. Whatever was happening here, it was clear that staying longer wouldn't get us any closer to the truth, at least definitely not right now. But as we turned to leave, the woman's voice cut through the silence one last time, sending a shiver down my spine.

"They never leave, they follow you everywhere."

she whispered, her eyes never leaving Khaja.

"You... you were there,"

she whispered, her voice trembling.

Khaja stood frozen, the woman's gaze piercing through him. Her voice, fragile yet filled with certainty, echoed in the small, sterile room, and each word landed like a blow. I could feel the tension rising in the air, thick and suffocating. The fluorescent lights above flickered slightly, casting eerie shadows on the walls, as if even the room itself was reacting to her words.

I wanted to say something, to ask her what she meant, but my throat had gone dry. There was something unsettling about her certainty. The way she stared at Khaja—like she knew him, like she had seen him before which made my skin crawl.

Khaja took a step back, his expression shifting from confusion to fear.

"I don't know what you're talking about,"

he muttered, but there was a tremor in his voice.

"I wasn't there. I've never been there. I don't know you."

The woman's trembling fingers pointed directly at him, and her voice, though weak, was filled with an unshakable conviction.

"You were there when the children cried. I remember you. You were watching..."

Her words sent a jolt of cold fear through me.

Children.

Crying.

I had heard those sounds—those eerie, disembodied voices in the apartment—and now she was tying them directly to Khaja. How could that be possible?

Khaja's face turned pale, his breath coming in short gasps. He shook his head violently, backing away from the bed.

"No, no... she's wrong. She's confused. She's sick, man. She doesn't know what she's saying."

I watched him, my mind racing, trying to process what was happening. I had known Khaja for years, he was my closest friend, the one person I trusted in all of this madness. But the way the woman looked at him, the way her voice dripped with certainty, made me feel as if we were standing on the edge of something terrible.

I took a step forward, my eyes locked on the woman.

"What do you mean?

What are you talking about?

What did he see?"

The woman's eyes flickered toward me, but only for a moment before they snapped back to Khaja.

"He watched when they disappeared... when they were taken away. I saw him. He didn't stop it."

A cold sweat broke out across my forehead, and I could feel my heart pounding in my chest.

Disappeared?

Taken away?

My thoughts spun in circles, grasping at the pieces of the puzzle.

Was she talking about the missing children? The ones from the building's dark past?

Or was she referring to the missing children's cases that were navigating towards the couple? Or was she refereeing to something completely different

Khaja was shaking now, his hands clenched into fists at his sides.

"I've never seen you before!"

he shouted, his voice cracking.

"I don't know you!

I wasn't there!

I couldn't have been there!"

But the woman didn't flinch. Her gaze remained steady, unwavering.

"You were,"

she said softly, almost sadly.

"You watched it all."

I turned to Khaja, my mind racing with a hundred questions.

"What is she talking about?"

I asked, my voice barely above a whisper.

"Khaja... is there something you're not telling me?"

Khaja's eyes were wide, his face pale as a ghost.

"I swear, I don't know what she's talking about,"

He said, his voice desperate, pleading with me to believe him.

"I've never met her before. I've never even been near their flat until we started investigating this! She's just... she's just crazy."

But the way he said it—his voice shaky, his hands trembling—it didn't reassure me. If anything, it made me more uncertain. The woman's words had struck something deep inside him, and it was clear he was terrified. But of what?

The woman's voice broke the silence again, and this time it was softer, almost a whisper.

"You can lie to him,"

she said, her eyes never leaving Khaja,

"But you can't lie to yourself. You were there. You let it happen."

Khaja let out a frustrated cry, running his hands through his hair.

"She's insane!"

he shouted, his voice cracking.

"I wasn't there! I couldn't have been!"

The room fell silent, the tension between the three of us thick and suffocating. I didn't know what to think. The woman was clearly unwell, but there was something about the way she spoke, something about the way she looked at Khaja that made me question everything I thought I knew.

And then she said something that made my blood run cold.

"They're still with you,"

She whispered, her voice barely audible.

The air in the room seemed to freeze, the weight of her words hanging heavy in the space between us. I turned to Khaja, my heart racing.

"What does she mean?"

Khaja shook his head frantically, backing away from the bed.

"She's mad, okay? She doesn't know what she's saying. Let's just leave. She is mistaking me."

But I couldn't move. Her words—They're still with you—echoed in my mind, filling me with a sense of dread I couldn't shake. Who was still with him?

Was she talking about the children whose voices we had heard in the apartment during their stay?

Before I could ask any more questions, Khaja turned and bolted for the door, his footsteps echoing in the hallway as he ran. I stood there, frozen, torn between following him and trying to get more out of the woman. But as I looked back at her, I saw something that made my decision for me.

She was smiling.

A small, knowing smile, as if she had just revealed a terrible secret.

Without another word, I turned and ran after Khaja.

"That's not possible! She's mad!"

The sound of Khaja's hurried footsteps echoed down the sterile hospital corridor, but I didn't follow him right away. I stood there for a moment, frozen, the woman's words ringing in my ears: They're still with you. Her smile had lingered in my mind, haunting and strange, as if she knew more than she was saying—more than we could understand.

I shook off the chill that ran down my spine and rushed after Khaja. I found him standing just outside the hospital's exit, his back to me, his body rigid as he stared out at the parking lot. The evening sun was casting long shadows on the pavement, but Khaja looked pale, as if all the blood had drained from his face.

"Khaja,"

I called out, walking toward him cautiously, my voice soft but urgent.

"What the hell just happened in there?"

He didn't turn around. His breathing was heavy, laboured, and when he finally spoke, his voice was raw with frustration and fear.

"She's mad. Completely insane. We shouldn't have come back here. I knew this was a mistake."

I came to stand beside him, watching him closely, trying to gauge his reaction. He was rattled, more than I had ever seen him before. His hands were trembling, and his jaw was clenched so tightly I thought he might crack a tooth.

"She recognized you,"

I said carefully, my own mind swirling with confusion.

"How is that possible? She looked at you like she knew you."

"She doesn't know me,"

Khaja snapped, finally turning to face me. His eyes were wide, frantic.

"I've never seen that woman in my life! She's just delusional, okay? You saw the way she was rambling before—she's out of her mind. She's been in that hospital for years, locked away because she's lost touch with reality. None of this makes any sense."

I nodded slowly, trying to process everything. What he was saying made logical sense—on the surface, at least. The woman had been confined to a mental hospital, muttering incoherently about things no one could understand. It wasn't unreasonable to think that she might be confused, that her mind had twisted events into something that didn't align with reality.

But there was something about her certainty, about the way she had looked at Khaja, that I couldn't shake. She had spoken with such conviction, and that final phrase—They're still with you—it was burned into my memory.

"Khaja, listen,"

I said, my voice calm but firm.

"She said you were there. That you watched. You have to admit, that's a pretty specific accusation. And it wasn't just random—she knew you. She was certain."

Khaja let out a harsh laugh, but there was no humour in it.

"She's delusional,"

he repeated, but this time his voice cracked slightly.

"She doesn't know what she's saying. People like that... they create stories in their minds. They make connections that don't exist. You can't trust anything she says."

I could hear the desperation in his voice, the fear bubbling just beneath the surface. He was trying so hard to convince me—and maybe himself—that what had just happened was nothing more than the ramblings of a disturbed woman. But it wasn't working.

"Then what did she mean when she said 'they're still with you'?"

I asked, pressing him.

"Who's still with you? Khaja, something's not right here, and we both know it."

Khaja's eyes flashed with frustration, and he took a step back, running his hands through his hair in agitation.

"I don't know!"

he yelled, his voice echoing in the empty parking lot.

"I don't know what she meant! It's just more of her insanity. She's making things up!"

He paused, his breathing ragged, and I could see the fear in his eyes. But it wasn't just fear of the woman's words—it was something deeper, something he was struggling to push down.

"She's wrong,"

he said again, quieter this time, his voice barely above a whisper.

"I wasn't there. I've never been there."

I stood there, watching him closely. His denial was strong, but there was something off about the way he was reacting—like he was trying to convince himself as much as he was trying to convince me. And the more he protested, the more I began to wonder if there was something he wasn't telling me.

"Khaja,"

I said slowly, choosing my words carefully,

"If there's something you're not telling me, something you're not sure of, you need to say it. Now's not the time to hold anything back."

He shot me a sharp look, his eyes filled with a mixture of anger and fear.

"I'm not holding anything back!"

he snapped.

"I don't know why she said those things. I don't know why she thought she recognized me, but she's wrong. I wasn't there. I swear to you."

I wanted to believe him. I wanted to believe that the woman's words were nothing more than the ravings of a troubled mind. But something deep inside me—something I couldn't quite explain—was telling me that there was more to this. And as much as I trusted Khaja, as much as I valued our friendship, I couldn't ignore the growing doubt creeping into my mind.

"Okay,"

I said finally, my voice calm.

"Okay, I believe you."

But I wasn't sure if I did.

Khaja let out a breath, his shoulders sagging slightly in relief.

"Good. We need to leave this place behind. This whole investigation—it's messing with our heads. We need to get out of here and forget about it."

But I couldn't forget. Not now. Not after everything we had uncovered.

As we walked back to the car, I glanced over at Khaja. His face was still pale, his expression strained, and I couldn't shake the feeling that something was terribly wrong. I didn't want to believe that my best friend could be involved in something so dark, but the woman's words had planted a seed of doubt, and it was growing with every passing second.

And as we drove away from the hospital, I realized that our investigation had taken a turn I hadn't anticipated. The mystery wasn't just about the couple anymore. It wasn't just about the strange occurrences in the building.

Now, it was about Khaja.

"What if Khaja had been part of this all along?"

The drive back to ABK township was shrouded in a tense silence. Khaja gripped the steering wheel, his knuckles white, his face tight with a mixture of frustration and fear. I glanced at him out of the corner of my eye, trying to read his expression, but his jaw was set, his eyes focused dead ahead. Neither of us said a word, but the weight of the conversation with the woman pressed down on us like a suffocating blanket.

I replayed her words over and over in my mind. You were there. You watched it all. They're still with you. I couldn't shake the sense that she knew something, that she had recognized something in Khaja that even he didn't fully understand. The more I thought about it, the more unsettled I became.

When we pulled into the parking lot of ABK township, the sun had dipped below the horizon, casting long, dark shadows over the building. The windows of the apartment complex loomed above us, dark and silent, as if the entire structure was watching us, waiting. I felt a chill crawl up my spine as I stepped out of the car, the cool evening air brushing against my skin.

Khaja slammed his car door and walked quickly toward the lift, not waiting for me. His steps were quick, almost frantic, as though he couldn't get inside fast enough. I hurried to catch up, but I couldn't shake the feeling that something had changed between us.

Inside the building, the familiar dim lighting and cold hallways felt even more oppressive than usual. We rode the elevator up to the 13th floor in silence, the hum of the machinery was the only sound between us. I could feel the tension radiating from Khaja, his body practically vibrating with pent-up frustration.

As we stepped out into the hallway, the door to the couple's old flat loomed ahead, just as it always did—silent, empty, but filled with a darkness I could feel. I stared at it, the woman's words echoing in my mind. They're still with you.

I couldn't help but wonder if whatever had haunted that flat, whatever had driven the couple to madness, was still there. Still lurking. Still watching.

"Khaja,"

I said quietly as we approached his apartment,

"We need to talk about what happened back there."

He shot me a sharp look, his eyes filled with anger.

"There's nothing to talk about,"

he said through gritted teeth.

"I told you already—she's mad. End of story."

But I couldn't let it go. Not after everything we had seen. Not after the way she had looked at him, as though he were the key to everything.

"You can't just dismiss this,"

I pressed, stepping in front of him as he reached for his door.

"What if she's not mad?

What if there's something you're not remembering?

Something from your past?"

Khaja's eyes flashed with anger.

"I told you, I've never seen that woman in my life. She's delusional. You're letting this whole thing get inside your head."

I took a step back, my mind racing. Maybe he was right. Maybe I was letting this get to me. But the doubt was there now, gnawing at the back of my mind, whispering that there was more to this than Khaja was letting on.

"What if there's something we don't understand?"

I asked, my voice low.

"What if this whole thing is bigger than we thought? The children, the voices, the disappearances... what if it's all connected? And what if you're part of that connection?"

Khaja's face twisted with anger, and for a moment, I thought he might actually hit me. His fists clenched at his sides, and his chest heaved with the effort of holding back whatever emotion was boiling inside him.

"Don't,"

he growled, his voice low and dangerous.

"Don't even suggest that."

I held up my hands in a gesture of peace, trying to calm the situation.

"I'm not accusing you of anything. But I can't ignore what she said. I can't ignore the way she looked at you."

Khaja shook his head violently, stepping back and running a hand through his hair.

"You're losing it, man,"

he muttered.

"You're starting to sound as crazy as she is."

But I wasn't losing it. I could feel the pieces falling into place, even if they didn't make sense yet. There was something here, something neither of us understood, but I started to see a connection. The missing children, the strange voices, the couple's madness... and now, Khaja's sudden involvement in it all.

What if Khaja had been part of this all along? What if, somehow, he had a connection to the events in ABK township, something he didn't even realize? The thought sent a chill through me, but I couldn't ignore it.

I watched as Khaja unlocked his door, pushing it open with more force than necessary. He stepped inside without looking at me, but before he could close the door, I placed a hand on it, stopping him.

"Khaja,"

I said quietly, my voice filled with doubt and concern,

"If there's anything—anything at all—you're not telling me, now's the time. We're in too deep for secrets."

He paused, his hand on the edge of the door, his face hidden in shadow. For a long moment, he didn't respond, and I could feel the tension hanging in the air between us. I could hear my own heart pounding in my ears, the weight of my words heavy in the silence.

Finally, without turning around, Khaja spoke, his voice barely above a whisper.

"There's nothing to tell."

Then, without another word, he slammed the door on my face.

Placing my hand on his door,

I stood there for a moment, staring at the door, my mind swirling with doubt and paranoia. Khaja was hiding something. I was sure of it now. Whether he knew it or not, whether he remembered it or not, it felt as if there was something from his past that tied him to the strange events in this building. And I was going to find out what it was.

"No matter, how dark your past might be, I will always be with you Khaja."

I spoke it mostly audible to myself.

But as I turned to walk back heading towards my apartment, a cold shiver ran down my spine. The building felt different tonight—heavier, darker. The air seemed to hum with a quiet, oppressive energy, and I couldn't shake the feeling that I was being watched.

I glanced back at the door to the couple's old flat, my heart skipping a beat. The hallway was empty, but the silence was thick, almost suffocating. And in the stillness, I could almost hear it—the faint echo of a child's voice, barely audible but unmistakable.

They're still with you.

CHAPTER VIII

The Dark Past Unveiled.

I knew there had to be more, buried somewhere in the past.
After our unnerving visit to the mental hospital, I couldn't stop thinking about the woman's words and Khaja's reaction. The questions were piling up faster than I could answer them, and the sense of dread was growing heavier with each passing day. I had come too far to stop now, and I knew that if I wanted to uncover

the truth, I needed to dig deeper—into the couple's past, into the building's history, and into the unsettling pattern that seemed to follow them wherever they went.

I spent the next few days buried in research. I combed through public records, local news articles, and old police reports, trying to trace the couple's movements before they arrived at ABK township. The more I uncovered, the darker the picture became. There was a trail, a disturbing pattern, that stretched back over a decade. Each time the couple moved, strange things happened—disappearances, unexplained noises, disturbances that left entire neighbourhoods on edge.

It wasn't easy finding information. The couple had kept a low profile, changing cities every few years, leaving just enough time for the whispers to fade before they reappeared somewhere else. But as I sifted through article after article, a clear pattern emerged. Missing children. Families reporting strange noises in the middle of the night—crying, laughter, whispers that didn't seem to have a source. It was always the same, no matter where they went.

And it always ended the same way: the couple vanishing just before things escalated.

I found a particularly troubling case from about eight years ago. It happened in a small town a few hours from here, a place where no one paid much attention to the news. The article was short, just a few paragraphs buried in the back of an old online archive. A child—a six-year-old boy—had disappeared from his home one night. The parents had been frantic, and the police had searched everywhere, but the boy was never found.

The article mentioned that the boy had lived in a quiet neighbourhood, in a house next to a couple who had recently moved away. The neighbours had described the couple as quiet, unassuming, but some had reported hearing strange noises coming from their house late at night. A low humming sound, like distant music, and what one neighbour swore was the sound of children laughing.

As I read the information, my gut twisted.

The boy had vanished just days after the couple left town. There was no evidence linking them to the disappearance, but the timing was too perfect to ignore. They had moved just before the search intensified, disappearing without a trace, just as they had done so many times before.

I leaned back in my chair, the weight of the evidence settling on me like a heavy blanket. The couple had been doing this for years. Wherever they went, children disappeared, families were torn apart, and entire communities were left in the dark, haunted by the unanswered questions.

I stared at the screen, the same sentence repeating in my head: They're still with you.

The woman's words took on a new meaning now, and I couldn't help but wonder if she had been referring to the children. Had the couple abducted children wherever they went, hiding them away, pretending they were part of their twisted, imagined family? Or was it something even worse?

I shook off the thought and clicked on another article, this one from a small town even farther away. *It was the same story*: Just weeks later, the couple moved out of town. a child disappeared without a trace, The police had questioned them, but they had no evidence to hold them. The couple had left, just like they always did, leaving nothing behind but whispers and fear.

I scribbled notes in my journal, trying to keep track of the dates and locations. There were gaps in the timeline, years where I couldn't find anything, but it was enough. Enough to know that this was no coincidence. They had been doing this for a long time, and somehow, no one had ever put the pieces together.

Until now.

As the hours passed, my obsession grew. I was no longer just trying to solve the mystery of the strange noises and the missing children. I was trying to understand how this couple had gotten away with it for so long—how they had managed to move from place to place, leaving a trail of horror behind them without anyone noticing. And, more importantly, what they were planning next.

I closed my laptop and leaned back in my chair, staring at the ceiling. I could feel the weight of the truth pressing down on me, but there was still so much I didn't understand. The couple's past was dark, but I needed more. I needed to find someone who had known them before they moved to ABK township, someone who could tell me what had really happened.

As I sat there, my mind racing, I realized that the answers were out there, waiting to be found. I just needed to dig a little deeper.

The clue was hidden in plain sight, something I should have seen earlier.

After spending hours combing through article after article, police reports, and town records, I had pieced together a disturbing timeline. But it still felt incomplete, like I was missing the most critical piece of the puzzle. Every story followed the same pattern: the couple moved into a new town, strange noises and children's voices were reported, then a child would disappear, and the couple would vanish before anyone could make the connection.

But there was one case that stood out. A small town called Tirupur, about a six-hour drive from ABK township, had been home to the couple about five years ago. They had lived there for a little over a year before moving away under suspicious circumstances—just days after a five-year-old boy disappeared. The boy's name was Anirudh. His case had gone cold after a few months, and no one had seen or heard from the couple again.

I had already read the article about Anirudh's disappearance a dozen times, but something nagged at me. I felt like I was missing something obvious. I reread the article one more time, scanning it slowly. That's when I noticed a small, almost throwaway detail I hadn't fully absorbed before the police had spoken to a neighbour who lived next to the couple. The article mentioned that the neighbour had raised concerns about the couple's strange behaviour—specifically, that the woman had an unusual fixation on children.

I leaned in closer to my screen, the words jumping out at me now. The neighbour, an elderly woman named Mrs. Mehta, had reported seeing the couple outside late at night, the woman often staring at children playing in the street, her eyes following them for too long. She had also mentioned hearing strange noises coming from the couple's home—noises that reminded her of children crying, though the couple had no children of their own.

I scribbled down her name and quickly searched for any contact information. Mrs. Mehta wasn't hard to find; she still lived in the same house, according to an old directory. Without hesitating, I grabbed my car keys and headed for the door.

The drive to Tirupur felt like it took forever, the scenery blurring past as my mind raced with possibilities.

Who was this woman?

What had she seen?

Why hadn't anyone followed up with her since the couple left?

As the town came into view, I felt a mix of dread and anticipation. I was close and now I got closer than I had ever been to finding the truth.

I parked a few blocks away from Mrs. Mehta's house, a small, aging structure tucked between newer developments. The yard was overgrown, the paint on the house chipped and fading. I hesitated at the gate, suddenly feeling a wave of doubt.

What if she didn't want to talk?

What if she was too frightened of what she knew?

But I couldn't turn back now. I had to know.

I knocked on the door, and after a few moments, it creaked open. A small, frail woman stood in the doorway, her face lined with age and her eyes sharp despite her years.

"Mrs. Mehta?"

I asked, trying to keep my voice steady.

She narrowed her eyes at me, clearly suspicious of an unexpected visitor.

"Who's that?"

I began, choosing my words carefully.

"I'm sorry to bother you, I'm looking into the disappearance of a boy named Anirudh from a few years ago. I read that you lived next to a

couple who were questioned about it. I was hoping you might be able to help me."

Her expression hardened at the mention of Anirudh, and for a moment, I thought she might close the door on me. But then she sighed, stepping aside to let me in.

"Come in,"

she muttered, her voice laced with weariness.

"I'll tell you what I know."

I followed her into the small living room, the air thick with dust and the smell of old furniture. She motioned for me to sit, then lowered herself into an armchair across from me. For a long moment, she didn't say anything, just stared at her hands, lost in thought.

"I remember them,"

she said finally, her voice quiet but firm.

"The couple. They were strange from the start, kept to themselves, but... she had this way about her. The woman, I mean. She was always watching. Watching the children."

Leaning forward slightly, I asked

"What do you mean, watching?"

Mrs. Mehta's eyes darkened.

"She would stand outside sometimes, just watching the children play in the street. At first, it seemed harmless enough. But then I noticed... she wasn't just watching. She was imagining. I could see it in her eyes—she was pretending those children were hers. She had this... hunger about her. Like she was longing for something she couldn't have."

A chill ran down my spine. The woman's obsession with children. It was starting to make sense now—the way she had fixated on the idea of having children, even though she and her husband had none. She had taken that obsession with her, from town to town, until it became something much darker.

"She didn't talk much to anyone,"

Mrs. Mehta continued, her voice growing softer.

"But one night, I heard something. Something strange. It was late—past midnight—and I heard noises coming from their house. It sounded like children crying. But they didn't have children."

She paused, her eyes clouding with memory.

"I told the police about it after the boy disappeared. They questioned them, but... nothing came of it. The couple left town not long after that. I always thought it was strange, the timing of it all."

I sat there, processing what she had told me. The woman had been watching the children in the neighbourhood, imagining them as her own. And then, one of those children had vanished.

It was becoming clear now. The woman's obsession with motherhood had driven her to the edge, warping her sense of reality. She had seen the children as hers to take, and her husband—he must have gone along with it, enabling her delusions, protecting her.

But what happened to those children after they were taken?

What happened to Anirudh?

"Do you think they... took him?"

I asked, my voice barely a whisper.

Mrs. Mehta didn't answer for a long time. When she finally spoke, her voice was filled with quiet resignation.

"I don't know what they did. But I know they were hiding something. And I know that boy didn't just disappear on his own."

Listening to her, I thanked Mrs. Mehta for sharing the information and I headed back, It felt as if, **The pieces began to fall into place, but the picture they formed was horrifying.**

Mrs. Mehta's words echoed in my mind as I drove back from Tirupur. Her account of the woman's strange fixation on the children and the chilling sounds of crying she had heard late at night gnawed at me. The deeper I dug, the darker the story became. I couldn't shake the feeling that I was on the verge of uncovering something far worse than I had imagined.

I spent the next several days sifting through police records, public archives, and anything I could find about missing children connected to the towns the couple had lived in. It was tedious work, and often the information was incomplete or vague. But there was a pattern—a trail of darkness that followed the couple, no matter where they went.

I leaned back in my chair, eyes burning from the hours spent staring at my laptop screen. My apartment felt cold and empty, the silence pressing in on me as I stared at the files spread out before me. Missing children. Unsolved cases. And in every town, neighbours reported the same things: **strange noises at night, a woman watching children with a hunger in her eyes, and then the couple vanishing just as soon as the police started to investigate.**

But there was one case, one chilling discovery that shook me to my core.

In a small, forgotten town called Mettur, I found a police report from ten years ago. It was an old document, yellowed with age, but still legible. The report detailed the discovery of the bodies of two children, buried in a shallow grave on the outskirts of town. The cause of death was never officially determined, but the report mentioned signs of physical trauma—bruises, cuts, broken bones.

The children had gone missing just weeks before the couple left Mettur.

My heart pounded as I read through the report. The connection was undeniable. The couple had lived in that town during the time of the disappearances, and just like in every other case, they had left abruptly. The police had questioned them, but without any solid evidence, they couldn't arrest them.

I stared at the screen, my stomach churning. Two dead children. This wasn't just about abduction anymore—this was murder. The couple had been taking children for years, and now I knew why they had always moved on so quickly. They weren't just hiding the children—they were killing them.

The realization hit me like a freight train. The strange noises, the children's voices we had heard in the apartment when the couple stayed, weren't just any echoes of some supernatural event in their own, they were real. The cries Mrs. Mehta had heard, the laughter that haunted the walls of ABK township... those were the children the couple had taken. And now, those children were gone.

I couldn't breathe. The weight of the truth pressed down on me, suffocating. This couple, these seemingly ordinary people, had been responsible for the deaths of children. Children who had trusted them, who had been stolen away from their families in the dead of night.

I couldn't get the image out of my mind—the woman, standing in the street, watching the children play, pretending they were hers. And when they weren't, she had taken them. She had taken them to feed her twisted delusions of motherhood, and when she grew tired of them, she had disposed of them like they were nothing more than broken toys.

The room spun around me as the horror of it all sunk in. I had been chasing a mystery, thinking I was uncovering strange occurrences or supernatural phenomena. But this wasn't some ghost story. This was real. And it was far worse than anything I could have imagined.

I sat in the dark, the only light coming from the screen in front of me. My hands trembled as I flipped through the pages of the police report, my mind racing. How had they gotten away with this for so long? How had they managed to move from place to place, leaving a trail of death behind them without anyone ever piecing it together?

But now I had pieced it together.

I couldn't sit here any longer. I needed to get out of the apartment, to breathe. I grabbed my jacket and headed for the door, my thoughts a whirlwind of fear and disbelief. The moment I stepped outside, the cold air hit me like a slap in the face, waking me from the nightmare that had taken root in my mind. But the nightmare wasn't over—it was real, and it had been lurking beneath the surface all this time.

I walked aimlessly, my mind replaying everything I had uncovered.

How many more children had there been? How many more towns had the couple visited, leaving behind broken families and unanswered questions?

And why had no one ever stopped them?

I knew the answer to that last question. The couple had been careful. They had chosen their victims carefully, moving from place to place, blending into the background like shadows. And each time they moved, they left no trace behind.

Except now that I had the trace.

The sound of children's laughter echoed in my ears, but I knew it wasn't real. It was the memory of that terrible night, the night we had heard the voices in ABK township. But now I understood what those voices were.

They were the ghosts of the children the couple had stolen.

I stopped walking, standing in the middle of the street, my breath coming in short gasps. I had uncovered the truth, but it wasn't the truth I had expected. This wasn't about spirits or hauntings—this was about a living, breathing horror. A horror that had been allowed to continue for years, unchecked.

I needed to tell someone. I needed to stop them before it happened again.

But as I stood there, staring into the dark, I realized with a sinking feeling that the only people who could stop them had disappeared. The couple had vanished once again, leaving behind nothing but their dark legacy.

And now, I was the only one who knew the full extent of their evil.

I couldn't ignore the doubts any longer. Khaja had to know.

The truth weighed heavily on me, an unbearable burden that I couldn't carry alone any longer. The more I thought about the couple's horrific past, the more my mind kept circling back to Khaja. The woman's haunting words at the mental hospital echoed endlessly in my head: **You were there.** I didn't want to believe it, but every piece of the puzzle seemed to lead back to him.

There was something about his reaction at the hospital that I couldn't shake. The fear in his eyes when she pointed at him, the way he shut down and tried to run. It wasn't just the ramblings of a madwoman that had scared him. Felt as if it was something deeper.

Something real.

I had to confront him. I had to know what he wasn't telling me.

That evening, I made my way to Khaja's apartment with a sense of dread hanging over me like a cloud. The air was thick with the weight of what I was about to do. My hand shook slightly as I knocked on his door, each thud feeling like a countdown to something inevitable.

Khaja opened the door, and for a moment, everything seemed normal. But the tension in his face told me he hadn't shaken off the encounter at the hospital. His eyes darted around nervously before finally settling on me.

"What's up?"

he asked, trying to sound casual, but his voice was strained. He knew something was coming.

"We need to talk,"

I said, stepping past him into the apartment.

Khaja hesitated for a second but then closed the door behind me. I could feel the walls closing in as I stood in the centre of the room, gathering my thoughts. How do you confront your best friend with something like this? How do you ask someone if they're hiding a dark connection to child abductions and murder?

"About what?"

he asked, sitting down on the couch, avoiding my gaze.

I took a deep breath, steeling myself for what I had to say.

"About what happened at the hospital. About what she said."

Khaja tensed visibly, his hands clenching into fists.

"We've already talked about this. She's insane. She doesn't know what she's talking about."

I shook my head.

"No, Khaja. There's something more. I've been doing some digging, and I found things—things that can't be ignored anymore."

His eyes flicked up to meet mine, and I saw it—the flash of fear, the look of someone who knows more than they're willing to admit. I pressed on.

"I found out about the couple's past. About the missing children. About the bodies."

I took a step closer to him, my voice shaking with both fear and anger.

"She wasn't lying, Khaja. They took children. They killed them. And somehow, you're connected to this. According to her words"

His face went pale, and he stood up abruptly, his eyes wide with panic.

"I told you, I don't know anything about that!"

he shouted, his voice cracking in pain.

"You're letting this get inside your head! She's just some crazy woman—she's been in a mental hospital for some time now!"

I shook my head, refusing to back down.

"You can't explain away what she said. She recognized you, Khaja. She knew you. And you can't stand there and tell me that it was just some random mistake."

He ran his hands through his hair, pacing back and forth in front of me.

"I don't know what to tell you, man! I wasn't there. I don't know those people! You're taking this too far."

I took a step toward him, lowering my voice.

"Look me in the eyes and tell me there's nothing you're not telling me. Tell me there's nothing from your past that ties you to them. To what happened."

Khaja stopped pacing and turned to face me, his eyes dark and troubled. For a moment, I thought he was going to come clean, that he would finally admit what I had suspected all along. But instead, his face twisted with anger.

"You think I'm involved in this?"

he growled, his voice low and soreness.

"After everything we've been through, you think I'm some kind of... of monster?"

I shot back, my own frustration boiling over.

"I don't know what to think anymore, But I know something's not right. Ever since we started this investigation, things haven't added up.

And now, after what she said, I can't ignore it."

Khaja stared at me for a long moment, his chest heaving with barely restrained emotion. The tension in the room was thick, and for a second, I thought he might hit me. But then his shoulders slumped, and he looked away, his voice suddenly quiet and tired.

"I don't know what she saw in me,"

he muttered, his eyes focused on the floor.

"I don't know why she said those things. But I swear to you, I had nothing to do with it."

I wanted to believe him. I wanted to believe that my best friend wasn't hiding some terrible secret, that this was all just a horrible misunderstanding. But the doubt was still there, gnawing at me, whispering that he wasn't telling me the whole truth.

"Then why did she recognize you?"

I asked, my voice barely above a whisper.

"Why did she say you were there?"

Khaja shook his head, his expression one of helpless confusion.

"I don't know. Maybe I remind her of someone. Maybe she's confusing me with someone else. Or maybe she just made things, I don't know."

I sighed, rubbing my hands over my face. The doubt hadn't gone away, but I could see that Khaja wasn't going to give me anything more. Either he was telling the truth, or he was hiding it so well that even he believed it.

"Okay,"

I said finally, my voice heavy with resignation.

"Okay, but something isn't right here, Khaja. And until we figure out what it is, I need you to be honest with me. No more secrets."

He nodded, his expression tense and tired.

"I've told you everything I know."

I didn't respond. The truth was, I wasn't sure if I believed him anymore.

As I turned to leave, the weight of the conversation settled over me like a heavy blanket. The doubts were still there, gnawing at the back of my mind, but I couldn't push Khaja any further. Not yet.

But I knew one thing for sure: this wasn't over. The woman's words, the couple's dark history, the missing children—it was all connected. And I was going to uncover the truth, no matter what it cost me.

They weren't just running from their past, they were planning something.

The confrontation with Khaja left me rattled. I wanted to believe him, but every instinct told me that there was still something hidden in the shadows of his mind—something he either couldn't or wouldn't face. I left his apartment with more questions than answers, but one thing was clear: **this couple wasn't finished.**

The evidence I had uncovered, the horrific trail of missing children and bodies, all pointed to one undeniable truth—they had done this before, and they were planning to do it again.

But where? And when?

The next few days were spent in a frantic spiral of research and dead ends. The couple had moved out from ABK township, but I was convinced they hadn't gone to mental hospital. They had a pattern, a twisted ritual that repeated itself every few years. First, they would move into a new place, lay low, and then the noises would start—the sounds of children crying, laughter at odd hours of the night. And then, when no one was watching, a child would vanish.

I couldn't let it happen again. Not this time.

The deeper I dug, the more unsettling my discoveries became. The couple had lived in at least five different towns over the past decade, and in every case, they left just before a child disappeared. But it wasn't until I came across a seemingly insignificant detail in one of the old reports that the true horror of their plan became clear.

It was in the case file from the town of Mettur, where the two children's bodies had been found. I had already gone over the report multiple times, but one small detail had slipped past me until now: the couple had been seen near a local school just days before the children went missing. At the time, it seemed like nothing—just a couple walking near the playground. But after everything I had uncovered, it took on a much darker meaning.

They were scouting.

The realization hit me like a punch to the gut. The couple wasn't just randomly abducting children—they were choosing their victims carefully, watching them, waiting for the right moment. They had been doing this for years, moving from town to town, planning each abduction with meticulous detail.

And I was certain they were doing it again.

But where?

I couldn't shake the feeling that they were still close by. ABK township had been their home for the past two years, and it was unlikely they had gone far. As I stared at the map on my desk, tracing their movements from one town to another, a chilling thought crossed my mind.

They always moved in circles.

The towns they had lived in formed a rough circle around the outskirts of the city, and every few years, they would return to the same region. It was as if they were following a pattern, each move carefully planned to avoid suspicion while still staying within their hunting grounds.

But this time, something was different. They had been at ABK township for two years—longer than any of their previous stays. And now, they had left suddenly, without warning. And to the aggravation, why did they go to mental hospital? Something had changed.

I leaned back in my chair, staring at the map, trying to piece it together. Why had they left? What were they planning?

Then it hit me.

They weren't just running from their past—they were preparing for something new.

My heart raced as the pieces started to fall into place. The couple hadn't fled because they were afraid of getting caught. They had left because they were ready to start their cycle again. And this time, they were going to take another child.

I grabbed my phone and dialled Khaja's number, my fingers trembling. He picked up on the second ring, his voice groggy and irritated.

"What is it now?"

he asked, clearly still upset from our earlier conversation.

"They're going to do it again,"

I said, my voice shaking.

"The couple—they're planning something. I found their pattern. They always scout local schools before they take a child. They did it in Mettur, and I think they're doing it again now."

There was a long silence on the other end of the line.

"Khaja, listen to me,"

I pressed, my voice rising with urgency.

"I don't know where they are, but I think they're still nearby. We need to find them before it's too late."

He asked,

"Too late for what?"

but I could hear the doubt creeping into his voice.

"For the next child,"

I whispered, the horror of the realization settling over me like a dark cloud.

"They're going to take another child, Khaja. And if we don't stop them, we'll never forgive ourselves."

Khaja was silent for a long moment, but I could hear his breathing quicken on the other end of the line. Finally, he spoke, his voice low and filled with tension.

"Okay. What do you want to do?"

I said quickly.

"I need you to meet me at ABK township, we're going to figure out where they went. I have a lead."

He hesitated, but then I heard him sigh. *"Fine. I'll be there in 30 minutes."*

As I hung up the phone, I felt a renewed sense of purpose surge through me. The couple's dark past was no longer a mystery—it was a warning. A warning that if we didn't act fast, another child would disappear, just like the others.

I grabbed my notes and headed out the door, my mind racing. I couldn't let them get away with it. Not again.

This time, we would stop them.

CHAPTER IX

The Missing Children.

I thought I had seen it all, but I was wrong.

Getting out of my flat, I thought, the weight of the truth had settled in, heavy and suffocating, but there were still gaps in the story—gaps I was desperate to fill. The more I uncovered, the more it felt like I was spiralling into a nightmare that had no end. The couple's crimes were worse than anything I could have imagined, and the thought that they were still out there, planning their next move, consumed my every waking thought. But there was one piece of the puzzle I hadn't fully explored: the missing children.

I couldn't stop thinking about them. Their faces, frozen in time in the grainy photographs I had found, haunted me. They were innocent kids, taken from their families, their lives cut short because of one woman's madness and a man's blind loyalty.

But how many children had there really been?

How many families had been destroyed by the couple's twisted obsession?

Driving my car, I headed towards the Khaja's flat, Khaja was already down at the parking lot, I took out all the documents of information I have gathered. Getting down the car,

"Khaja"

I waved at him, I thought to start our conversation, but the building atmosphere made me feel, as if someone is watching us, looking around, I said, lets go to your flat,

Khaja was startled looking at the amount of files that I was carrying, he didn't ask me anything while we were heading up in the lift, as soon as we reached 13th floor, I rushed myself into his flat, as I was constantly feeling, that someone was watching me, I rushed closing all the curtains,

Sitting down at the desk, I offered Khaja to sit along with me, Khaja staring at the pile of old police reports and articles spread out in front of me. He was astonished looking at the data I gathered. Pointing at them I said,

"Each one told the same, familiar story: a child goes missing, the police search but find no clues, and eventually, the case goes cold."

Stating it, I took a breath, and I began poring over the reports again, this time with a sharper eye. I had to find that thing which I was missing—something that would lead me closer to understanding the full scope of the couple's crimes.

Khaja was there sitting stock-still, I sifted through the reports, a pattern began to emerge. I had known about the major cases—the ones that had made headlines—but there were others. Smaller cases. Ones that had barely gotten any attention. And in every town the couple had lived in, there were disappearances that matched the timeline of their stay.

I flipped through the file from a small town in Tamil Nadu. The couple had lived there for six months before moving to ABK township.

The disappearance of a seven-year-old girl named Shruti had been reported during their stay. The case was eerily similar to all the others—Shruti had been playing outside, in front of her house, when she suddenly vanished. Her parents had only left her unattended for a few minutes, but in those few minutes, she was gone.

No witnesses. No clues. Nothing.

The report gave me the creeps, but I kept reading. The details were chilling. Shruti had been last seen near her home, and despite a massive search effort, no one ever saw her again. The police had questioned the neighbours, including the couple, but nothing had come of it. Like all the other cases, the couple had moved on before the investigation could dig any deeper.

I flipped to the next file, this one from another town in Andhra Pradesh.

A five-year-old boy, Rohit, had disappeared from a local park while his mother was distracted on her phone. Another child, another family destroyed, and the couple had left the town shortly afterward, their trail cold once again.

The more I read, the sicker I felt. The couple had left a path of destruction in their wake, moving from town to town, taking children and leaving behind only unanswered questions and broken families. I realized now that their crimes had been going on for much longer than I initially thought. Years, possibly decades.

It was overwhelming. I felt as though I was drowning in the weight of all these missing children. I looked at the faces in the photos—bright, smiling faces, filled with life and hope—and I couldn't help but wonder what had happened to them. What had those children gone through in their final moments?

Were they scared?

Did they cry for their parents, hoping someone would save them?

The thought made my heart race, and I had to force myself to breathe.

But there was something else that gnawed at me. None of the reports mentioned bodies. In the Mettur case, the two bodies had been found, but in the majority of the cases, the children were simply... gone. No traces. No remains. It was as if they had vanished into thin air.

How had the couple managed to make so many children disappear without a trace? What had they done to them? These were questions I couldn't answer yet, but I knew I was getting closer. The pieces of the puzzle were starting to come together, even if the full picture still eluded me.

I leaned back in my chair, the reports spread out in front of me like a map of the couple's atrocities.

There were too many names.

Too many faces.

Too many innocent lives stolen for reasons I couldn't fully comprehend.

I rubbed my hands over my face, exhaustion tugging at me. But I couldn't stop. Not now. Not when I was so close to the truth.

I glanced at the clock. It was late, but I still had time. I grabbed another file, this one from a small town in Karnataka. Another child. **Another disappearance. Another family torn apart.**

As I read through the details, one thing became clear: the couple had done this before. And if I didn't stop them, they would do it again.

I had to keep going. I had to find them. I had to stop them before another child disappeared.

After hours of scouring through police reports, news articles, and scattered documents, I was beginning to feel like I was hitting a wall. Every file told the same horrifying story—another child gone, another family destroyed, and the couple disappearing without a trace. But the deeper I went, the more I felt like there was still something I hadn't uncovered, something important that had slipped through the cracks of the initial investigations.

That's when Khaja pointed at it, a file, tucked away and nearly forgotten in the archives, collecting dust. It was from a case about seven years ago in a small town called **Thanjavur.** The name didn't ring any bells at first, but as I opened the file and started reading, a chill crept down my spine.

Both of us started looking into the case, it involved a missing girl—eight-year-old Neha. She had vanished from her neighbourhood one evening while playing with friends. The circumstances were all too familiar: no witnesses, no leads, just a child gone without a trace. The case had gone cold within a few months, and the file had been forgotten.

But buried deep in the file was something that the investigators hadn't given much attention to at the time—a witness statement from a neighbour's child, a boy who had been playing in the street the night Neha disappeared. His statement had been filed away as unreliable, written off as the imaginings of a child too young to understand what he had seen.

I skimmed through the notes, my eyes widening as I read his account.

The boy, who had been about nine years old at the time, had told the police that on the night Neha disappeared, he had seen

"*a shadow*" moving near the couple's house. He hadn't been able to make out the figure clearly, but he remembered hearing something—laughter. The sound of children laughing, coming from inside the couple's house.

At the time, the police had dismissed it as the couple had no children at that time, and there had been no signs of a break-in or struggle. The boy's statement had been categorized as imagination, a young mind playing tricks on itself after a traumatic event.

But now, knowing what I knew, it didn't feel like a child's imagination. It felt like a vital clue.

My heart pounding in my chest.

The laughter.

The couple's home.

The night Neha disappeared. It was all too much to be a coincidence.

I looked up from the file, my mind racing. If the boy had really heard laughter coming from the couple's house, then it meant one of two things: either the couple had taken Neha and were keeping her inside, or they were involved in something far more sinister—something that involved other children as well.

I couldn't shake the image from my mind: **the couple, inside their home, surrounded by the laughter of children that shouldn't have been there.**

I flipped through the rest of the file, looking for anything else that might help me understand what had really happened that night. But there was nothing—just the boy's statement, buried among pages of dead ends and inconclusive evidence.

The file had been forgotten, but now, I couldn't ignore it.

I needed to find the boy. I needed to know what he had really seen that night, and why no one had believed him.

I scribbled down his name—Arun Nair—and quickly searched for any contact information I could find. It didn't take long. Arun still lived in Thanjavur, now a young man in his early twenties. The thought of confronting him after all these years made me uneasy.

What if he didn't remember?

What if he didn't want to talk about it?

But I didn't have a choice. This was the lead I had been waiting for, the missing piece of the puzzle that might finally crack the case wide open.

I noticed Khaja was deep into his sleep, I didn't want to wake him up, I grabbed my keys and headed out closing the door as smooth as I can. Though I was still unable to get out of the statements made by the women pointing Khaja at the mental hospital, deep down I was still in a conflict among the thought that was raised by the sapling that women planted, and with a feeling in my bones that Khaja can never do wrong, I started driving towards Arun. With my mind spinning with questions.

What had Arun really seen that night?

Had he heard the children's laughter, or was it something more sinister?

And why had the mystifying couple left town so abruptly after Neha's disappearance?

As I drove toward Thanjavur, the sky darkened, the weight of the file and its hidden secrets pressing down on me. I couldn't shake the feeling that I was getting closer to the truth, but the truth was far more terrifying than I had anticipated.

The couple hadn't just taken Neha. There were others. And the laughter Arun had heard—it was real.

I reached Arun's neighbourhood just as the sun dipped below the horizon, casting long shadows across the streets. I parked outside a small, modest house, the place where Arun still lived. My heart raced as I walked up to the front door and knocked, wondering if he would even remember me—or, more importantly, **what he had seen that night?**

The door opened slowly, and a young man stood in the doorway, his face guarded, his eyes narrowing at the sight of me.

I asked,

"Are you Arun Nair?"

my voice being tense.

He nodded, crossing his arms over his chest.

"Yeah. Who are you?"

I quickly said

"I'm looking into the disappearance of Neha,"

watching his reaction carefully.

"You gave a statement to the police when you were younger. You said you saw something the night she went missing."

Arun's face darkened, his eyes hardening.

"That was a long time ago,"

he said quietly.

"The police didn't believe me. No one did."

I said, stepping forward slightly.

"I believe you, And I need you to tell me exactly what you saw?"

He hesitated, glancing back toward the inside of his house before stepping out onto the porch and closing the door behind him. He leaned against the railing, staring out at the darkening street, his voice low and steady.

"I heard them,"

he said, his voice barely above a whisper.

"The children. Laughing."

The impact of his words caused my stomach to churn.

"They were laughing, but when I looked, no one was there."

I knew this was my last chance. I had to follow the trail, wherever it led.

Arun's words hung in the air, as heavy as the darkness gathering around us. I stood on his porch, struggling to process what he had just told me. The laughter. The same eerie sound that had haunted me ever since I started this investigation. Hearing it from Arun, a witness who had nothing to gain from lying, made it all the more real. The terror that had been gnawing at the edges of my mind now seemed unavoidable.

I could see the unease in Arun's eyes, the years of doubt and dismissal weighing on him. He had held this story inside for so long, but it was clear he hadn't forgotten. The memory of that night was as fresh as ever, haunting him in the same way it now haunted me.

"What exactly did you hear that night?"

I asked, trying to keep my voice steady.

Arun looked down at his feet, as if the memory itself was too much to bear.

"I was just a kid,"

he began.

"But I know what I heard. It was late—well past when we usually stopped playing outside. I remember hearing Neha's mom calling for her, and that's when I started to walk home. But then... I heard the laughter. At first, I thought it was just the other kids playing, but when I turned around, no one was there."

He paused, his brow furrowed as he relived the moment.

"I followed the sound, thinking it was coming from behind the houses or in the alley. But it wasn't. It was coming from inside."

I asked,

"Inside where?"

my heart racing.

"The couple's house,"

he said softly.

"The house was dark, but I swear to you, I heard kids laughing in there. It was like... they were playing some kind of game."

My spine tingled with cold. This was the same couple, whose path I had been following, the same couple who had destroyed every community in which they had resided.

"Did you see anyone?"

I asked, already knowing what the answer would be.

He said,

"No,"

shaking his head.

"But I saw her—the woman. She was standing near the window, just staring outside, not moving. It was like she was watching something, but there was nothing there."

Arun's voice trailed off, and I could see the fear in his eyes, the fear that had kept him from talking about this for so many years.

"I ran home after that,"

he continued.

"I told my parents, but they didn't believe me. When Neha went missing, I told the police what I'd heard, but they said I was just scared, that I must have imagined it."

I took a deep breath, trying to steady myself. This was it. This was the piece of the puzzle I had been missing. The woman, standing in the dark, watching over something invisible, while the sound of children's laughter echoed through the house. It was a picture that didn't quite fit reality—more like a nightmare come to life. But I knew now that it wasn't a figment of anyone's imagination. Arun had heard it.

He had seen something that night, something that the couple didn't want anyone to know.

"Arun,"

I said slowly,

"did you ever see Neha again?"

He swallowed hard, shaking his head.

"No. She was gone after that. They searched everywhere, but she just vanished."

I clenched my fists, trying to push back the frustration and fear building inside me. The couple had been there, they had taken Neha, and no one had believed the boy who had heard her laughter just before she disappeared.

But there was something else that troubled me, something I hadn't fully understood until now.

The woman.

The way Arun had described her, standing at the window, watching as if she were lost in some other reality. I had heard stories like this before. People talked about her strange behaviour, her fixation on children, but this was different. It wasn't just that she was watching. She was listening, interacting with something—or someone—that no one else could see.

Could it be possible that the laughter Arun heard wasn't just a hallucination?

What if the couple had been using those children—Neha and others before her—in some way to feed the woman's delusions?

I had a horrible feeling in my stomach when the puzzle started to fit.

The couple didn't just take the children—they used them, twisted them into their dark, broken version of a family. The laughter wasn't some supernatural phenomenon. It was real in this case. And the children... they had been forced to play along in the woman's deranged fantasy until they were no longer useful.

And then they disappeared.

I looked up at Arun, who was still watching me carefully, waiting for my next question. But I had no more questions for him.

Not now.

I needed to follow this lead further, to uncover what had really happened in that house all those years ago.

"Thank you,"

I said, my voice tight.

"Thank you for telling me what you remember."

Arun nodded, but I could see the fear still lingering in his eyes. He had told me the truth, but the truth wasn't something that would give him peace. It was something far more terrifying.

As I turned to leave, Arun called out to me, his voice low and hesitant.

"Do you think she's still out there?

The woman?"

I paused, glancing back at him.

"I don't know,"

I admitted.

"But I'm going to find out."

I was losing myself in the darkness of this case, but I couldn't stop. Arun's words followed me long after I left his house. The sound of children's laughter, the woman standing at the window, the invisible horrors lurking in that house—all of it played on an endless loop in my mind.

Each step I took felt heavier than the last as I walked back to my car.

My thoughts were spinning in a chaotic blur, and the weight of the truth I had uncovered was starting to suffocate me.

I knew now that the couple's crimes went far deeper than simple abductions. They hadn't just taken children—they had trapped them in their twisted delusion, forcing them to participate in a sick, fabricated version of family life until they vanished without a trace. But how had they done it?

Where had those children gone?

What had the couple done to them?

I drove back to my apartment, the dark streets passing by in a blur, the only sound in the car the low hum of the engine. But in my mind, the laughter persisted, echoing in every quiet moment, as if it were following me. I knew it was all in my head, a product of my growing obsession with the case. And yet, I couldn't shake the feeling that it wasn't just a memory. It felt real. Too real.

By the time I reached my apartment, I was trembling. I could feel the investigation consuming me, taking over every part of my mind. I was losing sleep, barely able to think of anything other than the couple and the children they had taken. It had started as a mystery, but now, it had become something more—a gnawing darkness that threatened to pull me under.

I stumbled into my apartment, the silence wrapping around me like a suffocating blanket. I dropped my keys on the counter and collapsed onto the couch, rubbing my temples, trying to clear my mind. But no matter how hard I tried, the faces of the missing children, their innocent smiles frozen in time, refused to leave me. Their eyes seemed to follow me, accusing me of failing them. And then the laughter returned, soft at first, like the distant echo of a memory, but growing louder, sharper, until it filled the room.

I sat up, my heart pounding. The sound was so vivid, so real, I swear it was coming from the walls themselves. But I knew that couldn't be possible. It was just my mind playing tricks on me—wasn't it?

I stood up and paced the room, trying to shake the feeling that something—or someone—was watching me. Every shadow seemed to move, every creak of the floorboards set my nerves on edge. I had been chasing this mystery for so long, digging into the couple's past, uncovering more horror with each passing day, that now it felt like the horror was seeping into my life. I could no longer separate the investigation from reality.

The lines between what was real and what wasn't were blurring, and I was beginning to lose myself in the darkness.

I ran my hands through my hair, trying to steady my breathing, but the laughter continued.

I knew it wasn't real. It couldn't be. But it felt real, as if the children I had read about—the ones who had disappeared—were somehow still here, trapped in some liminal space, calling out to me for help.

I walked over to the window and stared out into the dark, empty street. The world outside seemed normal, oblivious to the horrors I had uncovered. But inside, my mind was unravelling. The weight of what I had learned was too much. The couple's crimes, their ability to disappear without a trace, the way they had manipulated those children—it was all too much.

I closed my eyes and tried to calm myself, but when I opened them, I saw something—movement, just beyond the edge of the streetlight's glow. A figure, standing in the shadows.

I froze, my breath catching in my throat. The figure was barely visible, just a silhouette against the darkened background, but it was there. Watching.

I blinked, and it was gone.

I backed away from the window, my heart racing. I knew it had to be a trick of the light, or my mind playing games with me, but the feeling of being watched lingered. It was as if the couple's presence had followed me, clinging to me like a shadow, refusing to let me go.

I sat back down on the couch, my hands shaking. I couldn't keep living like this. I couldn't let the investigation consume me like this.

But how could I stop?

Every time I tried to pull away, the faces of the missing children pulled me back in. They deserved justice. They deserved to be found.

But the more I uncovered, the more it felt like I was chasing shadows.

I glanced at the stack of files on my desk—the evidence I had gathered, the names, the photos, the unanswered questions—and felt a sinking sense of despair. The couple was out there, somewhere, and I knew that if I didn't find them soon, another child would disappear. Another family would be shattered, just like all the others.

I buried my face in my hands, trying to push away the growing sense of helplessness. I had never felt so lost, so unsure of myself. Every lead I followed seemed to end in darkness. Every clue only deepened the mystery. And now, the laughter was haunting me, following me wherever I went, as if mocking my inability to stop what was coming.

I stood up again, pacing the room. I couldn't give up. I couldn't let the couple win. But I was scared—scared of what I might find if I kept digging, scared of what would happen if I didn't.

As I paced, I heard a faint sound—a knock at the door.

I froze, my heart pounding in my chest. Who could it be at this hour?

I walked slowly toward the door, my hand hovering over the doorknob. For a moment, I hesitated, unsure of whether I should open it. The sense of dread that had been building inside me intensified, but I couldn't ignore the knock.

I opened the door.

No one was there.

I stepped outside, looking up and down the hallway, but it was empty. The only sound was the soft hum of the building's heating system.

But then I heard it again.

The laughter.

The truth was more horrifying than I had imagined. The laughter rang in my ears, echoing through the empty hallway like the whispers of a nightmare I couldn't escape. My heart raced as I stood frozen at the doorway, staring into the darkness, hoping to catch a glimpse of the person—or thing—that had knocked. But there was nothing. No one.

And yet, the sound lingered. Children's laughter. Soft, unsettling, and undeniably real.

I slammed the door shut, locking it, my hands trembling as I backed away from it. The investigation had become more than just a mystery. It was alive, infecting my thoughts, my senses, everything. I could no longer distinguish between reality and the shadows that haunted my mind.

I had to pull myself together. This couldn't be happening. The couple had left behind a trail of horror, but they were flesh and blood—human, not some supernatural force. The laughter was nothing more than a figment of my mind, an auditory hallucination brought on by stress. I was sure of it. I had to be sure of it.

But deep down, I wasn't sure at all.

I sat down at my desk, forcing myself to focus. The files were still scattered in front of me, mocking me with their unanswered questions. The faces of the missing children stared back at me, their eyes pleading for justice. And I had to give it to them. I had to push through the fear, the confusion, the madness, and find the truth.

I flipped through the reports again, scanning each one for something I might have missed. My mind raced as I connected the dots, each case pointing to the couple's chilling modus operandi: move to a new town, abduct a child, and vanish before anyone could piece together what had happened. But it wasn't just about the abductions. There was something more, something darker at play.

It was the laughter. It was the way every witness—whether they realized it or not—mentioned hearing children's laughter around the time of each disappearance. I hadn't noticed the pattern at first, but now, it was clear. In every case, there were reports of strange sounds, of laughter and children's voices coming from places where they shouldn't be.

It couldn't be a coincidence. It was all connected.

I grabbed the most recent file—the case of Neha, the little girl who had disappeared from Thanjavur. I read Arun's statement again, his account of hearing the laughter coming from inside the couple's house the night she vanished. The woman had been there, standing at the window, watching something only she could see.

I flipped to the crime scene photos. The house had been searched thoroughly, but there had been no signs of Neha. No traces of her anywhere. It was as if she had been swallowed by the darkness, taken into the same void that had claimed all the others.

But there had to be something. The laughter couldn't be a figment of everyone's imagination. And if it wasn't real in the supernatural sense, then the couple must have manufactured it somehow created it to maintain their sick fantasy.

I stared at the photos of the couple's house, trying to see beyond the surface, beyond the obvious. Then it hit me. There was one room the police hadn't fully examined in every case—a room they had dismissed as irrelevant: the basement.

In every house the couple had lived in, there had been a basement. It had been considered a storage space, filled with junk, nothing suspicious. But what if that was where the laughter had come from? What if the couple had used those basements to trap the children, forcing them to participate in their twisted version of reality?

My blood ran cold. I remembered a brief mention in one of the reports that the basement had been locked when the police arrived. The couple had claimed they'd lost the key, and the police, not suspecting anything, had broken in, finding nothing but old boxes and discarded furniture.

But what if the laughter—the voices of the children—had been coming from there? What if the couple had used the basement to keep the children hidden, to record their voices, to create the illusion that they still existed, even after they were gone?

I stood up, my body trembling as the horrifying realization settled in. The couple hadn't just taken children, they had created an entire fantasy world for themselves, using the laughter and voices of their victims to maintain their delusion. The children had been forced to play along, to be part of the couple's sick, twisted family. And when the children had outlived their usefulness, the couple had disposed of them, erasing all traces.

The laughter was real. It was the children's final cries, their desperate attempts to survive.

I collapsed back onto the couch, my head spinning. The truth was worse than anything I had imagined. The couple had been recording the children's voices, keeping their laughter alive even after they were gone, replaying it over and over as if the children were still there, still part of their make-believe world.

And now, I understood why the woman had recognized Khaja. He had seen her before, perhaps not in the way we thought, but in passing. She had noticed him, and her deranged mind had woven him into her fantasy, as if he had been part of her twisted family all along.

The woman wasn't just mentally ill. She was a predator, and her madness had driven her to commit unspeakable acts of cruelty in the name of fulfilling a delusion that had consumed her entirely.

I had been chasing shadows, but now I saw the horrifying truth. The couple wasn't just running. They were hiding. And somewhere out there, they were preparing to do it all over again.

But this time, I was going to stop them.

I stood up, grabbing the files and throwing them into my bag. I knew where I had to go next—to the house where Neha had disappeared, to the basement where the couple had locked away their secrets. The police had missed it before, but I wouldn't. Not this time.

As I headed for the door, the laughter echoed one last time in my ears, but this time, I wasn't afraid.

I was ready.

CHAPTER X

Confronting the Couple.

I knew this would be the most dangerous part, but there was no turning back.

The last few days had been a blur—relentless research, dead-end leads, and sleepless nights. But now, after everything I'd uncovered, I was close. Too close to walk away. The couple had been playing a sick game, moving from town to town, abducting children, and somehow evading capture for years. But their time was running out.

I had followed the trail of their crimes, piecing together the fragments of their twisted life, and I immediately reached the mental hospital, expecting them to be over there, I immediately grabbed my keys and headed to the hospital, where we met the couple last time.

As soon as I reached the hospital, I rushed myself to the ward, and looking at the empty bed made me feel my sweat, I ran towards the nurse who was working on the monitor, my restlessness being visible completely in my body, the nurse immediately responded,

"How may I help you?"

Steadying myself I held the edge of the counter, and asked,

"The couple, the couple in ward 4, where did they go?"

She immediately ran her data and said,

"They were discharged a couple of days ago."

I was shattered, the dread crawled over me, how could they be discharged?

Where might have they gone?

I immediately ran to the security guard of the hospital and asked him about the details of the vehicle that departed the couple of days ago.

I knew all these details were confidential which can't be shared with any individual who is a common man, but looking at me being worried, the security guard helped me with details, he showed the cc cam that was clearly displayed the car details that the couple had boarded. I thanked the security guard and headed back to my car.

I immediately dialed Khaja, he was the only one I could rely on, he immediately answered my call, saying,

"Where are you, man? And..."

with a concerned voice,

I know he has been worried about me, but I didn't have much time to explain the details so I interrupted him, even before he can finish his words, and said,

"Khaja, I need you to find me the details of a car, please hurry it."

Khaja didn't ask me anything, he immediately said,

"Okay, send me them."

I ended the call and texted him the numberplate details of the car that was boarded by the couple and started heading towards the city.

Just around 5 minutes after I sent the details to Khaja, he responded me with the co-ordinates of the couple where they are staying currently. Along with the information he also texted *"Wherever you are heading to, please be safe."*

I felt very bad as I got into the women's words and questioned Khaja. My heart was drowned with guilt, pulling my car to a side, I dialed Khaja and said,

"I am sorry Khaja, I hesitated to believe you, and I am going to end this soon."

I ended the conversation, I knew where they were, I accelerated my journey, the co-ordinates were directing me towards a remote house, hidden away on the outskirts of a town too small to make the news when another child disappeared. It fits their pattern perfectly isolated, inconspicuous, a place where they could hide and plan their next move.

I knew it would be dangerous to confront them alone, but I couldn't wait any longer. Every minute I hesitated was another minute that could cost a child their life. I needed to act now. The police had been too slow, too blind to see the truth all these years. But I wasn't going to let the couple slip through the cracks again. I had to face them myself.

As I drove toward the house, the tension in my chest grew tighter with every mile. The road was long and winding, the trees lining the sides of the road growing thicker and more menacing as I went deeper into the wilderness. The isolation of it all sent a chill down my spine, but I couldn't stop. I was committed. This was the moment I had been racing toward ever since I first uncovered the truth about the missing children.

I glanced down at the map as it was navigating me close to the destination, this was where they were hiding. This was where they had taken the children.

I kept driving, my mind racing with thoughts of what I might find when I arrived.

Would they be expecting me?

Would they deny everything, or would they try to flee? Every possible scenario played out in my mind, each one more unsettling than the last. But no matter how prepared I thought I was, nothing could have truly prepared me for what I would face when I finally saw them.

The road narrowed as I approached the edge of the woods, and soon, the house came into view. It was a dilapidated, crumbling structure, hidden behind overgrown bushes and trees, like something out of a forgotten horror story. The windows were dark, the roof sagging under the weight of years of neglect. But the place had a strange, eerie stillness to it. As if it was waiting for something—or someone.

I parked the car a short distance away, careful not to make any noise. My heart pounded in my chest as I stepped out, my legs shaky from a mixture of fear and adrenaline. I could feel the cold, biting air against my skin, but it was nothing compared to the chill running down my spine.

I approached the house cautiously, every nerve in my body on high alert. The silence was deafening. No birds, no wind, not even the sound of my own breath seemed to register in the oppressive quiet. It felt like the world itself was holding its breath, waiting for what would happen next.

As I reached the front of the house, I noticed something strange—a dim light flickering from one of the windows. They were here. I could feel it. But how would they react to seeing me?

Would they know why I had come?

I swallowed hard, trying to steady my nerves.

There was no going back now.

I raised my hand to knock on the door, hesitating for just a moment, my mind racing with all the things I wanted to say. I had prepared for this moment for so long, but now that I was here, standing on their doorstep, I wasn't sure if I was ready.

What would I find inside?

What if they were armed?

What if they attacked me?

But I couldn't think about that. Not now.

I knocked on the door.

The sound echoed through the house like a gunshot, breaking the stillness of the night. For a few agonizing moments, nothing happened. The silence stretched on, thick and suffocating. My pulse quickened, my hand shaking slightly as I waited for a response.

And then, I heard footsteps. Slow, deliberate, like someone taking their time, savouring the moment. The sound grew louder, closer, until finally, the door creaked open.

I held my breath.

There they were.

The woman stood in the doorway, her face illuminated by the faint glow of the light behind her.

She was exactly as I had imagined her—calm, composed, with that same unnerving smile I had seen in my nightmares. Her eyes locked onto mine, and for a moment, I couldn't breathe. There was something deeply unsettling about the way she looked at me, as though she knew exactly why I was there.

Behind her, the man appeared, standing slightly in the shadows, his face partially obscured. He was quiet, his expression neutral, but there was a tension in his posture, a readiness that made me uneasy.

For a long moment, none of us spoke. The air between us crackled with anticipation, like the calm before a storm. And then, finally, she spoke.

"We've been expecting you."

They were expecting me, but not like this.

Her words

"We've been expecting you"—hung in the air, thick and unsettling. My stomach twisted as I tried to comprehend what that meant.

Had they known I was coming all along? Had they been watching me, tracking my movements just as I had been tracking theirs?

Every hair on my body stood on edge.

She stepped aside, motioning for me to come in, her calm demeanour betraying nothing of the horror I knew lay beneath. The man behind her remained in the shadows, his expression unreadable, but there was something about the way he watched me that sent a chill down my spine.

I hesitated for a moment at the doorway. Every instinct in my body screamed at me to turn around and leave, to run far away from the nightmare I was about to walk into. But I couldn't. Not now. I had come too far, uncovered too much. And if there was even the slightest chance that another child could be in danger, I couldn't abandon this confrontation. I had to see it through.

I stepped inside, my heart pounding in my chest.

The house smelled of decay—rotting wood, dust, and something else I couldn't quite place. It was dark, with only a dim, flickering light from a single lamp in the corner, casting long, ominous shadows on the walls. Everything about the place felt wrong, like it had been frozen in time, untouched by the outside world.

The woman led me further inside, her movements graceful and deliberate, as though she was in complete control of the situation. She didn't seem the least bit threatened by my presence. In fact, she seemed almost... amused.

As we entered what looked like the living room, I got a better look at the man. He was tall and gaunt, his face pale and emotionless, his eyes cold and distant. He didn't say a word, just stood there, watching me with an intensity that made my skin crawl.

"Please, have a seat,"

the woman said, gesturing to a worn-out armchair near the centre of the room.

I didn't sit. I couldn't. My mind was racing with a thousand questions, and I needed answers—now.

"You know why I'm here,"

I said, trying to keep my voice steady, though my hands were trembling.

The woman smiled, a slow, unsettling smile that didn't reach her eyes.

"Of course,"

she said, her voice soft and soothing, as though she were speaking to a child.

"You've been searching for us for quite some time, haven't you?"

I swallowed hard, trying to push down the fear rising in my throat.

"What you've done... the children... I know everything."

The woman tilted her head slightly, her eyes narrowing as she studied me.

"Do you?"

she asked, her tone curious, almost playful.

"Do you really know everything?"

I clenched my fists, the anger bubbling up inside me.

"You took those children,"

I said, my voice trembling with rage.

"You abducted them, and you... you tortured them. And now, you're planning to do it again, aren't you?"

The room fell silent. For a moment, I thought the man would finally speak, but he remained still, his eyes fixed on me.

The woman let out a small laugh, the sound sending chills through my bones.

"Tortured?"

she repeated, her tone light, almost mocking.

"Is that what you think we did?"

I stared at her, my mind reeling. Was she trying to deny it? To twist the truth into something even more grotesque?

"They were my children,"

she continued, her voice soft and haunting.

"I loved them. I gave them a home. A family. Something their real parents could never do."

My blood ran cold. The way she spoke about them—it was as if she truly believed her own delusions, as if she saw herself as some kind of saviour, rescuing the children from lives of neglect and suffering.

"You kidnapped them,"

I said, my voice barely above a whisper.

"You stole them from their families."

The woman's smile faded, and her eyes darkened.

"Their families didn't care for them,"

she said coldly.

"They were lost, abandoned, left to fend for themselves in a world that didn't want them. We... we gave them a place where they belonged."

I shook my head, my heart racing.

"You're insane,"

I whispered.

"You're both insane."

At that, the man stepped forward, his presence suddenly more imposing. He still hadn't spoken, but the look in his eyes was chilling. He wasn't just a bystander in this. He was just as complicit, just as twisted.

The woman's gaze softened again as she turned back to me.

"We saved those children,"

she said, her voice almost tender.

"We gave them something they never had before.

A family. A mother."

I felt sick. I had expected denial, excuses, maybe even rage. But this—this was something far worse. This wasn't just madness. It was a deeply ingrained delusion, one that had driven them to commit unspeakable horrors.

"You didn't save them,"

I said, my voice shaking with anger.

"You destroyed them."

The woman's smile returned, but it was different now—colder, more sinister.

"You don't understand,"
she said softly.
"You've been looking for monsters, but what you'll find is a family. A family that would do anything to stay together."

I took a step back, my mind spinning. I had come here to confront them, to get answers, but now, standing face-to-face with the couple, I realized that nothing they said could make sense in any rational way. They were lost in their own twisted reality, where love and cruelty had become one and the same.

The woman's eyes gleamed in the dim light as she watched me, her smile widening.

"You've come all this way, and now you're here,"
she said, her voice almost a whisper.
"You're part of the family now, too."

My heart stopped. I realized in that moment that I had walked into a trap. They hadn't just been expecting me—they had been waiting for me.Their truths were worse than I had imagined.

I stood frozen in the centre of the room, their words sinking into me like ice. The woman's voice, soft yet sinister, filled the space, wrapping around my mind like a web of lies. But these weren't lies, were they? No, in her mind, every word she spoke was the truth. And that made it all the more terrifying.

She turned her gaze toward the man, who had been silent up until now.

"He doesn't understand,"
she said, almost sympathetically.
"He thinks we're the villains in this story."

The man finally spoke, his voice low and rough, like someone who hadn't used it in years.

"They always do,"
he said, his eyes fixed on mine. There was no remorse, no guilt in his expression. Just emptiness.

I took a step back, trying to distance myself from their suffocating presence.

"You... you took those children,"

I said, my voice wavering, struggling to keep the anger from crumbling into fear.

"You took them and you... you tortured them."

The woman shook her head slowly, as if disappointed in me for not understanding.

"Tortured?"

she repeated.

"You keep using that word, but you don't know what you're talking about."

Her tone was condescending, like she was speaking to a child who had misunderstood something simple.

"I gave them love,"

she continued, her voice growing softer, more wistful.

"I gave them a home, a place where they were wanted. They were my children."

I couldn't believe what I was hearing. My mind raced as I tried to process the horror of her words.

"You're delusional,"

I whispered.

"You kidnapped them. You took them from their real families, and you—"

the man interrupted,

"Their real families didn't care,"

his voice sharp.

"They left those children to suffer, to be forgotten."

I looked at him, anger rising in my chest.

"So, you think that gives you the right to take them? To imprison them?"

The woman smiled, a sad, pitying smile.

"They were already prisoners in their own homes,"

she said softly.

"Their parents didn't love them. Not like I did."

I wanted to scream, to shake her, to make her see what she had done. But I knew it was pointless. Her mind was too far gone, twisted by years of delusions that had become her reality.

"You destroyed their lives,"

I said, my voice trembling with anger.

"You didn't save them."

The woman's smile faded, her expression hardening.

"You don't know anything,"

she said coldly.

"You think you understand, but you don't. You're just like the others, always so quick to judge, to label us as monsters."

She took a step closer to me, her eyes burning with something dark, something I couldn't quite place.

"But we weren't monsters,"

she whispered.

"We were their parents. We were the only ones who truly loved them."

I could feel the bile rising in my throat, my body trembling with disgust.

"You killed them,"

I said my voice barely above a whisper.

"You killed those children."

The woman's eyes narrowed, and for the first time, I saw a flicker of something—rage, maybe? Or fear? It was hard to tell.

"They were part of my family,"

she said, her voice dangerously low.

"I would never hurt my family."

The room seemed to close in around me as her words sank in. She truly believed what she was saying. In her mind, she hadn't killed those children—she had given them a family, a twisted, perverse version of what a family was supposed to be. And in that delusion, she had justified every unspeakable thing she had done to them.

The man remained silent, standing behind her like a ghost, his eyes never leaving mine. I could tell he was the more practical of the two, the one who had carried out the physical acts while the woman lived in her fantasy. But he was just as guilty. He had let her madness infect him, had allowed her delusions to justify the atrocities they committed together.

And now, standing before them, I realized something chilling—they were proud of what they had done. They didn't see their actions as crimes. To them, it was all part of some greater purpose, a warped vision of love and family that had driven them to abduct and murder.

"You took them,"

I said again, my voice shaking.

"You took those children, and you—"

the woman interrupted,

"They weren't taken,"

her voice rising slightly, her calm façade cracking.

"They were given to me."

My heart pounded in my chest.

"What do you mean?"

I asked, dread creeping into my voice.

The woman's eyes gleamed with something dark and triumphant.

"They were given to me,"

she repeated.

"Their parents... they didn't want them. They didn't care. They let me take them because they knew I could give them something better. A real family."

I stared at her in horror, the weight of her words crashing down on me.

"You're lying,"

I said, though my voice lacked conviction.

"No parent would ever give their child to you."

She smiled again, that same eerie, unsettling smile that made my skin crawl.

"You'd be surprised,"

she said quietly.

"People can be convinced of anything if they believe it's for the best."

I felt sick, my body trembling with the realization of what she was saying. Had she convinced the parents to give up their children? Or had she simply manipulated them, taken advantage of their desperation? Either way, it was monstrous.

"You're sick,"

I whispered, stepping back from her.

"Both of you."

The man finally spoke again, his voice low and deliberate.

"We gave those children what no one else could,"

he said.

"We gave them a place to belong."

I shook my head, my mind reeling.

"You took everything from them,"

I said.

"Their lives, their futures. You didn't save them—you destroyed them."

The woman's eyes narrowed again, her calm exterior cracking further.

"You don't understand,"

she said, her voice shaking with anger.

"You'll never understand. I did what I had to do. I loved them."

The room was suffocating now, the weight of their twisted logic pressing down on me, making it hard to breathe. They truly believed they had done something noble, something right. But all I could see were the faces of the children they had stolen, the lives they had snuffed out in their delusional quest for a *family.*

The woman took a step toward me, her eyes locked on mine.

"You think you're here to stop us,"

she said, her voice soft but menacing.

"But you're too late. You can't stop us. Not now. Not ever."

I never thought it would come to this.

Her words- **You can't stop us**-echoed in the room, chilling me to the bone. There was no reasoning with them. No appeal to logic or morality could penetrate the dense fog of their madness. And as I stood there, watching the woman's calm façade crack further, I realized something terrifying: I wasn't in control anymore. They were.

The tension in the room had reached a breaking point. I could feel it in the way the woman's eyes darted from me to the man, the way her breathing had quickened. Something was about to snap, and I knew I had to be ready for it. My mind screamed at me to leave, to get out before things turned violent, but I couldn't. I had come too far. I had to see this through.

"You think you've won,"

the woman said, her voice shaking with barely restrained fury.

"You think you can come here and take everything from me?

You have no idea what you've walked into."

I took a step back, my heart pounding in my chest. Her calm exterior had vanished, replaced by a wild, desperate energy that made the air in the room feel thick and oppressive. The man, too, was on edge, his posture rigid, as if he was waiting for some unspoken signal.

"I'm not here to take anything from you,"

I said, my voice tense but controlled.

"I'm here to stop you from hurting anyone else."

The woman's eyes flashed with rage.

"Hurting?"

she spat, her voice rising.

"You think we're the ones doing the hurting? We gave those children a home. We loved them. We protected them from a world that didn't care about them."

I shouted,

"You murdered them!"

being unable to hold back my anger any longer.

"You took them from their families, twisted their lives into some sick fantasy, and then you-"

she screamed,

"They were mine!"

her voice shrill and unhinged.

"They were my children! You don't get to take that away from me!"

Before I could react, she lunged at me, her face contorted in fury. I barely had time to step aside as she clawed at me, her nails raking the air just inches from my face. Her movements were wild, and erratic, driven by a madness so deep it felt like she was no longer human. She was a predator, and I was her prey.

I stumbled backward, trying to keep my balance as she lunged again, this time catching the sleeve of my jacket and yanking me forward. Her strength was shocking, fuelled by pure, unbridled rage. I twisted free, my heart hammering in my chest, but she was relentless, her eyes wide with fury, her breath coming in ragged gasps.

The man remained in the shadows, watching the scene unfold with a strange, detached calm. He didn't move to help her, didn't try to stop her. It was as if he was waiting- waiting for the right moment to step in and finish what she had started.

"You won't take them from me!"

the woman shrieked, her voice breaking as she lunged at me again. This time, I wasn't fast enough. She slammed into me, knocking me backward into the wall. The impact sent a shock of pain through my body, but I barely had time to register it before she was on top of me, her hands clawing at my throat.

I struggled against her, my vision blurring as her fingers tightened around my neck. I could feel her nails digging into my skin, the pressure cutting off my air. Panic surged through me as I fought to free myself, my hands flailing as I tried to push her away.

In the chaos, I managed to grab hold of her wrists and twist her hands away from my throat, gasping for air as I shoved her back. She staggered, her eyes wild and unfocused, but she wasn't done yet. She came at me again, screaming incoherently, her rage blinding her to everything else.

"Stop!"

I shouted, my voice hoarse.

"Just stop!"

But she didn't stop. She couldn't stop. The madness had consumed her completely, leaving nothing but a feral, uncontrollable fury in its wake. I received a call from Khaja during that time, I wasn't in a state to pick up his call, so I dodged her next attack, stumbling toward the center of the room, trying to put some distance between us. I glanced at the man, hoping absurdly that he might intervene, but he stood frozen, his eyes locked on the woman as if he was waiting for her to finish what she had started.

Suddenly, she grabbed something from the table-a heavy glass vase- and swung it at me. I barely managed to duck, the vase shattering against the wall behind me. Glass shards flew through the air, cutting across my arm, but I didn't have time to think about the pain. I had to defend myself.

She was on me again, her hands swinging wildly, her nails slashing at my skin. I could feel the sting of each blow, the hot blood dripping down my face and arms, but adrenaline was keeping me on my feet. I fought back, shoving her away with everything I had, trying to create space between us.

But she wouldn't stop. She was relentless, like a wild animal, her movements fuelled by a madness that seemed to give her inhuman strength.

And then, in the midst of the chaos, the man finally moved.

I saw him out of the corner of my eye, stepping forward with slow, deliberate steps. His expression hadn't changed, but there was something dangerous in the way he moved, like a predator stalking its prey.

I had a split second to react. He was reaching for something-something in his pocket, something that glinted in the dim light.

A knife.

My heart stopped.

He was going to kill me.

The woman lunged at me again, and I had no choice but to throw her off with all my strength, sending her crashing into the table. She screamed in frustration, but I barely heard it. My focus was on the man, on the knife in his hand, on the cold, emotionless look in his eyes as he stepped toward me.

I backed up, my mind racing. I had to think. I had to act. But my body was already bruised and bleeding, and I wasn't sure how much longer I could fight.

The man raised the knife, his movements calm and deliberate, and I knew I was out of time. The horror wasn't over, but the nightmare was beginning to end.

The man's knife glinted in the low light, each step he took toward me feeling like a countdown to something inevitable. I backed up, my breath quickening, the sound of my heartbeat pounding in my ears. The woman, bruised and bleeding, struggled to pull herself up from where I had thrown her, her shrill voice muttering incoherent words, lost in her madness. But it was the man I feared now. His cold, detached expression as he moved closer, knife in hand, made my skin crawl.

I had seconds less to react. My mind raced for a solution, for anything that would give me a chance to survive. My body ached from the struggle, and blood dripped from the cuts on my arms and face. I felt weak, worn down by the relentless attack from the woman, but I couldn't give up now. This had to end here, one way or another.

"Stop!"

I shouted, my voice raw and desperate.

"You don't have to do this!"

The man's expression didn't change. He kept coming, his eyes locked on mine, the knife steady in his hand.

I looked around the room, my eyes darting from the broken glass to the scattered furniture, searching for anything I could use to defend myself. And then I saw a shard of glass from the shattered vase, large enough to use as a weapon, just a few feet away.

With no other option, I lunged for the glass shard, grabbing it and turning just in time as the man swung the knife at me. The blade missed by inches, but the momentum threw him off balance for a moment. I didn't hesitate. I slashed at him with the shard of glass, catching him across the arm. He recoiled, blood dripping from the fresh wound, but his face remained eerily calm as if the pain didn't even register.

"You're not getting out of this,"

I said, my voice trembling.

"It's over."

The man's eyes narrowed, his grip on the knife tightening.

"It's not over,"

he said quietly, his voice almost a whisper.

"Not until you're gone."

He lunged at me again, and I barely managed to block the attack with the shard of glass. The impact jarred my arm, sending a sharp pain shooting through my body, but I held my ground. I had to. There was no other choice.

We struggled, the knife slashing through the air, the glass shard barely keeping him at bay. My strength was fading fast, but the adrenaline kept me moving, kept me fighting. I couldn't let him win. I couldn't let them escape after everything they had done.

In the chaos of the struggle, I heard a noise behind a low, desperate groan. The woman. She had crawled closer, dragging herself across the floor, her eyes wild with rage and madness. She reached for the knife, her hand outstretched, but before she could grab it, I kicked it away, sending it skidding across the floor.

"No!"

she screamed, her voice cracking with fury.

"You won't take them from me! You can't!"

The man's face twisted in anger as he lunged at me with renewed fury, his movements more frantic now that his partner had been disarmed. I dodged his next attack, my body barely able to keep up, and slashed at him again with the glass shard, catching him across the chest this time. He staggered back, blood pouring from the wound, but he didn't stop.

"You're insane,"

I whispered, barely able to catch my breath.

"We did what was necessary,"

the man hissed through gritted teeth.

"We gave those children a life-something no one else could."

I spat, my voice trembling with anger.

"You killed them, you didn't save anyone."

The man lunged at me one last time, but I was ready. I sidestepped his attack, using every ounce of strength I had left, and drove the shard of glass into his side. He gasped, his eyes wide with shock and pain as he stumbled backward, the knife slipping from his hand and clattering to the floor.

For a moment, everything seemed to stop. The man swayed on his feet, blood pooling around him as he struggled to stay upright. His eyes locked onto mine, and for the first time, I saw something resembling fear flicker across his face.

He collapsed to the floor, gasping for breath, his hand clutching at the wound in his side. The woman, still on the ground, let out a scream sound so raw and filled with rage that it cut through me like a knife.

"No!"

she cried, crawling toward him, her hands shaking.

"No, no, no! This isn't how it ends!"

I stumbled back, my hands trembling, the glass shard slipping from my grip as I tried to steady myself. My body ached, my vision blurred, but it was over. It had to be over.

The woman reached the man's side, her hands covered in his blood as she tried to stop the bleeding, her mind still clinging to her delusion.

"It's okay,"

she whispered to him, her voice soft and broken.

"We're going to be fine. We're going to be a family again. Just like before."

But the man was already gone.

I stood there, numb, watching as the woman cradled his lifeless body, her mind fractured beyond repair. The house, once filled with their twisted delusions, now felt eerily empty, as if the madness had finally drained from it, leaving only silence and death in its wake.

The woman's sobs grew quieter, her body shaking with the weight of her grief, but I knew there was no redemption here. There was no saving her. She had been lost to the darkness long ago, and now, it was all catching up to her.

Sirens wailed in the distance. The police were finally on their way, though it felt like a lifetime too late. I should have called them sooner, and should have waited for backup, but I knew that if I had, more lives would have been lost. The couple would have fled, disappearing into the shadows to start again somewhere else.

But now, it was over.

I sank to the floor, my body trembling, the adrenaline finally wearing off as the pain and exhaustion set in. The horror of everything I had witnessed, everything I had fought against, began to weigh on me. It wasn't just the physical wounds-it was the emotional toll. The weight of all the children who had suffered because of this couple. The lives lost, the futures destroyed.

And yet, there was a part of me that felt hollow. The woman had been right about one thing: this wasn't over. The children might be gone, but their ghosts would remain. The memory of their laughter, twisted and haunting, would follow me for the rest of my life.

The woman's sobs faded into silence as the sound of footsteps approached. The police. They would take her away now, but it didn't feel like justice. It didn't feel like enough.

Because no matter what happened next, nothing could undo the horrors that had been unleashed in that house.

CHAPTER XI

The End.

It felt over, but something inside me refused to let go of the horror.

The sirens cut through the night air, growing louder as they approached the house. Red and blue lights flashed against the darkened windows, casting long, distorted shadows across the walls. I collapsed on the floor, watching the scene unfold, my body trembling with exhaustion and adrenaline. I should have felt relieved. I should have felt like it was over. But the truth was, it didn't feel like the nightmare had ended at all.

My clothes were soaked with blood—some of it with mine, some of it with theirs. The couple who had haunted my every waking thought for weeks were finally subdued, the woman sobbing in the corner, clutching the body of the man, her twisted partner in crime. She rocked back and forth, her hands stained red, mumbling incoherently. Her madness had consumed her completely, leaving nothing but an empty shell of the person she once was. The man lay lifeless on the floor, his eyes still open, staring vacantly into the distance.

I wanted to feel something—relief, closure, anything—but I couldn't. Instead, all I felt was a hollow numbness, like I had stepped outside of my own body, watching it all from somewhere far away. The chaos had ended, but the weight of everything that had happened pressed down on me, suffocating me.

The front door creaked open, and a group of officers entered the house, their footsteps heavy against the old, rotting floorboards. They moved quickly, their radios buzzing with instructions I couldn't quite hear. Two of them rushed toward the woman, pulling her away from the man's body, while others secured the area. She didn't fight them, didn't even seem to register their presence. Her eyes were vacant, lost in a world of her own, a world where her delusions had been real and the horrors she had inflicted were justified.

I was still crushing onto the floor, my eyes half closed, being unable to move, I heard a familiar voice,

"Hey...!"

The voice felt as if it was pathing towards me, though it was a casual word, it was carrying the concern and distress...!

My sight fixed on the woman, I noticed her being unable to move or speak as they took her away. She looked so different now, her eyes wide but empty, her body limp as they led her out into the night. Just hours before, she had been a force of rage, a whirlwind of violence and madness. Now, she was nothing but a broken woman, haunted by the demons of her own making.

The man, though—he wasn't going anywhere. His body lay crumpled on the floor where I had left him, a pool of blood spreading out beneath him like a dark, ominous stain. The officers barely glanced at him as they worked, treating him as though he were already part of the past, something to be cataloged and filed away as evidence.

It felt as if someone was trying to wake me up,

"Wake up, open your eyes."

Turning my head slowly, I noticed the face, it was Khaja, holding me, he called for help,

"Officers"

One of the officers approached me, his face grim.

"You alright?"

He asked, his voice steady, professional, as if he had seen scenes like this a thousand times before.

I opened my mouth to respond, but no words came out.

Was I alright? I didn't know. Physically, I was bruised and bleeding, my body aching from the fight. But it was something deeper, something I couldn't quite put into words. The numbness that had settled over me like a fog wouldn't lift.

The officer nodded as if he understood.

"We'll take it from here,"

he said.

"You should get checked out by the paramedics. It's over now."

Soon I was rushed out to the ambulance, paramedics checking me.

Though I was lying semi-conscious, all my thoughts were still on the house.

The house, once filled with the oppressive energy of the couple's madness, now felt eerily quiet, as if it had exhaled for the first time in years. The walls, the broken furniture, the scattered pieces of their twisted life—all of it remained, but the terror that had clung to every corner seemed to have vanished the moment the police arrived.

But the horror hadn't disappeared. It was still with me, gnawing at the edges of my mind, refusing to let go. I could still hear their voices—the woman's screams, the man's cold, detached words. I could still see the faces of the children, the ones they had taken, their laughter echoing in my ears even though I knew I'd never hear it again.

But it didn't feel over. Not really. I watched as they took control of the scene, cordoning off the area, cataloguing evidence, all while the woman's cries faded into the night. And yet, despite the calm that had settled over the house, something inside me refused to believe it was truly finished. The nightmare might have ended for them, but for me, it was just beginning.

As I started getting back into my consciousness, I slowly stepped outside, the cold night air hitting me like a slap to the face. The officers were circulated throughout the area, it sensed as if they were expecting me to talk, but I wasn't ready to talk to them. I needed a moment alone. I walked toward the edge of the yard, the grass damp beneath my feet, and looked up at the sky. The stars were out, clear and bright, as if nothing terrible had just happened.

But I couldn't escape the feeling that the horror I had uncovered would stay with me forever. The couple might be gone, but their twisted legacy—what they had done to those children—would never truly fade.

I closed my eyes, taking a deep breath. It was over. It had to be over.

But the fear, the horror—it wasn't going anywhere.

The truth was out, but the scars it left were deeper than anyone could have imagined.

Sitting on the steps of the ambulance, I could hear the murmur of voices behind me. The police were inside the house, piecing together the couple's twisted plan, uncovering the evidence I had feared might never come to light. Every now and then, I caught fragments of their conversations—mentions of documents, hidden compartments, things I hadn't seen when I was inside. I couldn't bring myself to go back in. Not yet.

I had done what I came to do. I had confronted them, and uncovered the truth behind the disappearances, the children. But now, as I sat in the cold night air, it felt like I was watching everything unfold from a distance, disconnected from the reality of it all. Khaja was there standing right next to me, with tears dripping from his eyes, anger being held in his fists, he was there, standing silent.

A detective, one of the lead investigators, walked over to me. His face was drawn, his eyes tired but focused. He had the look of someone who had seen too much but wasn't allowed to feel it.

"We've found enough to put the pieces together,"

he said, his voice steady but laced with something darker.

"They were planning to leave the country, weren't they?
Dubai?"

I nodded, though my throat felt tight like speaking would reopen wounds I was trying to hold closed.

"They were going to fake their mental illness,"

I said, my voice quieter than I'd intended.

"Disappear once everything had settled down, once people had stopped asking questions."

The detective ran a hand over his face, shaking his head.

"They nearly got away with it,"

hc said, his tone laced with frustration.

"We've found flight tickets, documents—everything was ready for them to leave within the week. They had everything in place. If you hadn't stepped in..."

He didn't need to finish the sentence. I knew what he was going to say. If I hadn't been there, if I hadn't forced the confrontation, they would have vanished, slipping away into a new life while the horrors they left behind faded into unsolved mysteries. The thought made me sick.

"They were meticulous,"

the detective continued, pulling out a small notebook from his pocket.

"We've found detailed journals—mostly hers—about the children. Names, dates, where and when they took them."

He paused, his face grim.

"It's worse than we thought."

I felt the bile rise in my throat, but I forced myself to stay calm. I had known it was bad. I had seen it in their eyes, heard it in their words. But hearing the confirmation, knowing that there were records—actual records—of their crimes, made it all feel so much more real. Too real.

"How many?"

I asked though I wasn't sure I wanted to hear the answer.

The detective hesitated for a moment before speaking.

"At least six children, from different towns across the region. But there could be more. We're still going through everything."

Six. Six innocent lives were taken by their twisted need for control, for whatever sick version of a family they thought they were creating. And there could be more.

I stared down at my hands, still smeared with dried blood, my mind reeling. They had been so close to getting away with it. All of it. The lies, the abductions, the murders—it had all been part of a carefully constructed plan, hidden behind their act of insanity. And no one had seen it.

"They used their madness as a cover,"

the detective continued as if reading my thoughts.

"Played the part of the disturbed, mentally ill couple. Neighbors thought they were harmless. Doctors believed their stories about hearing children's voices, about seeing things that weren't there. And all the while, they were hiding in plain sight."

The weight of his words settled over me like a heavy blanket. It made sense now—how they had managed to evade capture for so long. They had used their delusions as a shield, hiding their crimes behind the mask of mental illness, manipulating everyone around them into thinking they were victims of some terrible, untreatable disorder.

But it was all an act. A performance they had perfected over the years, designed to keep anyone from looking too closely, from asking too many questions.

I clenched my fists, the anger bubbling up inside me again. They had been so methodical, so calculated in their cruelty. And the worst part was, they had nearly succeeded.

"They were smart,"

I said, my voice tight.

"They knew exactly what they were doing."

The detective nodded.

"Yeah, they did,"

he agreed.

"But not smart enough to get away forever."

A silence fell between us, the weight of everything hanging in the air. I could hear the distant voices of the other officers, the sound of evidence being cataloged, and the clicks of cameras taking photos of the scene. It felt clinical, cold like the life and death that had happened in that house was being reduced to numbers and facts, stripped of the horror that still clung to me like a second skin.

I looked up at the detective, my voice hoarse as I asked the question that had been burning in my mind since the confrontation.

"Why didn't anyone stop them sooner?"

He sighed, his shoulders sagging under the weight of the question.

"People like them... they know how to work the system,"

he said, his voice laced with frustration.

"They hid behind their illness, which made everyone around them believe they were the victims. And the kids they took... a lot of them came from troubled homes. Runaways, kids nobody was really looking for. They slipped through the cracks."

He shook his head, his expression grim.

I felt a wave of anger and sadness wash over me. The children—their lives had been deemed unimportant, their disappearances dismissed because no one had been there to fight for them. And the couple had taken full advantage of that, using it to build their sick world, believing they could get away with it.

"They won't get away with it now?"

I said, though it sounded more like a question, the words felt hollow. The couple might have been caught, their plan exposed, but the damage they had done would never truly be undone.

The detective nodded, but his expression remained solemn.

"No, they won't, but that doesn't change what they did. Doesn't bring those kids back."

he said.

I looked away, the weight of his words pressing down on me. He was right. Nothing could change what had happened. The truth was out now, the couple's plan laid bare for everyone to see, but the scars they had left would never heal.

As the detective turned to walk back into the house, I stayed where I was, staring at the stars above, feeling the cold night air biting at my skin. The couple might be gone, their twisted plot exposed, but the fear, the horror—it would always be there.

No one told me that surviving the horror would feel like this.

The sun was beginning to rise, casting an eerie light over the scene. The once-dark house stood silent, now nothing more than a crime scene for investigators to comb through. The flashing police lights felt like a memory already, as if the chaos of the night had been swallowed up by the approaching dawn.

I sat on the edge of the ambulance, my hands wrapped around a cup of water that I hadn't touched. My throat was dry, my skin sticky with the dried blood from the confrontation, but none of it mattered. The paramedics were talking nearby, but I couldn't hear their words. I couldn't shake the feeling that even though the night was over, something darker was still alive inside me.

The weight of everything—the faces of the missing children, the brutality of the couple's actions, the madness in the woman's eyes as she lunged at me—hung over me like a storm cloud. I kept thinking I'd feel relief once they were caught, once the truth came out, but the more I thought about it, the hollower I felt.

What was supposed to be closure didn't feel like it. It didn't feel like anything. The house was quiet now, the police were taking the couple away, and the truth was laid bare for the world to see. And yet, I was still haunted by the ghosts of everything that had happened.

Khaja said, in his utmost comforting tone,

"Come, let me drive you."

He helped me get into the car, and as the car started heading back, I knew I was going distant from the place, but I was still stuck within the loop. I could still hear their voices—the woman's twisted words as she tried to explain her crimes as if she had been saving those children instead of destroying their lives. I could still see the man's cold, emotionless eyes as he watched me, calculating, preparing to strike. But worst of all, I could still hear the children's laughter, echoing in my mind like a song that wouldn't stop playing, no matter how hard I tried to push it away.

And it wasn't just the laughter. It was their faces, too. The missing posters I had seen in towns across the region, the reports of runaways and disappearances, the names of the children they had taken. I had read about them, and searched for them, but nothing could have prepared me for the guilt that came with knowing I hadn't been able to save them.

Six children. That's what the detective had told me. Six innocent lives were stolen, taken from their families, and their futures snuffed out by the couple's twisted fantasies. And that number could still rise.

I should have felt victorious. I had uncovered the truth, I had stopped them before they could take another child, but all I felt was a gnawing emptiness inside me. Because I hadn't saved the others. They were gone. And there was nothing I could do to bring them back.

I glanced up at the house, now surrounded by crime scene tape and officers going in and out. I couldn't bear to go back inside. The thought of walking through those rooms again, of seeing the remnants of the couple's twisted life, made me sick to my stomach. I had spent weeks chasing this mystery, but now that I had uncovered it, I wished I could forget it all.

But I couldn't.

The faces of the children—their names, their stories—would follow me. They were etched into my mind, into my very soul. I hadn't known them, but I felt like I had failed them all the same.

I wasn't a detective. I wasn't a hero. I was just a person who had stumbled into this nightmare, and now I was stuck carrying the weight of it with me. The horror of what the couple had done wasn't something that could be undone by their arrest. It wouldn't disappear just because they were behind bars.

It had become a part of me.

I thought about the parents of those children. The ones who had been left behind, still waiting for answers, still clinging to the hope that their children would come home. How could I face them?

How could I tell them that their children had been taken by monsters and that there was no happy ending?

The tears welled up in my eyes before I could stop them. I hadn't cried once through this whole ordeal, not when I had found the clues, not when I had uncovered the couple's secrets, and not even when I had fought for my life in that house.

But now, sitting in the car, experiencing the stillness of the early morning, the tears came, silent and heavy.

I tried to wipe them away before Khaja could see, but it was no use. The grief was too much, the weight of it crushing me from the inside. I felt like I was drowning in it like I couldn't breathe under the pressure of everything that had happened.

No one had warned me about this. No one had told me that surviving something like this didn't feel like survival at all. It felt like losing a piece of yourself, a piece you could never get back.

Looking at me as I was lost in my own thoughts, Khaja pulled his car, stepping out for a moment, maybe he thought I needed some space, but I was still lost in the faces of the children I hadn't been able to save. The laughter in my head was relentless, mocking me, reminding me that no matter how much I had uncovered, I hadn't been able to change the past.

As the car stopped, he got out of the car, I opened the door, sitting in my seat, putting my legs out enough they could touch the ground, I leaned forward, my elbows resting on my knees, and stared down at the ground. I didn't know how to move on from this. I didn't know how to pick up the pieces and go back to my life like none of this had happened.

I didn't want to be the one who carried these stories. I didn't want to be the one who had to remember. But now, it was all I had. These weren't just headlines in the newspaper anymore. They were real, and they were part of me.

Looking at our car being pulled out, the police vehicles approached us, as soon as the vehicles stopped, an officer got down from the vehicle and said,

"Sir, we need you to follow us, our head would like to meet you."

We nodded, and as Khaja entered the car, I closed the door, buckling myself, I closed my eyes, trying to block out the memories, trying to find some kind of peace in the midst of all the chaos. But there was no peace to be found. Not yet.

Maybe not forever.

The case was closed, but there were still so many questions left unanswered.

We drove straight to the police station, following the guards in front of us. The sterile brightness of the police station contrasted sharply with the dark memories I carried with me. I sat in a small, cold room, waiting for the detectives to return. The walls were bare, and the air felt stifling, filled with the quiet hum of computers and the occasional click of a door shutting down the hall. It was the kind of place where facts were dissected, where human lives were reduced to files, reports, and case numbers.

I had been in this room before concerning my projects or research, but today felt different. I wasn't here to uncover any more truths. I was here to demand answers.

The couple had been taken away, their reign of terror ended, but my mind wouldn't let me rest. The more I thought about everything

I'd uncovered, the more questions gnawed at me. How had they gotten away with it for so long?

How had no one noticed the children disappearing?

How had the system failed them over and over again?

The door creaked open, and Detective Harish, the lead investigator, stepped inside. He carried a thick folder, the weight of which seemed to echo the weight of the case itself. He gave me a brief nod as he sat across from me, placing the folder on the table between us. He looked tired—more so than the last time we'd met—but there was a cold professionalism in his eyes that told me he was ready to tie up the loose ends.

"We've gone through most of the evidence now,"

he said, flipping open the folder and spreading out some of the documents in front of me.

"It's... overwhelming, to say the least. As per the records, the couple had been operating for nearly five years. The children they took, the journals, the flight plans—all of it points to a highly calculated, premeditated operation."

He paused, glancing at me, waiting for my response. I felt the knot tighten in my stomach. Five years. Five years of terror. Five years where children were taken, and no one had stopped it.

"How did it go on for so long?"

I asked, my voice rougher than I intended.

"How did no one notice?"

Harish sighed, rubbing a hand across his face.

"It's not easy to admit, but the system failed,"

he said, his tone heavy with resignation.

"Most of the children they targeted came from troubled backgrounds—runaways, orphans, kids who were already slipping through the cracks. There were reports filed here and there, but nothing that ever stuck. They were good at covering their tracks."

I could feel the anger bubbling up inside me.

"But those kids had families—people who loved them. How could this happen?"

I demanded.

"How could they just disappear, and no one... no one looked harder?"

Harish nodded slowly.

"You're right,"

he said quietly.

"People did care. But the couple was smart. They knew how to manipulate the system. They chose their victims carefully—children who didn't have strong support systems, who were already on the margins of society. It made them less likely to be found. And when there were investigations, the couple played the role of innocent bystanders, mentally unstable but harmless. It worked for a long time."

I clenched my fists under the table. Every answer felt like a punch to the gut. The thought that these children had been abandoned by the very people who were supposed to protect them made me sick.

"I don't understand,"

I said, trying to keep my voice steady.

"How could this couple—just two people—pull this off for so long?

There had to be warning signs. People must have noticed something."

Harish flipped through the documents, pulling out a few pages that looked like reports.

"There were signs,"

he admitted.

"A few neighbors reported hearing strange noises, but nothing concrete. And when the couple visited doctors or counselors, they used their mental health diagnosis to explain away their behavior. It was all part of their plan."

I felt a wave of frustration wash over me.

"So, because they seemed mentally ill, people just... ignored the rest?"

Harish met my eyes, his expression serious.

"Mental illness is complicated,"

he said.

"*It can mask a lot of things. And in this case, they used it to their advantage. They were seen as victims of their own minds, not as perpetrators. And that made it easier for them to hide what they were really doing.*"

It felt like every layer of this case was wrapped in some new form of tragedy. The couple hadn't just fooled their neighbors or the police—they had fooled an entire system. A system that should have caught them. A system that should have protected those children.

"*But it's not just about them,*"

I said, the frustration evident in my voice.

"*It's about the kids. Their families. How many of them went to the police and were turned away because no one believed their kids were worth looking for?*"

Harish's face tightened.

"*Too many,*"

he said, his voice quiet.

"*Too many cases were dismissed as runaways. And once a child is labeled a runaway, it's harder to get resources to look for them. It's one of the cracks they slipped through, and it's something we're trying to fix.*"

I shook my head, the weight of it all pressing down on me again.

"*They slipped through the cracks,*"

I repeated, my voice bitter.

"*But why didn't anyone try harder to fill those cracks?*"

The room felt smaller, more claustrophobic, as the silence stretched between us. Harish looked down at the folder, tapping the edge of the papers with his fingers.

"*You're right,*"

he said finally.

"*We should have done more. But cases like these—they're complicated. They're not always black and white. There were failures, on many levels. But now, we have the truth. We have the evidence. The case will go to trial, and they'll pay for what they did.*"

I stared at him, feeling a sense of emptiness wash over me.

"But what about the families?" I asked quietly.

What about the ones who lost their children? What about the ones who are still waiting for answers?"

Harish's expression softened.

"We'll reach out to them," he said.

"We'll do everything we can to give them closure. But for some of them... it may never feel like enough."

I stood up, unable to sit still any longer. The room felt stifling like the walls were closing in. I needed air, and space to think. The truth was out, but it didn't feel like justice. It felt like a hollow victory, one that came too late for too many.

As I made my way to the door, Harish called after me.

"You did the right thing," he said, his voice steady.

"You stopped them."

I didn't respond. I wasn't sure I believed him.

The horror had ended, but the fear would never truly go away.

The wind was cold against my face as I walked away from the police station. The dawn had fully broken now, the pale light of the morning casting long shadows on the empty streets. My body felt heavy, weighed down not just by the exhaustion of the last few days, but by the emotional burden of everything that had happened. The couple was in custody, their plan exposed, the children's fates revealed. Yet there was no sense of victory in me. It felt more like a hollow resignation like I had merely survived the storm without knowing how to rebuild in its wake.

Khaja was still there, standing near the car, giving me a warm smile as if he were trying to comfort me.

Days passed, and the world outside moved on, unaware of the horrors that had been uncovered in that small apartment. People were walking their dogs, sipping coffee in cafes, talking on their phones as if nothing had changed. And maybe, for them, nothing had. But for me, everything had.

To Be Continued..

Days did check off, everyone in the ABK township lived their life as usual, Khaja got back to his day routine, but somewhere deep down, I still holded the guilt of suspecting Khaja. I was unable to go back to ABK township for couple of days after the incident. As I got healed from the injuries, I headed to meet Khaja. Just as I headed into the ABK township, people started talking, I can clearly see their eyes being on me, the watchman being startled, his restlessness was visible in him body moments, as I headed towards the lift, people over there started conversating,

"Look, he was the guy, who found the couple."

With me ascending the floor through lift, I was nervous about how would Khaja respond with my visit?

Is the pattern still alive?

I had no answers for any of my questions. Entering on to the 13th floor, I made my way to the Khaja's flat. I encountered the mysterious flat, being locked, I took a

moment, I stared at it, with a hope that everything is over, and I headed back on my way to Khaja's flat. Standing in front of the door, I rang the bell, I could hear his voice,

"Coming,"

Saying it, he opened the door. Looking at me standing at unease,

"what's with that face? And since when did you start ringing the bell?"

Saying it, he headed back inside, but I was still standing outside of the door, he noticed it, looking back, he paused his walk.

"what's wrong with you? Why aren't you coming in?"

Hearing to him, I was speechless, he invited me with no void, I slowly entered the flat, my eyes filled with tears of guilt, I said,

"I am so sorry, Khaja."

Khaja stepped towards me, and said,

"It was done, let's leave it where it was supposed to be,"

Taking a moment, turning his head back facing the kitchen, he continued,

"You know what? You came on the right time, I was preparing a new beverage, let's try it out."

It felt welcoming, he was the same Khaja, who is joyous. We spent that day playing video games, chatting and watching movies together which indeed created a push. After a long time, I stayed that night at Khaja's place. The next day morning as I got down into the parking lot, I noticed the watchman being stressed, I approached him and,

"Are you okay?"

I asked.

He didn't respond for a moment. His hands being shivered, his eyes checking the

surroundings as if he was checking whether he can say or not.

Noticing his nervousness,

"Uncle, the couple are gone from here, they are under police custody, and everything is solved."

Watchman being silent till then, as soon as heard me, he emphasised,

"No, the 13th floor mystery is not over yet, there is still a lot."

What was he saying?

What does he mean by there is still more? What was he talking about? With all the questions firing in my head,

"What are you talking about? And ..."

Even before I can finish my questions, he said,

"If you want to know what I am talking about, meet me at the café round the corner tomorrow, before my shift."

I asked,

"Cafe? Why at the cafe?"

He paused for a moment and replied,

"They are watching, they can see you, it is not safe to talk here."

Saying it, he didn't even turn back, making me stay within my thoughts, he left the place. I didn't know what he wanted to say. Was it connected to the same couple? Who are watching? Why isn't it safe down here? All I could do was wait till I meet him at café.

The next day I went to the café mentioned by the watchman, I reached there around 11:00 AM, The café looked balanced with people, few near the coffee counter, and few at their tables. I noticed a table at a corner near to the glass door around the entrance, which can seat 2 people. I headed towards the table, pulled the chair, and rested myself in the chair, I found a newspaper lying on the coffee table, I grabbed it within the glance, I was expecting at a corner about the news that can cover the incident of the couple being caught, I started flipping through the pages, as I almost finished the paper, there was no article, no post or no story about the incident. How can this happen? How come there is no news about it?

"You cant find what you are looking for in the paper."

Hearing to the words I shifted my eyes from the paper and looked up from the top corner of the paper, and it was the watchman. How does he know what I was looking for?

Putting the paper, I gestured him to sit, he was wearing a blue shirt with a black trouser, hat on his head and a bag being pressed between his hands. He was nervous. He pulled his chair with his eyes looking around the glass door, he took his hat slowly from his head and took his seat, making sure the bag he brought was secured.

"So?"

I asked, with my face expressing all the curiosity. He took a moment, he pulled the bag that he brought and placed on the table. *"you are the first one to drive this long in this journey, now I can only rely on you.."*

What was he saying? Rely on me? *"No one else could have come this far, alive."*

He stressed when he said alive. *"Uncle, what are you trying to convey? What is that thing which you can only rely on me? And.."*

He interrupted me even before I could anymore questions, pointing at the bag, he said,

"This, bag, isn't just any bag, it is a just a tiny key to the upcoming concealed dark,"

What was he saying? What dark is he referring? What else is concealed?

"There is more than you discovered in ABK township, it is deeper than you can ever imagine,"

He continued, I was in a dilemma whether to believe him or not? And I asked,

"If this is about ABK township, why can't we have the conversation in the building itself, who is hearing us?"

The watchman being worried, he looked out again, leaning forward onto the table, he said,

"They observe your every move,"

He said it as if the "they" he was referring to, were just around us. He slowly opened the bag that he bought, and pulled out a paper, it was more like a chart, folded multiple times, putting his bag aside, so that the table is making space for the paper to be spread across the table. He took out his spectacles from the pocket of his shirt and putting it on, he started opening the paper, the unfolding revealed that it was not just any chart, but a blueprint.

"Blueprint?"

I spoke out, more like amused. *"Keep your voice down."*

He said by putting his finger on his lips, looking around.

"What is this blueprint?"

Listening to my question, he rotated the layout so that I can look into it clearly, just to the right corner below the chart, it mentioned as "ABK township". And I knew, it belongs to the building, but to make sure if I was correct, I asked,

"Does this belong to the building, ABK township"

I emphasised, he simply nodded and pointed at the layout that was marked as "layout of 13th floor." Looking at layout I asked,

"what is it about the layout?"

He slowly pointed at the Khaja's flat, and moved his finger towards the elevator.

Following his moment, I noticed, that the flat 03 doesn't exist on the map.

"Where is the flat?"

He sighed, and signalling to keep my voice low,

"That is what I was about to say,"

How come the flat 03 which is just beside to Khaja's flat in real doesn't exist on the blueprint?

"look, whatever I am showing you, is very confidential, we saw your strength, even they saw it, I guess."

Who are they? Is he referring to the couple? Or who is he referring to?

"if this is very confidential, then why are you telling me this?"

He didn't respond to that question, his eyes were speaking as if they were trying to convey as if I am the only hope.

"Can you describe more, can you tell any observations of yours? Any inputs that you can give?"

Breaking the silence, he said,

"I have observed the pattern, it started even before the couple had entered, no matter who the tenants were, where was their past stay, they always stayed anonymous, and left strange, they never stayed long," Breaking his words, I asked,

"All the same, all the tenants who ever resided in that flat were the same?" He nodded gently,

"Yes, they all were."

Though I was seeing the plan, my mind was hanging with the question, how come the flat is not on the map, we cross it regularly, we saw the couple staying there, how come it doesn't exit, I immediately asked,

"Was the flat built after the construction?" He immediately denied,

"No, I checked through the renewed plan details as well, there was no sign of this flat existence." Looking at the map, I said,

"So you are saying, there is a flat 03, which doesn't exist according to the official records but it is still present physically." Folding the papers, he nodded.

"Does anyone else knew about it?"

"no" It was his quick response. As he was getting, he started packing his bag in a panic way.

He stood grabbing his hat, folding his reading glasses and putting it back in his pocket, he said,

"I don't know whether you will be following the case or not, looking at your smart and bravery, I felt that you, only you can solve this, Now, it is all in your hands, you have to finish this journey, and let me warn you, this journey is definitely not going to be an easy one. And you'd have to confront it."

All his words were heavy, but I knew the depth of the unfinished mystery, that I have started.

I stood up being confused and I didn't know how to answer him so I just nodded.

He started heading back, and I collapsed into the chair, resting my head between my arms, my elbows on my knees, I was tired,

mentally. Rubbing my face, I saw a keychain that was dropped at the place where the watchman sat, I had the keys, thinking they belong to the watchman I headed towards him, I started giving my voice,

"uncle,"

He didn't notice me, as he was already outside the glass door, I rushed and opened the door, I saw him stepping forward to cross the road, on a snap, a truck travelling at full speed, horning loud, crushed the watchman. Infront of my eyes, I saw him being hit by the truck, he fell down to the ground, with blood bursting from his body, the truck didn't stop, not even to see whether he was alive or dead, which made me feel, that this wasn't any accident, but it was planned. But who can hold grudge on a simple watchman? It took a moment for me to get back to my senses. I rushed to the watchman, his face was completely disturbed,

"Uncle, uncle, can you hear me?"

I tried checking his pulse, I can clearly feel his heart beat dripping down, blood flowing out, I started hearing to an alarm, it was coming from the watch that was on the wrist of the watchman, the alarm ticked 13:03, and he was no more.

a person whom I met just a couple of minutes ago was now no more, my shirt with his blood leaving the mark of his existence, I remembered the words he said "you are the only hope" was still alive. Holding the keychain he left behind, I placed it in my pocket, Being unable to hold myself, I rushed towards the 13th floor in ABK township, reaching the floor I stood facing the 03 flat, which typically didn't exist officially, and it scared me even more, my hand started reached the door, as soon as I was about to open the door, my phone started vibrating in my pocket, pulling my hand back, I reached my phone. I saw a notification from the lock screen, it was a text message, from an unknown number, I tried ignoring, but it chimed again, opening my phone, I tapped on the message.

"We are watching you."

"Mind your steps."

Looking at the message, my hands started trembling, I looked around, searching if anyone was watching me, I found no one around me, taking a deep breath, I texted back,

"Who is this."

I was waiting for the reply, and after a couple of minutes, my phone buzzed again, with a sense of shiver, I opened the message, it stated,

"To be continued.."

What does it mean? What is this leading to? It felt as if I am boxed, with the BGM echoing and making me remember Christopher Nolan. And the message it was still alive.

To be continued..

To The Reader!

The events that had unfolded in the past few months felt like a lifetime ago, yet their grip on me was stronger than ever. As I sat in the quiet of my apartment, the shadows of everything I had uncovered still crept in around me, filling the space between the walls and my mind. It had been weeks since the couple had been arrested, their twisted plot exposed, but the fear—the real fear—still lingered.

When I started this journey, my fears had been of the unknown. Ghosts. The supernatural. Things that couldn't be explained. But now, after everything, I realized that fear wasn't about the unknown at all. The unknown was simply a mirror, a blank canvas where our minds painted the darkest images we could imagine. What terrified me most now wasn't what I couldn't see, but what I had learned to see clearly.

The couple had been human. They looked like any ordinary people. Friendly neighbors. Harmless eccentrics. That was the real horror—how easily they had blended in, how effortlessly they had masked the cruelty inside them with the banality of everyday life. There had been no shadows lurking in the corners of their apartment, no flickering lights or cold spots. Just them.

Fear had always seemed like something distant, a looming cloud of what-if scenarios. But now I understood that fear was intimate, close to the bone. It wasn't some phantom chasing us down dark hallways; it was within us. In our minds. In our everyday lives. It was in the people we passed on the street, in the faces we barely noticed, the ones who hid their darkness behind smiles and pleasantries.

I sipped my coffee, feeling the cool ceramic against my palms. The drink tasted like nothing—just warm liquid to fill the void. Even the mundane things felt different now. The colors of the world had shifted ever so slightly, the warmth of the sun was no longer comforting but instead casting strange, elongated shadows I couldn't ignore.

What I had uncovered had changed me. Fear wasn't a monster anymore, something lurking outside of myself. It was woven into the fabric of the world I lived in, part of the human condition. It was rooted in what people were capable of when no one was watching.

I used to think that fear was something to be conquered. Once I understood the truth behind something, the fear would go away, replaced by rationality and clarity. But now I saw the truth more clearly than ever—fear wasn't something to eliminate. It was something to understand. It was what kept us alive. It was what kept us from falling into the very madness I had witnessed in that couple.

I had stared into the heart of darkness, and it had looked back at me. Not as a supernatural force or a faceless horror, but as human beings—fragile, broken, terrifyingly real.

I leaned back in my chair, the creak of the wood the only sound in the room. Outside, the city continued to move forward, oblivious to the terror that had unfolded, oblivious to the way my world had shifted. People went about their lives, making plans, laughing, and worrying about the mundane problems of the day. But for me, the concept of "normal" had changed. It had become an illusion, something fragile and easily shattered.

I could no longer fear the unknown. That part of me had died somewhere in the middle of uncovering the couple's twisted secret. But I had gained something new in its place—a deeper understanding of what fear really was. Not something external, but something internal. A reflection of our deepest doubts, our darkest instincts. Fear wasn't something to run from. It was something that could never truly be escaped.

In the end, it wasn't the couple's madness that haunted me. It was the realization that the real monsters didn't come from myths or legends. They lived in the apartment next door.

"I returned to ABK township, thinking that seeing it again might finally bring me peace. I was wrong."

A part of me thought that revisiting ABK township would bring closure and that walking through those familiar halls one last time would release me from the grip of the memories. But as I approached the entrance to the apartment complex, the weight in my chest grew heavier, not lighter. The building stood tall, imposing, yet completely ordinary. It was a structure like any other in the city, yet to me, it held the darkness of everything that had unfolded within its walls.

I hesitated for a moment at the gate, watching as people came and went, completely unaware of the horrors that had been exposed here. A young couple walked by, holding hands, laughing. An elderly man shuffled past with his groceries. Life went on, unchanged, as if the nightmare that had once lived in this place had never existed.

I took a deep breath and stepped inside, the cool air of the lobby hitting me like a wave. Nothing had changed. The marble floors still gleamed, and the elevator doors still opened and closed with a quiet hum. The air smelled faintly of cleaning supplies, fresh and sterile as if trying to wipe away the stains of the past. But no amount of disinfectant could erase what I knew had happened here.

I pressed the button for the elevator, feeling the cold metal under my finger. When the doors slid open, I stepped inside, and suddenly, it all came flooding back—the nights I had stood here with Khaja, listening to the sounds of children crying from the apartment next door. The uneasy glances we had exchanged, the questions we had been too afraid to ask. It seemed so far away now, like a story I had read in a book instead of something I had lived through.

The elevator jolted slightly as it ascended to the 13th floor. My heartbeat quickened, the familiar dread creeping back in. I didn't want to feel afraid, not after everything I had learned, everything I had faced. But the building itself seemed to hold on to the fear, as if the walls had absorbed it, leaving faint echoes that only I could hear.

When the doors slid open, I stepped out into the hallway. It was empty, quiet. Too quiet. And yet, standing there, it still felt like they were here. I could almost hear the faint sounds of the children's voices, the soft cries that had haunted me for so long. My mind played tricks on me, conjuring up the past as if it were happening all over again. I knew it wasn't real, but the weight of the memories pressed down on me like a lead blanket.

I took a step closer to the door, my hand trembling slightly as I reached out to touch the cold metal of the handle. It was locked, but even if it hadn't been, I wasn't sure I could have brought myself to go inside. I didn't need to see the empty rooms. I didn't need to feel the suffocating air of that apartment again. The darkness wasn't in the walls. It was in the memories that still lived inside me.

The apartment was just a shell now, empty and lifeless. But to me, it would always be more than that. It would always be the place where I had come face-to-face with the darkest parts of human nature. The place where the lines between sanity and madness had blurred, leaving me questioning everything I thought I knew about people, about fear, about myself.

I turned away from the door, my heart still racing, and walked back down the hallway. I could hear the faint hum of the elevator as it descended, carrying someone else to a different floor, a different life, unburdened by the knowledge of what had happened here. For them, this was just another building, another place to live. For me, it was a graveyard of fear, a monument to the darkness that had once thrived here.

I stepped back into the elevator, watching the numbers descend. Each floor felt like a small victory, putting distance between me and the memories, but no matter how far I went, I knew I couldn't escape them completely.

By the time I reached the lobby, I felt a hollow sense of defeat. I had come here for closure, but what I found was that closure didn't exist, at least not in the way I had imagined. The fear wasn't something that could be left behind. It was part of me now, part of this place. The shadows had taken root, and they would stay with me, no matter how far I tried to run.

I walked out of the building, the sun brighter now, casting long shadows across the street. As I turned to look at ABK township one last time, I realized something: the building hadn't changed. It was still just bricks and mortar, a place where people lived their lives, oblivious to the horrors that had once taken place within its walls.

But I had changed.

And that was something I could never undo.

The Lingering Dread

The Unanswered Questions

"There were still pieces of the puzzle that didn't fit, things I would never fully understand."

As the days passed and I tried to return to some semblance of normal life, one thing became painfully clear: there were still too many unanswered questions. The couple was gone, their twisted lives laid bare for everyone to see, but I couldn't shake the nagging feeling that I hadn't uncovered everything. There were gaps in the story, shadows that remained untouched by the light of truth.

I'd replay the investigation in my mind, trying to make sense of the parts that didn't fit. We knew they had taken at least six children, but were there more? There had to be. The way they operated, so careful, so methodical—it was hard to believe they hadn't left more victims in their wake. And then there was the question of why. What had driven them to such madness? Their inability to have children was only part of the story. What was the deeper reason for their descent into this kind of horror?

I spent hours poring over news reports, and police updates, trying to find something—anything—that might explain the missing pieces. But the more I searched, the more frustrated I became. The facts were there, but the answers weren't. The couple had been clever, hiding their tracks, and manipulating the system. But their motives? Those were harder to untangle.

I thought back to the journals we had found in their apartment. The meticulous notes the woman had kept, tracking the children's lives as if they were part of some grotesque experiment. She wrote about them with a cold detachment, yet there were moments where her words took on a twisted tenderness as if she believed she was caring for them, saving them from a world that didn't want them.

Was it madness? Or was there something more to her delusions?

I couldn't stop thinking about the day we visited the mental hospital. The way she had looked at Khaja—like she recognized him like there was something she knew that we didn't. What had caused that reaction? Was it simply part of her fractured mind, or was there something more behind it? I had never mentioned it to Khaja. It didn't seem right to burden him with more questions, and more uncertainty, but it haunted me.

I'd lie awake at night, staring at the ceiling, my mind racing with possibilities. I couldn't escape the feeling that we had only scratched the surface of the couple's darkness. What else had they hidden? What other secrets were still buried in the walls of ABK township?

I had come to understand that fear of the unknown wasn't just about what couldn't be explained—it was about the things we refused to accept. The things we didn't want to see. The more I dug into the couple's past, the more I realized that not everything could be neatly wrapped up in a case file. Some parts of their story would always remain hidden, unanswered.

There were moments when I thought about going back—about reopening the investigation myself, pushing for more answers. But what would that accomplish? The couple was gone, and the horror they had inflicted was finally exposed. Yet the questions lingered, like a splinter in my mind. It wasn't just about the number of victims or the details of their crimes. It was the why. Why had they done it? What had pushed them over the edge?

I'd never know for sure.

There was a part of me that hated that—the part that needed to understand everything, that needed to tie every loose end into a neat, logical conclusion. But life didn't work that way. Some mysteries stayed unsolved. Some questions remained unanswered. And I had to learn to live with that.

The police had closed the case, content with the evidence they had. But for me, it didn't feel finished. There were still too many gaps, too many threads that had yet to be pulled. But maybe that was the nature of fear. It thrived in the spaces between what we knew and what we didn't. It lingered in the shadows of uncertainty.

I looked back at the notes I had scribbled in the middle of sleepless nights, the articles I had printed out, and the police reports I had combed through. They sat in a messy pile on my desk, a testament to my obsessive need to understand what had happened. But no amount of evidence would ever truly explain it. The couple's motives, their madness—it was beyond comprehension.

And maybe that was the most terrifying part of all.

Somewhere, in the darkest corners of my mind, I knew I would always be haunted by the questions I couldn't answer. The faces of the children, the couple's twisted logic, the unanswered why. It would stay with me, lingering at the edges of my thoughts, a reminder that not everything could be understood. That fear didn't always come with an explanation.

I closed my notebook, knowing that I couldn't keep searching for answers that didn't exist. But even as I tried to let go, the questions remained. Some part of me would always wonder if we had missed something—if the horror we had uncovered was only part of a larger, more terrifying truth.

I stood by the window, looking out at the world beyond. The sun was setting, casting long shadows across the streets. I thought about all the things we couldn't see, the mysteries we didn't even know were there, and I realized something: sometimes, it wasn't the answers that mattered. It was the questions themselves. They were what kept the fear alive, what kept us looking into the darkness, searching for the light.

But in this case, the light would never come.

"The fear never really leaves. It just learns to live in the shadows."

Life continued after the investigation was closed. On the surface, everything seemed to return to normal. The city moved on, the headlines faded, and the story of the couple became just another dark chapter in the endless cycle of news. But for me, things weren't so simple. The fear, the trauma, and the questions—they didn't disappear. They lingered in the background, quiet but persistent, like a shadow that never fully goes away.

I learned to live with it. In the mornings, I'd wake up and go through my usual routine—coffee, work, errands, small conversations with friends and family. Outwardly, everything seemed fine. But the shadows of what had happened stayed with me, woven into the fabric of my daily life. Every time I heard a child's laugh, I'd feel a pang of sorrow, remembering the children who hadn't been saved. Every time I saw a couple walking down the street, I wondered what darkness they might be hiding behind their smiles.

The world had taken on a new, darker hue. It wasn't that I had become paranoid or fearful of everything around me. It was more subtle than that. I had become more aware of the fragility of normalcy. I had seen how easily the line between good and evil could blur, how people could hide their true nature behind the veneer of everyday life. That awareness stayed with me, like a shadow at the edge of my vision, reminding me that the world wasn't as safe or as predictable as I once believed.

There were nights when I couldn't sleep when the memories of everything I had uncovered would replay in my mind. I'd see the couple's faces, their cold eyes, their twisted words. I'd hear the voices of the children, their cries echoing in my head. In those moments, the fear would creep back in, reminding me that the darkness I had faced wasn't something that could simply be left behind. It was part of me now.

But I had learned to live with it.

I had learned that fear wasn't something that could be conquered, as I once naively believed. It wasn't something that could be banished with logic or understanding. It was something that had to be managed, something that would always be there, lurking in the shadows. And that was okay. Fear wasn't the enemy. It was a reminder of everything I had faced, of the strength I had found within myself.

There were days when I could almost forget. When the sun was shining, life felt normal again. On those days, the fear would fade into the background, barely noticeable, just a faint echo. But it was always there, waiting. A sudden noise, a stray thought, and it would come rushing back, pulling me into the darkness for a moment before I could regain control.

I had learned to live in the spaces between fear and normalcy, between the light and the shadows. It wasn't easy, but it was necessary. The fear wasn't going anywhere, and neither was I. We had reached a sort of truce. I wouldn't let it control me, but I wouldn't pretend it didn't exist either.

Every so often, I'd find myself standing by the window, staring out at the world, watching people go about their lives, unaware of the shadows that lingered around them. I wondered if they knew. If they felt it too—that quiet, ever-present sense of dread that hid in the corners of the world. Or if they lived their lives blissfully unaware, never questioning the safety and stability they believed was theirs.

I envied them sometimes. The people who hadn't been touched by the darkness. The ones who could walk through the world without feeling the weight of fear pressing down on them. But then I'd remind myself that I had survived. I had faced the darkness and come out the other side. I had uncovered the truth, and while it hadn't set me free, it had given me something else—perspective.

I knew now that fear was part of life, part of being human. It couldn't be avoided or erased. It could only be faced, managed, and lived with. And that was okay. I didn't need to be fearless. I just needed to keep going, to keep moving forward, even when the shadows followed me.

Because in the end, that's what survival was—learning to live with the fear, the trauma, and the uncertainty. Learning to carry the weight of everything I had seen, everything I had uncovered, without letting it crush me.

I glanced at the mirror, catching a glimpse of my reflection. I looked the same as I always had, but I knew I wasn't the same person who had started this journey. The fear had changed me, but it hadn't broken me. And that was enough.

I took a deep breath, feeling the familiar weight of the shadows around me. They were still there, as they always would be. But I had learned to live with them. They didn't control me. They didn't define me.

They were just... there.

And I could live with that.

And just when I thought it was over, something happened that made me question everything once again.

Weeks had passed since my visit to ABK township, and I had finally begun to settle into the rhythm of everyday life again. The shadows were still there, but I had learned to live with them. I had come to terms with the fact that not every question would be answered, not every mystery fully solved. It was enough that the couple was gone, that their twisted game was over. Or so I thought.

The message was from an unknown number.

We haven't forgotten you.

I stared at the screen, my heart skipping a beat. My first instinct was that it had to be some kind of prank. A mistake. But as I read the words again, my blood turned to ice. The message was too specific, too deliberate. It wasn't a coincidence.

I looked around the room, suddenly feeling the weight of the walls closing in on me. The shadows that I had learned to live with, the ones I thought I had come to terms with, suddenly felt darker, more oppressive. I tried to calm myself, to think logically. The couple was gone. They were in custody. There was no way this could be connected to them.

But as I read the message again, a creeping sense of dread settled in the pit of my stomach.

I tried to reason with myself. Maybe it was just a random message. Maybe it was nothing. But deep down, I knew that wasn't true. The words felt too deliberate, too familiar. There was a part of me that had always feared this—that the darkness I had uncovered wasn't fully behind me. That it would find a way to come back.

I quickly typed a reply, my fingers shaking slightly as I hit send. ***Who is this?***

I stared at the phone, waiting for a response, my heart pounding in my chest. Minutes passed. Nothing. The silence was deafening, each second stretching into an eternity. I told myself it didn't matter, that it was probably just some sick joke. But the unease gnawed at me, growing with every moment of quiet.

Finally, I set the phone down and stood up, pacing the room. I couldn't shake the feeling that something was wrong, that this message was a sign. I walked to the coridor, staring out at the quiet street below, searching for any sign that I wasn't alone. Everything looked normal. People walked by, cars drove past. Life went on as if nothing had changed.

But everything felt different now.

I turned back to the phone, half-expecting another message to appear, but the screen remained blank. I wanted to believe that this was just paranoia, that the shadows of my mind were playing tricks on me. But I couldn't shake the feeling that the past wasn't as far behind me as I had hoped.

I thought back to all the unanswered questions, the loose ends that hadn't been tied up. Could there have been more people involved? Others who had been part of the couple's twisted game, watching from the sidelines? The possibility had always been there, lurking in the background, but I had chosen to ignore it. I had wanted so desperately for everything to be over, for the nightmare to end.

But now, I wasn't so sure.

I picked up the phone again, scrolling through the messages, looking for anything that might explain the source of the text. But there was nothing. Just those chilling words, hanging in the air, unanswered.

We haven't forgotten you.

I knew I couldn't ignore this. I couldn't pretend it was nothing. The fear that had been lying dormant inside me had been reignited, and now it burned brighter than ever. There was no escaping it. The message had opened a door I thought I had closed, and the darkness had rushed back in.

I sat down on the edge of the bed, my hands trembling slightly. I didn't know what to do. Who to call? What to think. I had faced the worst of human nature and uncovered the truth behind the terror that had consumed ABK township. But now, it felt like that terror wasn't finished with me.

As the night deepened and the shadows grew longer, I realized something: the fear had never really left. It had been waiting for the right moment to return, hiding in the dark corners of my mind, biding its time. And now, it had found its way back.

I stood up, pacing the room once more, trying to shake the feeling of dread that had settled over me. I didn't know who had sent the message or what it meant, but I knew one thing for certain.

The nightmare wasn't over.

Not yet.